PRETTY GIRL COUNTY

ALSO BY LAKITA WILSON
Last Chance Dance

FOR YOUNGER READERS
Sparkle
Be Real, Macy Weaver

PRETTY GIRL COUNTY

by
Lakita Wilson

VIKING

VIKING
An imprint of Penguin Random House LLC
1745 Broadway, New York, New York 10019

First published in the United States of America by Viking,
an imprint of Penguin Random House LLC, 2025

Copyright © 2025 by Alloy Entertainment LLC
Last Chance Dance excerpt copyright © 2023 by Alloy Entertainment LLC

Penguin Random House values and supports copyright. Copyright fuels creativity, encourages diverse voices, promotes free speech, and creates a vibrant culture. Thank you for buying an authorized edition of this book and for complying with copyright laws by not reproducing, scanning, or distributing any part of it in any form without permission. You are supporting writers and allowing Penguin Random House to continue to publish books for every reader. Please note that no part of this book may be used or reproduced in any manner for the purpose of training artificial intelligence technologies or systems.

Viking & colophon are registered trademarks of Penguin Random House LLC.
The Penguin colophon is a registered trademark of Penguin Books Limited.

Visit us online at PenguinRandomHouse.com.

Library of Congress Cataloging-in-Publication Data is available.

ISBN 9780593525647

10 9 8 7 6 5 4 3 2 1

Manufactured in the United States of America

BVG

Edited by Kelsey Murphy   Text design by Jim Hoover
Text set in Marion

This book is a work of fiction. Any references to historical events, real people, or real places are used fictitiously. Other names, characters, places, and events are products of the author's imagination, and any resemblance to actual events or places or persons, living or dead, is entirely coincidental.

The publisher does not have any control over and does not assume any responsibility for author or third-party websites or their content.

The authorized representative in the EU for product safety and compliance is Penguin Random House Ireland, Morrison Chambers, 32 Nassau Street, Dublin D02 YH68, Ireland, https://eu-contact.penguin.ie.

*To the Prince George's County Memorial Library System,
especially the Fairmount Heights branch and Spaulding,
who kept books in my hand
and stories in my heart growing up.*

Thank you.

PRETTY GIRL COUNTY

1
Sommer

GIRLS LIKE REYA Samuels *always* come from Prince George's County. If she were from Montgomery County, where generational wealth flows like water, the other rich Black girls would be calling her over-the-top for driving around in that flashy pink Audi. And if she came from Fairfax County, she'd be one of the only Black girls with money—period.

But here in Prince George's County? Girls like Reya Samuels are expected to flaunt their money—encouraged even—because most folks around here didn't start out that way. It's a whole thing to show everyone you've finally made it.

Imagine, huge homes sitting on honest-to-goodness golf courses, *multiple* luxury cars tucked inside three-car garages, catered backyard barbecues. Here in PG? Almost everyone you know is chasing a check or running up the bag.

"Sommer," my dad likes to say, "never make assumptions about someone's pockets. Some of those people living in those big houses don't have enough left over for furniture."

I'm not convinced that's exactly true. Back when everyone's parents made them invite the entire class to birthday parties, I've personally witnessed the following: furniture that doesn't slide across the floor when you bump into it, original artwork on walls, *live-in* housekeepers.

Some say Prince George's County, Maryland, is a place of infinite possibility. And I guess that's sort of true. Every day, there's another Black doctor, politician, or entrepreneur moving into a neighborhood tucked away behind ornate cast-iron gates. Practically every time I scroll socials there's a new "started from the bottom" post featuring a kid from my high school hanging out in the bowling alley in their basement, or lounging on an inflatable flamingo in their Olympic-size swimming pool.

Me, personally? I know *nothing* about this kind of life.

I live in PG County, too—except I started from the bottom and I'm still there.

Shall I introduce you to Seat Pleasant, Maryland, where our cast-iron gates are significantly smaller—and attached to our windows? Where bus stop benches provide seating for the overworked and beds for the unhoused? Where dead-end streets become football fields and someone's grandma runs a corner store out the side window of her house?

In Seat Pleasant, swing sets are dangling metal chains without rubber seats. Basketball hoops are missing backboards, and

PRETTY GIRL COUNTY

kids are more likely to climb the hills of an evicted neighbor's furniture than a jungle gym because no one's coming to rebuild the playgrounds.

I may be attending the same high school for talented and gifted students that Reya Samuels does, but trust and believe, we are *not* the same.

Not anymore, at least.

Which is why I don't pay Reya any mind when she walks to the podium in the middle of lunch to remind everyone to come out for the Annual School Fashion Show auditions next period.

"Just so you know, I've convinced teachers to issue thirty-minute passes for any student who wants to audition. How's that for school spirit?!" she says in that fake pep rally voice of hers.

Thunderous applause immediately rips through the cafeteria, showering the stylish queen bee with gratitude and reverence.

Listen, Reya Samuels and that two-hundred-dollar cashmere sweater she's rocking well into the month of April just aren't relatable enough for my applause. She's busy lording over the cafeteria, offering the student body an opportunity to participate in a carefree after-school activity.

Meanwhile, I'm sitting at the cafeteria table closest to the trash cans with my friends Amara and Reed, working like a dog on an extracurricular side gig so I'll be able to afford college come fall. I got into my dream school, Spelman, but even with financial aid, paying for everything is going to be a stretch. Food, books, transportation to and from the ATL . . .

This side hustle and my shifts at my dad's bookstore will put a tiny dent in it all, but let's keep it real, until I'm rocking the white dress at New Student Orientation, there's no guarantee I'll have enough money to go.

"The *Sims* developers put out a new game patch last night, so we need to update any glitchy inventory before our subscribers start complaining," Reed announces.

Back in middle school, I was a diehard *Sims* gamer—willing to lose sleep and sanity to keep my *Sims* characters well cared for. But when I linked up with Amara and Reed sophomore year, they showed me how to turn my obsession into dollars. After they taught me basic graphic design skills, we began designing cute custom clothes for characters and charging superfans a subscription fee to access our inventory.

We don't bother recreating any of that preppy mess that comes with the base game, either. We specialize in replicating high-end designer drip. Oversize Balmain sweaters. Hellessy bell-bottom jeans. Jordan sneaker dupes. Platinum Cuban link chains. Diamond-encrusted Patek watches. Moncler *erry*thing.

We reel customers in with the designer dupes, then I sprinkle in the real gems—my original concepts. Leather over-the-knee boots. Faux fur bucket hats. Belts with seat belt buckles. Glittery accessories. All by Sommer Watkins.

Kids and adults alike flock to what we're offering, since finding custom content by and for Black gamers is rare in the gaming community. So far, we have over three hundred subscribers—*easy* money, since the three of us love creating new content.

PRETTY GIRL COUNTY

Except on patch day, when the *Sims* developers update the game and drama breaks loose, forcing us to scramble to ensure our CC doesn't glitch. Our subscribers don't want to hear that we have frivolous stuff on our plate, either—like passing calculus or finishing high school. If they paid their hard-earned $2.99 a month, then they expect playable merch—no excuses.

Amara, who is sitting across from me, pulls up Sims 4 Studio on her laptop. "Reed, you search for any broken code strings, and I'll go behind you and fix them."

I pop a french fry dripping in melted cheese in my mouth and turn on my iPad, ready to pitch in wherever I'm needed. "Should I send out an announcement that an update is coming?"

Reed shakes his head. "Amara and I can handle updating the old stuff. Sommer, you should keep working on the new collection. We promised we would have the School's Almost Out drop by the end of the week."

Enough said.

We all get busy with our individual tasks. Amara, who refuses to wear her glasses, squints while she runs her finger across her laptop screen. Reed's typing fast. I'm sketching a designer top that caught my eye in these very halls last week.

I am so absorbed trying to get a sleeve just right that I pay very little attention to someone behind me yelling *"Go long, bro!"* until a brown leather football sails over my head.

Then someone's muscular, two-hundred-pound body crashes into my back, shoving me into the table and knocking the wind out of me.

My chili cheese fries fly all over the table, and my open milk carton spills, sending a chocolate stream straight for Amara's motherboard. She screams and starts swatting the milk back in my direction. Reed swoops up both laptops but trips over the fallen football on his escape from the table. He falls on his butt hard with both laptops still intact. He holds them up over his head like prize trophies.

That's when I realize my iPad is sailing toward the table's edge—and after that, to the cold, hard cafeteria tile.

"Somebody get my tablet!" I scream. I can't afford my own laptop like Amara and Reed. And I haven't quite figured out how to jailbreak my school-issued Chromebook. My iPad is literally all I have to work on content for our business.

The kid who crashed into me in the first place dives for the iPad, catching it just as it falls from the table's edge, and walks it back over to me.

"My bad, Sommer."

I grab my tablet from him and mumble a quick thanks before realizing whom I'm sending gratitude to.

Sean "Sauce" Levi. The male version of Reya Samuels, right down to the good looks, popularity, and very deep pockets.

"Is this yours?" he asks, handing me my sketching stylus from under the table.

I stop myself from biting my bottom lip. "Oh, um, yeah." Our fingers graze as I take my time getting it back from him.

Listen, I know I just talked all that mess about Reya. If we want to get technical here, I *should* detest Sauce for the exact same reasons.

PRETTY GIRL COUNTY

But . . . he's just so *fine.*

And unlike me and Reya, we don't have personal beef.

His friend Bryce shouts, "Yo, Sauce! What's taking you so long? Run that ball back, bro!"

Just like that, I'm reminded why my secret crush on Sean is weird.

Sean and Reya are part of an obnoxious little group I like to call the Brat Pack. There's Sauce, of course. Then there's Marlon, a judge's son. Azadeh, whose mom is a popular journalist for *The Washington Post.* Bryce, who's the weather lady's kid. And the "it girl" herself, Reya Samuels, whose mom is a successful lawyer turned reality TV star. Every single kid in that friendship circle comes from a family with money. And they're all champ.

Before you go "Aww, they're all *champs,* way to go" . . .

No. In PG County, *champ* is being or doing something that would irk the average person.

Case in point? Reya—who's still over there working the room, inviting kids to audition for the fashion show in that hot cashmere sweater—didn't turn around once while my friends and I were falling over iPads, laptops, and spilled milk.

Like she didn't live in Seat Pleasant herself five years ago. Like we weren't next-door neighbors practically our entire lives or mixing and matching our outfits to stretch the limits of our wardrobes. Like we didn't spend every day out on my front porch after school until her mom's career took off and they ran away to Bowie and never looked back.

You know what? *Forget* Reya Samuels. If all it takes are a

few designer bags and a luxury car to make her forget a day-one friendship, she can stay over there in her fancy new zip code.

Revisiting all that old drama, I almost forget Sauce is still standing here staring at me.

"Thanks for helping, but I'll finish the rest." I try to wave away him and this flirty energy.

But he continues to linger. "Are you sure?"

"Yeah, I've got it." I walk over to grab a mop leaning near the trash cans. "This whole fiasco was so uncalled for." I slap the mop down over my spilled milk. "If you had broken my tablet, then what?"

Sauce gets this look on his face like he's shocked I'm not swooning over his kindness. "I would've bought you a new one, of course . . . just like I'm about to buy you another school lunch." He pauses a moment. "So, um, does the lunch lady take Apple Pay?"

So champ.

See what I mean about these rich kids? Even my secret crush has his flaws. So out of touch with us average folks, he needs help purchasing a regular school lunch.

Before I can encourage Sauce to go on over there and try paying cranky Ms. Crowder with digital cash, someone yells out, "Hey yo, Sauce! Lunch is here, bro!"

That gets Sauce's attention. He looks over at the side cafeteria door, where his friends usually accept their DoorDash orders. Then, forgetting all about my fallen lunch tray, I watch as Sauce dips out to go dine with Academy of Health Sciences elite.

"*Sauccccceeeeee*, I hope you catch these Carolina Kitchen bags better than you caught that ball," Bryce goes, clapping him on the back.

I shake my head and try to convince myself I don't even really like hot dogs and that I can probably make it until dinner on the few fries I already ate. I pick up my tablet and stylus and start sketching again, annoyed that for a tiny moment, I gave Sauce a few cool points for helping me clean up a mess he basically created. While I'm over here applauding him for doing the bare minimum, he's just as self-centered as the rest of his friends.

To be fair, it's probably all he knows. Sean "Sauce" Levi is not only the king of the Brat Pack, but also heir to a dynasty. His great-grandfather brought his family's now-famous Mumbo Sauce recipe from Chicago to DC in the 1960s and used it to start a takeout restaurant in the heart of Washington, DC, where they dripped the special sauce on everything from chicken wings to french fries. Once the popularity of the sauce spread across the nation's capital, and every eatery from Chinese carryouts to Polish hot dog stands began copying the hot sauce/ketchup mix, Sauce's parents decided to bottle the family recipe and begin distributing it in stores.

Now, most stores in the DMV—DC, Maryland, Virginia— carry Sauce's family sauce. Seriously, it is shelved everywhere from Walmart to Whole Foods, and now Sauce's family lives in Potomac Overlook, a superexpensive gated community at the National Harbor. Please don't ask me to describe how fabulous his house looks. I only go to the Harbor during the "Free Movies on the Potomac" in the summer.

I thought my literal run-in with Sean would be the end of it, but suddenly he's back. "Ayo, Sommer. You want my lobster roll instead?"

On impulse, I get ready to say, with major attitude, "No, I *don't* want your charity lobster." But the smell of hot butter hits my nostrils, and I get real with myself. How often does this school offer seafood on the menu?

I hold out my hand. "Fine. Hand it over."

Sauce takes his time unrolling the red-and-white-checkered paper and laying it out in front of me. He places the lobster roll in the center, then sets down a plastic fork-and-knife pack and a little lobster bib.

"You don't need all this since the lobster meat is technically already out of its shell, but it's here, in case you want it."

I smile a little at the gesture. "Thanks."

I'm seconds away from sinking my teeth into a buttered roll when . . .

"Yo, is that my *sweater*?" Sauce asks. His eyes have landed squarely on my tablet.

Cringe. Cringe. *Cringe.*

Welp. Now my special lunch is ruined by emerging embarrassment.

"Uh . . . what?" I mumble, trying to cover up the screen with my hand—even though anyone could tell this is a replica of the long-sleeved Balmain shirt Sauce had on last Wednesday.

"It looks really good. I didn't know you could draw." Before I can stop him, Sauce reaches over me and my newly acquired

PRETTY GIRL COUNTY

lobster to pick up my tablet. "Yo . . . and what's this?" He just starts scrolling like it's perfectly normal to snoop around on somebody's personal electronic advice.

Evidently Amara and Reed think Sauce's invasion of privacy is perfectly normal, too. Because Amara says, "We create custom content for *The Sims.*"

Sauce looks at me. "I only have *2K*. Can I purchase this Balmain skin for that?"

I wipe a little lobster butter off my lips. "My stuff only works on *The Sims.*"

"*But* you can always subscribe to our Patreon." Reed pulls up a QR code. "Just $2.99 to support . . ."

I shoot Reed a dirty look. Why the heck is he trying to strong-arm three dollars a month from the richest kid in school? But when Sauce pulls out his phone and signs up for our five-dollar VIP subscription, I am grateful for my friend's initiative.

"Thanks, Sauce."

Sauce shrugs. "It's cool . . ." He starts walking back to his table but stops to look back at me. "Let me know if you want to draw another one of my outfits. I just bought these Amiri jeans that might blow your brand up."

All right now, simmer down . . . This isn't The Sauce Show.

Out loud, I say, "I'll keep that in mind."

When Sauce finally walks away, Amara is all over me. "Something's definitely sizzling between you and Sauce!"

"Yeah, right!" I polish off the last of my lunch. An innocent crush is one thing. But I'm not about to lose my mind over free lobster. Amara and Reed recently transitioned their friendship into a relationship. But that's not me—not right now.

"Reed, please tell our friend Sommer here that friend zoning someone as cute as Sauce should be a crime," Amara says.

"Definitely a misdemeanor," Reed says. "If you *do* ever decide to give love a chance, we could call you two the Sommer of Sauce."

"Okay, I'm going to have to stop you right there." I grab a cheesy fry off Amara's plate, the only one that survived the mess. "Just because you two decided to take a chance on falling in love two months before graduation, doesn't mean I want to." I shake my head. "Unless I win the lottery, I literally can't afford to date until college."

Not to mention, dating my ex-best friend's new best friend? As cute as Sauce may be, no way am I inviting *that* drama to my doorstep.

2
Reya

THE BRAT PACK?! Who said that? And *champ*? Like, be for real. You can't call a group of National Honor Society kids who participate in every major club on campus, from drama to lacrosse, who volunteer outside of the required twenty-four community service hours needed for graduation, who were literally featured in *The Washington Post* for stopping the party of the year to save an endangered bird, *brats.*

For the record, I'm the one who found that poor sedge wren flopping around in a bush suffering from a broken wing. Yes, I *had* been locked in a steamy lip-lock with a girl I'd just met when I discovered the bird. But that doesn't change the fact that when my eyes eventually landed on the poor thing, I immediately unglued my lips from the finest girl I'd seen all week and forced Sauce to cut the music.

"We have to call the zoo or something," I suggested.

"Nah," said Bryce, shaking his head. "Wildlife Services is the better option. They'll home it with a licensed volunteer wildlife rehabilitator."

"Is that a thing?" Marlon said, perking up. "Man, I've got to google how to sign up for *that*."

The next thing you know, Wildlife Services was rescuing the injured wren, Marlon was inquiring about how he could volunteer with them over the summer, and Azadeh's journalist mother had come over from next door to see why the Wildlife van was parked out in front of my house. Long story short, my friends and I were in the paper the following Sunday for our good deed.

Now, does that sound like a pack of brats to you? I think *not*.

So what if we like to party? Who cares that our clothes are pricey? What does it matter that we prefer to order in lunch instead of settling for basic cafeteria food?

All that matters is we're good people.

Wealth doesn't make you *champ*. Treating people poorly does. If my memory serves me correctly, I can't ever remember a time when my friends had an unkind word about anyone. And not only are we kind, we give back. Currently, I'm donating my time and energy to a cause worthy of my expertise—AHS's Annual School Fashion Show.

Okay, I know what you're thinking. *Oh, the girl with the Chanel bag in three different colors wants to direct the school fashion show, huh? How cliché . . .*

Let me tell you something. Under normal circumstances, I

PRETTY GIRL COUNTY

wouldn't need another extracurricular under my designer belt.

But I've been wait-listed.

Yes, you heard right. Wait. *Listed.* At the Fashion Institute of Technology—the Dior of all fashion design programs. After a flurry of calls to admissions, someone finally got back to me with a bit of feedback from the fashion department panel. Something about needing to see more of my voice shine through in my work. Whatever *that* means.

"Just so you know," the admissions counselor whispered to me over the phone, "the fashion department panel usually takes another look at portfolios over the summer, as students drop off the acceptance list."

That's all I needed to hear.

I refuse to accept a lukewarm *maybe* when I deserve air-horns, confetti, and a gold-trimmed acceptance letter. So, I'm redesigning everything, elevating my fashion game, and breaking records on how fast I come off that wait list once FIT takes a second look.

Think of this as my own personal "buy one, get one free" special. While I'm curating a 2.0 collection for the FIT panel, AHS will get to experience a Reya Samuels fashion show experience.

After last year's fashion show director failed to read the room by throwing nothing but size two models on the runway in unoriginal designer knockoff pieces, *someone* had to make things right this year.

So here I am, sitting with Azadeh and Sean, holding auditions.

15

"Remember, we're judging on walk and charisma only," I warn my friends as I cross another wannabe model off the list. "I *don't* want a repeat of what happened last year."

Sean immediately looks offended. "Why are you looking at us? We weren't on the fashion show committee last year."

Azadeh eyes me as I pull up the Notes app on my phone and add a few more items to my already pages-long to-do list for the show. I can feel her choosing her next words carefully. "Do you think you might be taking this fashion stuff a little too seriously?"

I squint at my friend. "You had your dad install Gucci seats in your Jeep last year. Trust me, you care about fashion as much as I do."

"Yeah, because it looked cool. Not because I spent hours researching the origins of every fashion house in Italy before selecting fabric for my car's interior." Real concern shows in Azadeh's face as she stares me down. "You're acting like your life will be over if you don't get into one school. You do have other options."

"Those other schools don't even begin to compare to FIT," I snap. Then I simmer down, because I know Azadeh is only trying to soften the blow in case things don't go exactly as planned. But she doesn't get it. I refuse to settle for a backup. I'd rather work hard to get what I really want.

Sean leans over to wrap an arm around my shoulders. "If you want to go to FIT, you're getting in. Your determination is unmatched."

Sean's words of encouragement make me feel slightly better.

PRETTY GIRL COUNTY

He knows me better than almost anybody. *I* also know *him* better than anybody else, which is why I refuse to call him "Sauce"—my bro is *so* much more than a secret family recipe.

"You already asked your mom to help with promo, right?" Sean asks. "Once FIT finds out your brand is about to be on TVs everywhere, you're in."

Love her or hate her, you've probably heard of my mom. Does the name "Angelica V. Samuels" spark any strong emotions? As in a Housewife from *that* show. Listen, I'm not sure my mom should've slung a glass of champagne in her castmate's face, either. But the moment *did* go viral and it secured Mom's spot on the second season of the Potomac edition of the franchise.

But back to auditions.

Kids from every grade and clique are strutting their way down the makeshift runway I've thrown together using masking tape on cafeteria floor tile, doing their best to impress me. Every so often, some out-of-touch freshman will eliminate herself immediately by ogling Sean instead of perfecting her walk.

After cutting the tenth freshman, I stand up and face the crowd lined up near the stage. "My rules at the beginning of auditions were pretty clear," I say, jumping into director mode. "Fashion is *life*. Fashion is self-expression. Walk like your life depends on it."

As if in answer to my prayers, a gorgeous junior with hair cut close to her scalp and a razor-sharp lightning-bolt side part struts down the runway.

PG County isn't called "Pretty Girl County" for nothing.

Seriously, everywhere you look—beauty, style, charisma. I don't ask to have an endless stream of baddies cross my path on the daily; it just happens.

Calling ourselves "pretty" isn't all about vanity, either.

You know how your grandparents probably hip-bumped at a house party in the 1960s and '70s while chanting "Black is beautiful"? Positive affirmations, created for us by us, have always been Black people's way of pushing back against the world's negative stereotypes.

Pretty Girl County? Basically, a "hey, girl, I see you" in a world that often forgets to find the beauty in our existence.

"What's her name?" I whisper, still stuck on the girl gliding toward me.

Azadeh taps her tablet screen, looks up, then scrolls. "Harmony Weeks."

When Harmony reaches the end of the runway, she reveals a cute set of dimples.

Sean grabs my phone and starts typing. "I'll just go ahead and add her to your top choices list, Reya," he says with a chuckle.

Normally, I would just march over, spark up a conversation, and have a date locked in for the weekend in minutes. But *professionalism.* I can't risk innocent flirting being misinterpreted as playing favorites . . . or even worse, abusing my power as director of one of the biggest school productions of the year.

So, I keep my wandering eye to a minimum and get back to work. Once everyone's had a chance to strut the runway and my friends have helped me narrow the top picks down to

PRETTY GIRL COUNTY

a solid twelve models, I thank everyone for coming and grab my things.

"There's so much more to do and only six weeks to pull it all off," I groan. I have to design and construct twenty pieces, figure out how to announce the student models in a *dramatic* way so that they will feel special about being chosen, and then stage the show of a lifetime.

"Breathe, Reya," Azadeh instructs. "We're here to help you, remember?"

I take a moment. "You're still walking in the show, right?" I ask my friends. "You both promised—"

Sean crosses his heart with his finger. "Have I ever broken a promise?"

"Good, thank you," I say. I look down at my list, scrolling through my notes and initial thoughts on design. "Now I just need to figure out how to make my line really special so it stands out to the admissions officers."

Sean pauses a beat. "Hey, Reya, if you need help . . ."

"Yeah?" I prompt.

He starts messing with his phone. "You know that girl Sommer?"

A swirly feeling hits my stomach immediately. "Yeah . . ." I say cautiously. I've never broken down the actual beef between Sommer and me, but Sean knows things are weird with us.

"She drew a picture on her tablet that looks *just* like a shirt I had on last week. I think she makes, like, little computer clothes for video games or something." He shows me a blurry image—looks like he only had two seconds to snap a picture of

19

Sommer's tablet. "Maybe she could help you with your outfits for the show and FIT."

I study Sean's fuzzy photo, even though I didn't need proof to convince me of what I already know. Of *course* Sommer is still out there sketching fire designs.

It's nice to know that one thing hasn't changed over the years. But the idea of talking to Sommer—of asking for her help—makes me briefly consider popping an antacid tablet to ease the mixed emotions swirling behind my belly button.

I contemplate changing the subject, or pretending like I didn't hear Sean at all. But he knows me too well. I don't brush off good ideas. And I am heading to Seat Pleasant this afternoon anyhow to pick out some fabric for the show. Maybe I can fit in an extra stop . . .

"The next time I see her, I'll ask her about it," I assure him.

After all, I'm Reya Samuels. I make things happen.

Even when they seem impossible.

3
Sommer

YES, PRETTY GIRL County is a whole thing in our area. But let's get one thing clear. There are at least two types of pretty girls in this county.

You have the pretty girls like Reya with the all-expenses-paid lifestyle. Their parents are doctors, judges, and business owners, and they are happy to foot the bill for luxury cars and rotating designer wardrobes. It's all tiny golf club sets as toddlers, diamond earrings in middle school, and fancy cars on sixteenth birthdays. An after-school *job*? For what?!

As you might have guessed, I do not fall into that category. Instead, I'm standing here at the bus stop, in this blazing heat, because my parents share our one family car and I need to get to work.

In addition to not having a car, I'm one of those pretty girls who *don't* have a glam squad at their sweet sixteen. I'm shopping at Wigs Beauty Supply for two packs of hair if I want a little extra length and volume, and thrifting in Montgomery County anytime I can get a ride going that way. If seeing a repeated outfit irritates your eyes, I suggest you grab a little Visine and keep it moving. My makeup is convenience-store affordable. I don't get my nails done every week. And no, I will *not* be waiting in line when the newest J's drop. My whole aesthetic is giving cute on a budget.

Now I step closer to the curb and crane my neck. "Where is the bus?" I complain. Hundreds of cars whiz by on Route 202, but so far, no Metro bus in sight.

Last year, I took a regular school bus to school, but at the beginning of this school year, a stop wasn't scheduled for me. When Mom called the bus lot to complain, they told her to call the school board. When she called the school board to complain, they told her to call the bus lot. Since no other students from my neighborhood attend AHS, my case kept slipping through the cracks, and Mom was forced to get me one of those Metro student cards. So far, I've only had to put money on it once, because every time students board, the bus driver waves us on through.

Normally it's just me standing here, but some days a few students from Largo, the regular high school across the street, wait for the bus here, too. Or just use the space for hanging out.

Like this kid Octavius.

Today he keeps looking over at me—making it completely obvious he wants to ask me something. But I stare straight

PRETTY GIRL COUNTY

ahead, then down at my phone like I don't notice him.

No offense, but even if I had time to date, it wouldn't be with a boy like Octavius. He's from my neighborhood, too. But from the looks of things, it doesn't appear that he has any plans to do anything other than hang out with his crew after graduation. He still goes to school, which is more than I can say for some of the boys he runs with. But I never see him carrying his Chromebook case, a pencil, or anything school related.

Sometimes while we're standing here, kids walk over to dap him up—which *could* be a friendly greeting, or maybe a code for something else. Based on who Octavius runs with—most likely the other thing.

Anyway, we're both standing here in awkward silence when a pink car comes speeding up, nearly jumping the curb, to stop right in front of us. We don't have time to step back properly before Reya's sticking her head out of the driver's side window. "Hey, Sommer, can I talk to you a second?"

I raise a brow. Reya must be trying to get the attention of a different Sommer. The last time I checked, we haven't spoken a word to each other in years.

Luckily the C22 finally comes screeching up, and I figure that's the end of that. I don't say a thing, I just board the bus as soon as the double doors open and slide into a seat at the front, where the senior citizens normally sit. Octavius heads to the back.

When he passes me, he shakes his head like, *Cold.* But I don't feel guilty about ignoring Reya in the least.

23

While everyone's clearing the aisle, a beeping horn catches my attention. I look outside, and Reya's pulled her Audi around next to my window. This close, I can see that she's wearing a white silky baby tee and a blond bob wig. Long, dangly iridescent stones hang from each ear on a single wire, giving the appearance of floating gems. Even I have to admit her look is on point, not that I would ever tell *her* that.

Avoiding eye contact at all costs, I scroll through songs on the music app on my phone until the bus lurches forward on Central Avenue. As we ride, the landscape quickly transforms from rows of townhomes crushed together to older homes, apartment buildings, and a strip of old warehouses that have been boarded up as long as I've been alive.

Even with SZA blasting in my ears, I feel someone sit down beside me. Octavius.

He reaches over and pulls one of my earbuds out my ear. "Yo, why is your girl following the bus?" He points out my window, and there's Reya, keeping pace in the next lane over.

Octavius is laughing, but I don't find a *thing* funny about her behavior right now. "She is *not* my girl," I say with a sniff.

Once, a long time ago, Reya and I were best friends. We did everything together—we slept over at each other's houses, walked to school together, ate every lunch together. Most importantly, we drew together—creating elaborate sketches for clothes and even sewing prototypes. But when we were in middle school, Reya's mom got rich, they moved to Bowie, and Reya dropped me faster than a boiling cup of Oodles of Noodles.

PRETTY GIRL COUNTY

Shaking his head, Octavius stays seated next to me for the rest of the ride, which is fine—it's not like we haven't known each other forever. The bus rumbles on another fifteen minutes or so, until it stops across from the shining star of our neighborhood, Grand Rising, the bookstore my dad owns.

Black people don't read? Tuh. Last year's store sales say otherwise. Now, if the expenses to run the store weren't so high, we'd actually have something to show for our efforts.

"Next stop," the bus driver yells out, "Addison Road and MLK."

Octavius and I check our seats to make sure we haven't left anything behind before we get off. Then he gives me a quick wave goodbye before going on his way toward Seat Pleasant Drive. I hold off a second to check my surroundings for Reya.

Good. No sign of that pink car anywhere. Hopefully the bus lost her somewhere between Carmody Hills and Central Gardens.

The second-best part of graduating in two months? Losing Reya for good.

Today I'm on register, and Dad's newest junior associate, Carmen, is busy opening up a shipment of Beverly Jenkins romances. Carmen is a senior, too, but she goes to Charles Herbert Flowers High, or Flowers for short. Her parents just moved here from Baltimore because one of them got a job working for the government in downtown DC. If that were me, I'd be stressing over changing schools right before graduation, but Carmen's been pretty chill about the move.

About an hour into my shift, a commotion near the front forces me to look up. The bell at the top of the door jingles and a hurricane whirls in, nearly knocking over the carefully curated selection of new releases at the front of the store.

My stomach sinks. I guess the bus didn't lose Reya after all.

In her arms is the biggest bundle of fabric I've ever seen in my life. "Can I use your bathroom, Sommer?"

"I don't know . . . *can* you?" I cross my arms and stare at her. For pettiness's sake.

Reya dumps her fabric on the counter and lets out a huge breath, blowing her blond bangs off her forehead. "Come on, Sommer, please. It's an *emergency.*" She pauses a moment to lock her knees together and let out two short oohs. "I stopped for a sweet tea on the way to the fabric store, and I didn't have time to . . ."

She squeezes her eyes shut again, does a little knee swirl, and lets out a third panicky ooh.

Realizing this is a code yellow situation, I point to the back. "Just go, before this turns into a problem and I need to clean up near the biographies." I raise an eyebrow. "You remember where the bathroom is, right?"

Putting bodily functions over book sales is my way of showing her grace. The jab is to let her know I haven't forgotten a thing.

Dad, who has been working on payroll at a table behind the counter, looks up and raises an eyebrow. "Was that little Rey-Rey?"

PRETTY GIRL COUNTY

I frown at the old nickname. "Sure was."

"Now, *that's* a face I haven't seen in forever . . ."

Tell me about it.

Dad goes back to working on payroll, Carmen ducks off into the Science Fiction section, and I try to get back into my sketching, but the toilet flushes a moment later and Reya comes back out, wiping her damp hands on her jeans. She gives me one of those fake beauty pageant smiles.

"Okay, so I know things got a little hectic back there, but I actually stopped by for more than your restroom," she says.

"Hopefully to check out our new releases!" Dad chimes in. "Nice to see our Rey-Rey back in Seat Pleasant supporting Black business."

I shoot him a warning glance. Because, please, sir . . . simmer down.

But Reya takes Dad's kindness and runs with it. Her amber eyes sparkle when she goes, "I don't mind purchasing a book, Mr. Watkins. You know I *always* loved Grand Rising."

Dad nods in Carmen's direction. "Well, let's have our newest junior associate help you find something interesting."

Reya simply waves her hand and goes, "A cute paperback related to fashion would be nice, thank you."

I'm not feeling the way she doesn't bother turning around while addressing Carmen. We exchange a glance across the store, then I launch into my own version of "customer service."

"Actually, we have a nice, thick limited edition coffee table book on fashion on our Special Reads display. I think *that* would be perfect for one of our oldest customers." I don't mention it's the most expensive book in the store. "Little Rey-Rey" will find out soon enough.

"Sounds perfect." Reya keeps her focus on me. "Sommer, I actually came in to ask you something important."

I want to tell her that I want to ask her something important, too. Like "Why can't your Brat Pack friends help you with whatever you're about to ask me?" But I'm not rude, so I just go, "What's up?"

"So, um, Sean saw one of your sketches and thinks it might be really great if you help out with the fashion show—"

My heart skips a beat when she mentions Sauce. But I keep my composure. "Sauce and I don't even know each other like that. Are you sure he wasn't referring to some *other* poor unfortunate soul from the ghet-*toe*?" I sprinkle a little extra seasoning on that last word so the intent burns on the way down.

Reya's smile wobbles just enough to warm my hardened little heart. "Come on, Sommer. Don't act like that . . ."

Humph.

I put my elbows on the counter this time and lean in close. "How am I acting, Reya?"

Reya drops her head for a moment. When she looks back up at me, the sparkle has faded from her eyes. "I don't know, like you have a problem with me or something."

How can she stand there and act all innocent? She *knows* what she did—I certainly don't need to remind her.

She picks at her cuticles, and I see that one thing, at least, hasn't changed. She always did that when she was stressing.

PRETTY GIRL COUNTY

"You wouldn't believe how much stuff is going on right now. I don't even know what I'm going to do about college next year. FIT wait-listed me and I can't go anywhere else."

Now, *this* gets my attention. "Wait . . . what?" I know Reya and I aren't on the best of terms these days, but I still have a heart. "You didn't get accepted *anywhere?*"

Reya isn't just a talented fashion designer. She also maintains a 4.2 GPA. It's hard to imagine any school rejecting her.

I'm seconds away from softening up, just a smidge, cutting her a little slack, when her entire demeanor flips.

"Well, *no.* I still have acceptance letters from Delaware State and Howard. And you probably already heard Bowie State accepted me early and offered me a full ride, plus stipend—"

My right eye starts twitching again as she blathers on.

"—but why eat hot dogs when a gold-flecked center cut filet is on the menu?"

Okay, that's enough.

"Reya, I'm not about to let you stand in a Black-owned bookstore and disrespect three beloved HBCUs like that."

I mean, if she wants to get marched up out of here by her little Louis Vuitton collar, just say that. I look back at Dad for assistance, and sure enough, he's already frowning.

"Yeah, Reya. I'm really surprised to hear you talking like that."

I'm not.

Of course, Reya tries her best to play off the disrespect. "You know I don't mean it like *that*, Mr. Watkins. But a Black girl trying to make a name for herself in fashion? Almost impossible. Brand names get you noticed in that world. I walk into rooms with a degree from FIT in my hand and people will notice."

I watch Dad chew on Reya's words. "I feel what you're saying, young queen, but when you're lifting up one brand, try not to knock down all the others."

I try to come up with an extra two cents to throw in, but then Carmen arrives with the coffee table book.

"This one's about the history of textiles. It could help you explain how you came up with some of your pieces for your fashion show," she says, looking proud about her bookish find.

Reya takes a look at the front cover, then *finally* up at Carmen. In seconds, she goes from completely oblivious to batting her lashes. "Thank you *sooo* much. I'll check this out whenever I get a little downtime."

Carmen scans Reya from head to toe. "I like your jeans, especially that pattern near the stitching," she says. "Did you do that yourself?"

Reya smiles until her dimples pop. She sticks out her right leg, giving Carmen a better view of her jeans. "This here is all me."

Carmen grins and my heart sinks. Now, I've gotten to know Carmen pretty well since she moved here and she's a cool girl with—I thought—excellent judgment. But if she's into Reya Samuels? Absolutely *not*.

Suddenly, I'm beginning to regret allowing Reya access to our bathroom.

I take the book from Reya and scan the barcode on the

PRETTY GIRL COUNTY

back. "To answer your original question, Reya, no, I *won't* be helping you with your fashion show stuff."

For a second, Reya looks a little taken aback that I have the audacity to tell her no. But then in a blink, she's back to pageant pleasantries. "But Azadeh's mom knows an entertainment editor at *The Washington Post* who might run a story on the show. And I'm planning to ask my mom about having the *Housewives* cameras follow her to our show. This could be a really good look for everyone involved."

I snatch a bag from under the counter and stuff her new book in. I raise an eyebrow. "I'm sure that's going to be really wonderful for you, but I'm not interested."

"Why not?"

"I have my own stuff going on, Reya. I don't have time for anything like that," I say, steering Reya toward the door. "Thanks for the purchase, and don't forget to follow our store's new Instagram page."

When the door jingles closed behind Reya, I let out a sigh of relief.

Carmen looks up from where she's now unloading another shipment of books in the New Fiction section. "That was pretty harsh, Sommer."

I take the box cutter out of Carmen's hand and stab the box right at the seam, sliding the blade down the clear packing tape until a stack of Elizabeth Acevedo novels smile up at me. "I won't go into details because I don't spill my friends' business, even if we're not close anymore. But just trust me on this one, she deserves my shade."

31

"Oh yeah?"

"I'll just say that we were close when we were younger, but not anymore. And I'm not shedding any tears over it."

"I mean, she seems a little bougie, but nothing too outrageous." Carmen raises a brow. "You don't think people can change?"

I level a look at her. "That's actually my biggest issue with Reya. People do change. But not everybody changes for the better."

4
Reya

THAT WAS FLIRTING, right? That was *definitely* flirting. No one makes a comment about a barely there pattern on a swatch of denim in the name of selling books.

That bookstore girl was definitely fine and *most certainly* shooting her shot.

Unlike Little Miss Thirsty at auditions today, Bookstore Bae seems cool . . . and just my type.

Speaking of bookstore girls . . . just the thought of my interaction with Sommer makes me cringe as I take Exit 19 toward Bowie. I'm not perfect, okay? I never, *ever* said I was above being called out. I know I made some mistakes when I moved from Seat Pleasant. But Sommer did, too. That year when I moved? It was hard. And Sommer wasn't there for me. Can you blame me for making new friends?

Anyhow, she didn't have to treat me like a complete stranger. We used to be friends.

I'm *still* thinking about everything fifteen minutes later as I pull up at my house, a large three-story brick house with white columns out front. Cutting the engine, I grab my pile of newly purchased fabric from the back seat and fix my face before sticking my key in the door. I don't need a million questions from my mother. Not today.

"Your favorite daughter is home!" I yell as I kick the front door closed with the toe of my Cole Haan flats. Dang, that door is heavy. Sometimes, taking this all in—the extra-tall ceilings, the huge rooms, even the bathroom attached to my bedroom suite—is still unbelievable. But hey, Mom did work her butt off to get us here, so I'm not going to act like I *don't* deserve luxury.

Mom comes out of the den holding a laptop under her armpit and a stack of manila folders in her hand. Her messy bun may be held together by a huge hair clip with ballpoint pens sticking out of the top, but her Brooks Brothers blazer, crisp and custom tailored to her figure, is giving wealthy heiress.

Mom sets her folders down on the coffee table and takes some of the fabric out of my hands. "I don't know how you plan to get all these outfits made in a few short weeks," she says, dumping her pile on the couch. "You sure you're not putting too much on your plate, baby?"

I give my mother a peck on the cheek, then shake my head. "I'm a Samuels woman. We get things done."

Mom nods. "True."

PRETTY GIRL COUNTY

I nod at the stack of folders on the coffee table. "Working on a new case?"

Yes, Mom's on TV now. But by day, my mother is a well-respected attorney who represents a few local celebrities and entrepreneurs. Early in her career, she won a huge settlement against an insurance company and the payout single-handedly wiped out her student loans and bought us a one-way ticket out of Seat Pleasant. Now she runs her own boutique firm with several associates working for her.

"Just going over a few client contracts, nothing major." Mom grabs her phone. "Remember that little tussle I got into with Geneva Steed online?"

"Yeah."

"Well, you know, while I think I held my own pretty well, there's a certain section of the internet that thinks my clapbacks were a little outdated. Now, I've been researching Urban Dictionary for the last few weeks, and I just wanted to run a few phrases by you. Do you and your friends ever use the term 'green bubble struggle' for people who don't have iPhones? I think Geneva may have owned an Android phone at some point . . ."

I raise an eyebrow. "If you want to know the truth, Mom, I actually think clapbacks in general are a little outdated."

My mother chews on that for a second. "Maybe you're right. There were some judgmental comments in my DMs the night the champagne toss aired. Okay, new idea. What if I have a signature nickname?" She does a rainbow motion with her hands. "The Potomac *Princess.*"

35

"But we live in Bowie," I point out. Some people call Bowie the Potomac of PG County. But I don't see any NFL players and movie stars living in *my* neighborhood. Potomac is the wealthiest city in Montgomery County. Not even Mom's new lawyer money is paying for a home out there.

But I should have known Mom would find the perfect loophole to set her plans in motion. "We're no longer *just* residents of Bowie, Reya," Mom goes, smiling. "We're also proud renters of a Potomac Airbnb. For filming."

I walk over to my mother and smooth back a lock of her hair. "Listen, Mommy. Just keep it cute, and everything will be fine. You did good last season, just don't go too far with things, and you'll be fine."

I stifle a sigh, realizing the same advice could be applied to me. My mom frowns in concern. "Everything all right, baby?"

"Yeah, why wouldn't it be?"

"I don't know. You look a little . . . *down*."

Shrugging, I decide to just go on and spill my troubles. "Well, I stopped by Grand Rising on the way home from the fabric store—"

Mom suddenly turns to me. "The bookstore? What were you doing in Seat Pleasant?"

"Pleasant things, of course—you know me." I wink at Mom, but she doesn't look amused.

"Don't get cute, Reya. Seriously, why were you there?"

A little irritated with all the questioning, I quickly give my mother the rundown. "Well, I needed to get fabric, but I also

PRETTY GIRL COUNTY

wanted to stop and see Sommer." Even saying her name out loud gives me the stomach swirls.

"I didn't know you two were friends again." Mom frowns. "Couldn't you have just called her?"

"It was just as easy to drop by the store." This is why I don't tell my mom anything. She always has a hundred questions. "Plus, I found out Etta's has all the designs they carry at the Joann in Bowie, except cheaper." I shrug. "I'm probably going to start shopping there from now on."

Mom gets a funny look on her face. "I'm not building all these income streams for you to have to worry about *cheaper*, Reya. Come on, now."

I blow out a long breath. "So saving money is a problem now?"

"I never said it was a *problem*. I'm just saying . . . you're driving a luxury car around like every single person in the world can afford one." Mom brushes imaginary dust from my right shoulder. "You're the one who *had* to get vanity plates and your car custom painted. Some people, in certain places, notice things like that. Those same people also tend to notice when a young girl is driving the custom-painted car *alone*."

"You really think someone's going to try to carjack me for a pink car?"

"It could happen, Reya." Mom googles something on her phone, then holds out her screen for me to see. "Crime is way up all over the county, but in Seat Pleasant, things are getting out of hand."

I make a face. "I was just there and it was fine."

But Mom shakes her head like she doesn't want to hear all that. "I *know* things aren't fine over there." She taps her phone screen. "Sixteen arrests last month? It's getting bad these days."

"Mom, we lived there only like five years ago."

"Exactly. *Years* ago," she says sharply, then smooths down the lapel of her blazer. "I didn't work this hard to move us out here for nothing. You understand what I'm saying?"

Not really.

Don't get me wrong, I love our new lives. I love this house and this neighborhood. I love the little jogging paths woven through all the parks. I love shopping in stores without bulletproof glass surrounding the counter.

Shoot, I love getting an allowance.

There was a time when Mom was still in law school that we didn't know how we were going to come up with grocery money. Now a direct deposit hits my CashApp every Friday. I do love my new life, here in Bowie. But what's so wrong with hanging out in my old neighborhood every now and then?

"Did you hear me, Reya? I feel safer when you're close to home."

Something about her tone makes me feel strange, like this is about more than simple helicopter mom stuff.

Mom's looking at me like she's in desperate need of validation, so I give it to her. "Yeah, I hear you."

"Good." Mom kisses me on the forehead. "Now take that fabric on up to your room and put it *neatly* away. Don't just toss it anywhere like you usually do. The cleaning lady is coming tomorrow and the last thing I want her to see is a messy house. I'm not about to have Edwina talking mess about us at her dinner table."

We share a laugh as I scoop the fabric back up in my arms and take it upstairs.

I'm still feeling a little iffy about Mom trying to control my life, but once I set my things down in my room, my brain immediately shifts to the next big thing. I pull my MacBook out of my bag and open it up at my desk. First, I follow the Grand Rising IG account, because I never miss an opportunity to support a Black business. Then I scroll their followers list to find the girl. I find her social media page in less than two minutes. Carmen—*that* was her name.

I send her a follow request so that she'll notice and follow me back. Then I get into my next point of business. I pull up Sommer's Patreon on my phone, then transfer the website to my laptop so I can see everything on a bigger screen and start scrolling.

Digital knee boots. Sketched-out jean jackets with rhinestones. Feathered boas. Fendi bag dupes. All of it amazing.

"Just like back in the day," I whisper at the screen. Sommer and I didn't live anywhere near Bowie or Potomac when we were younger. But we lived next door to each other in Seat Pleasant, and we were best friends. I can't tell you how many times we sat on each other's porches, sketching designs and dreaming big about changing the world with our creations.

Right then and there, I decide Sean's right. Sommer should be working on this project.

She's clearly holding a grudge about everything that happened between us. But I just have to figure out how to get through to her. One thing I've learned from watching my mother in the courtroom and on TV is that everyone has their price.

I just have to find Sommer's.

5
Sommer

THE NEXT MORNING, I'm sitting on a lumpy couch in the school lobby, waiting for Amara and Reed to show up. I'm sure they're somewhere, holed up in a quiet corner of the school, kissing each other's faces off. But we need to keep working on our designs—and this little pocket of time is a rare free moment in our busy schedules.

I should be using it to get a jump on my next set of sketches, but I can't stop thinking about next year. So instead, I'm using a Post-it note I've tacked to the front of my iPad to tally every possible expense I'll start incurring at Spelman in the fall.

Here's the deal. I got into Bowie State—on a full ride. Dad was through-the-roof happy when I got the letter. He even drove me around the campus so I could get a feel for walking around like a college freshman, earning my bachelor's degree for free.

"For *free*, Sommer. You'd better put a smile on your face, baby girl. Because not many places are giving away a college degree for free."

I did put a smile on my face. But secretly, I'd always had a different hope for college, and it didn't involve putting on a red sweatshirt and becoming a Bulldog. And Dad's reaction when I got *that* acceptance letter . . . well, let's just say it was different.

"Spelman?!" he shouted when I told him. "Fifty-thousand-dollars-a-year Spelman?!"

"Well, it's not *quite* fifty thousand—"

"I know it's somewhere around that price."

"But, Dad, they're giving me financial aid—"

"They just oughta be, for fifty thousand dollars a year!"

The fact that Spelman's financial aid package didn't cover all the expenses didn't help the situation.

My mom, the sweet angel that she is, interjected on my behalf. "You know how much Spelman empowers young Black women, Keith," she said, rubbing his shoulders. "Shoot, *I'm* empowered, and I've never stepped foot on that campus. Maybe Sommer can put in some extra hours at the bookstore."

When Dad softened under Mom's gentle touch, my hope began to rise. In the end, my parents and I reached a compromise. If I worked for at least half of everything that Spelman didn't cover, Mom and Dad would see to it that I became a Jaguar.

This entire senior year, I've been putting in as much over-

PRETTY GIRL COUNTY

time at the bookstore as I can without jeopardizing my grades. Plus, I've been earning my extra income from *The Sims*, but there is just so much to pay for. I glance back down at my list.

Books (can get many through libraries)
Bus tickets
College gear
Snacks
Bedding

The list goes on and on, as does the total cost, which is creeping into the four figures. How does anyone *afford* all this?

On the other side of the hall, someone starts banging on one of the vending machines, interrupting my impending panic attack. Sauce is shoving his shoulder into the side of the machine, grumbling about "the machine eating my dollar."

As cute as he is, it's taking everything in me not to roll my eyes over him of all people groaning over a lost dollar.

Sauce eventually gives up, swipes his card, and grabs the drink from the bottom of the vending machine. When he looks up, he catches me looking over at him and gives me a head nod.

I try to pretend I'm waving to someone behind him, to play the entire situation off. I doubt he buys it. The only group directly behind Sauce would be the Brat Pack, and I go out of my way to ignore them as much as possible.

For as long as I've been attending this high school, the same groups of kids have occupied the same spaces while waiting for first bell.

43

Naveen Mahadevan and Michaela Green, the two frenemies vying for valedictorian, compete in an intense chess game in one of the empty unlocked classrooms. The jocks hang out in the student parking lot until three seconds before the bell rings. The baddies crowd the bathroom mirror, getting their looks together. The Brat Pack chills by the bank of vending machines in the main hall. And my friends and I sit on a lumpy sofa against the wall.

No one bothers anyone. No one randomly chills in another group's territory. Absolutely *no one* crosses our carefully curated boundaries.

Now that I've broken hallway protocol, Sauce takes this as his cue to abandon his vending machine post and venture over onto lumpy couch row.

I'm not about to awkwardly stare him in the face as he walks over here, so I look down. I anxiously run through a bunch of far-fetched reasons why he's approaching me, but by the time he sits down next to me, there's really only one obvious answer.

Reya. I *know* she asked him to beg on her behalf.

"Hey, Sommer," he says as he drops something small and cold onto my lap.

A green bottle of Mountain Dew.

So, she put him up to bribing me with gifts, too?

Deadpanning him, I pick the soda up and toss it back at him. "Nah, I'm good."

Sauce gets a funny look on his face. "You don't want it?"

I shake my head. "You really don't have all the facts on

PRETTY GIRL COUNTY

how everything went down between Reya and me. You're cool and all, but please try not to insert yourself in ex–best friend business."

"I'm not . . ." Now Sauce looks genuinely confused. "Sommer, seriously. When I swiped my card, the first soda fell down with the second one. I saw you looking over, so I thought you might want one. That's it." He tucks the soda under his arm. "But if you don't want it, I'll just give it to Bryce or something."

Now I feel silly for jumping to conclusions. "No, wait . . . I'll take it." I wiggle my fingers in his direction.

Sauce smiles and hands me back the soda. Then he just kind of sits there . . . like he's waiting for me to take the first drink.

"I think I'll wait to open this," I tell him. "We've been tossing it back and forth to each other like a hot potato." After we both chuckle, I go, "But thanks for the drink, though."

He holds up his hands. "Okay, but since we're on the subject. Come on, now. Whatever happened between you and Reya is probably irrelevant by now. You're cool. She's cool. You're both talented at fashion stuff. Why wouldn't you be down to help her get into FIT? You probably know more than anybody how long she's been chasing that dream."

I'm torn between telling him to mind his business and finding it sweet he cares about his friend so much. If only Reya had that kind of compassion.

While I'm thinking about how to answer him, Sauce taps my soda bottle. "Have a drink on me and think about it, okay?" He flashes me that cute smile. "And I'll try my best to stay out of ex–best friend business."

I bite the inside of my lip to keep from blushing.

"But, uh, the next time I'm thirsty, you've got me, right?" he says.

I look away so he can't tell I'm losing an uphill battle to keep it cool. "Um, sure."

"Aight, bet." Sauce gives me a final nod, then heads back down the hallway.

While I'm waiting for my carbonated drink to settle down, I glue my eyes to the back of Sauce's chiseled physique. I can't lie. Even when he's being nosy, he looks good. His second-period weight training class is really doing its job.

I force myself to snap out of it. I'm not messing with Sauce. Or with Reya.

The truth is, I'm still feeling a way about her coming into the store last night, like we haven't been on a friendship break the last five years. Why should I spend what little free time I have helping a girl get even more things she doesn't deserve?

I can't lie and say Reya isn't talented. But her self-centered ways overshadow the good parts.

Still.

Sauce might actually be right. I know how much this would mean to Reya. Even when we were little and designing clothes for our dolls, she was talking about FIT.

"It's my dream school, Sommer," she told me back then.

But not all dreams come true. I certainly know that better than anybody. Maybe it's time Reya learned it, too.

6
Reya

DO I CARE that it's been an entire school day and Carmen still hasn't accepted my follow request on Instagram? Nope! Did you *think* I would care? Because I don't. I never did. I never will. I—

A ball of anxiety suddenly surges through my belly, causing me to maybe, accidentally kick the locker closest to my size six Off-White sneakers.

Azadeh, who's been taking way too long applying her lip gloss, looks at me like I've grown two heads. "You *do* know this is a public school, right? You dent that locker, and it will remain that way until our grandchildren attend this school."

She's right. I take a deep breath and put my foot back on the floor where it belongs. "I'm just frustrated. Can you believe Carmen still hasn't accepted my follow request?"

Azadeh leans in to get a closer look at her lips in her locker mirror. "Maybe she doesn't accept follow requests from accounts she doesn't recognize."

The absurdity of that statement makes my right eye twitch. "My profile picture is clear as day. We just saw each other yesterday. Trust me, she knows it's me sending the request."

"Well, maybe she's been busy with school stuff all day. Give her a minute." Then Azadeh does this shoulder shrug thing, like her advice is perfectly acceptable.

The problem is, I don't want to wait. "She's the one who started things with the comment about my jeans!"

"Okay, what's that supposed to mean?"

"It means, she got the ball rolling. The least she can do is keep up, after I make the next move."

Azadeh pauses her makeup routine to make a face. "Okay, first of all, calm down. Maybe she's just a friendly person."

"Her compliment did not read as 'just friendly.'" I catch Azadeh's eyes in her locker mirror. "There's electricity between us. I know these things."

It's not like I'm going to chase Carmen around if she doesn't respond to my social media request. On principle alone, I refuse to drown in a sea of cringey behavior because I can't keep my thirst at bay.

But going from polite bookstore pleasantries to being left in someone's requests longer than necessary is going backward.

"I'm honestly surprised you care this much." Azadeh begins coating her lashes with mascara. "The Reya *I* know would've moved on from that hours ago."

PRETTY GIRL COUNTY

"But she's so *cute*." I swing the locker door away from Azadeh's face so she can pay a little attention to me. "I'm serious. This time it was different."

Azadeh manhandles her locker door from my grasp and resumes her primping. "Just give it some time, Reya. If she likes you, she'll make it known."

I'm just about to check socials again to see if a certain someone finally followed me back when I notice Sommer walking to her locker.

Well, if I can't make headway with one bookstore girl, I may as well try my luck with the other. I make a beeline for her.

"*Hey*, boo!" I say in my brightest "don't you want to help me?" voice. In the moments today when I haven't been stressing about Carmen, I've been thinking about how best to get Sommer on my team. The trouble is, I don't know this version of Sommer. All my memories of her stop in eighth grade, when we were just on the cusp of entering high school. I have no idea how to best get on eighteen-year-old Sommer's good side.

"Hi," she says flatly.

"Did you think any more about helping out with the fashion show?" I ask.

"I think I told you yesterday that I already have a lot going on, Reya." She doesn't even turn to look at me, just continues piling books into her backpack.

I nod slowly. "I did detect a bit of . . . resistance in your tone yesterday, Sommer. But you have to know adding your ideas to the fashion show is only going to help put more eyes on your content. I looked up your Patreon yesterday and your stuff is

49

great. I even had some ideas about how to bring some of them to life."

She's about to put her tablet into her backpack when I reach out to grab it. "Let me show you what I mean," I say.

"If you don't hand me back my tablet right now—" Sommer starts, her eyes narrowing.

When I look down at the screen, it's not her sketches I'm looking at, but a purple Post-it note containing a long list with a dollar amount circled three times.

"What is this?" I ask.

"Nothing!" Sommer snatches the tablet back. She appears ready to bite my head off, but she can't hide the worried look in her eyes. It's the same look she wore when her dad said he was laid off as a delivery person at FedEx and thinking of opening his own business. Like she isn't sure how everything's going to fall into place.

Sommer and I may not be as cool as we were back in the day. But even when I didn't have much, I still wrapped my arms around her shoulders and told her everything was going to be okay.

That's when it clicks. The days of only being able to help with a cheap hug are over. I have the *money* now to fix things—or at least help ease her worries.

"I don't expect you to help me for free," I blurt out. "Your work is amazing, and your time is valuable. If you help me, I'll pay you what you're worth."

"Oh yeah?" Sommer says, trying—and failing—to sound disinterested. "And what's that?"

PRETTY GIRL COUNTY

I type a number onto my phone's Notes app and hold it up for her.

Her eyes go wide and she nearly drops her tablet. "Wait, are you serious?"

"There's nothing I am more serious about than FIT," I say.

For a split second, Sommer's expression softens, and it's like we're young and friends again. Like I'm showing her a sketch and she's encouraging me to add just one more design element. But the moment passes, the look fades, and it's back to business. A transaction between strangers.

"So, when do we start?" she asks.

I grin. "How about now?"

Sommer checks the time on her phone. "I have to work."

"I'll give you a ride—we can talk on the way." I pause briefly. "It'll also be nice to see that cool girl who works there again . . . What's her name? Carmen?"

Sommer stares at me for so long, I can legit feel the rejection coming. But then she narrows her eyes and turns up the corner of her lips. "If I tell you no, will you chase my bus again?"

"Of course," I answer with a wide grin.

I gesture toward the door, where my car is parked in the lot. As I lead Sommer outside, I tally up this small victory. And if Carmen just so happens to be working this afternoon . . . well, maybe I'll have another to add to the list soon enough.

7
Sommer

OKAY, I KNOW what you're thinking. I sold out.

Trust me. If you'd seen that number, you would have, too.

No, money doesn't heal betrayal and the pain of losing a friend, but it *can* make my transition to college a little less panic-inducing. With more money coming in, I'll have more time to study instead of always worrying about my next side hustle.

At least this is what I tell myself as I settle into the passenger seat of Reya's Audi.

All this time, I assumed the inside of Reya's car was just as pink as the outside. It *is* her favorite color. But no. The exterior paint job may be over-the-top, but she's kept the inside regular.

Since I'm not used to riding around in sports cars, I take the opportunity to enjoy this moment. No public bus lurching every time the driver stops to pick up or let someone off. An

PRETTY GIRL COUNTY

extra Stanley water bottle for guests to sip on while riding. A sound system so crystal clear, I can hear notes in SZA's music I've *never* heard through my cheap headphones.

When Reya drives past my regular bus stop, I slouch down in my seat, even though she has tints. Something just feels a little wrong about me getting to enjoy the cool comfort of a luxury vehicle while Octavius stands at our stop, melting like a Hershey bar left out in the sun too long.

When we're a safe distance away from the stop, I close my eyes and sink into the passenger seat's lumbar support. I have to stop myself from sighing out loud.

"Okay, so we should probably talk about our collab," Reya begins. "I was thinking that maybe you could do a digital lookbook or something of some of my designs. And I'd like to get your eyes on my portfolio so you can tell me what I'm doing wrong." She pauses. "You always *were* good at telling me like it is."

I give her a quick side-eye. Her cheeks are perfectly contoured, and an emerald-cut diamond stud shines on her ear.

I'm not a fan of this new version of my ex–best friend. But I can't pretend Reya doesn't have great style. I'm still surprised FIT didn't take her.

"Did they tell you why you're on the wait list?"

She shrugs. "Something about voice, whatever that means."

I force back an eye roll. "It means they can't tell who you are by looking at your work." The petty side of me would've tacked on "They aren't the only ones." But you know what? Not going there.

53

"Do you really think my help will matter?" I ask skeptically. "I barely know who you are these days, either."

Yes, I sketch, but I've never wanted to be a real designer. And not that I want to talk myself out of a paycheck, but I don't know how making a digital version of her designs will move the meter.

"You know me, Sommer. I live in Bowie and wear nicer clothes, but come on, I'm still *me*."

I shrug, not fully convinced. It's been five years since she left. I barely know Reya 2.0. "So, what's your plan?"

"The fashion show is six weeks out. I've hired the models, taken their measurements, and done some initial sketches. I purchased some of the fabric, and Mrs. Keyes says the best students from her home-economics class can help me with sewing. Hopefully, I can submit my designs, footage from the show, and a digital lookbook to the committee to show them how much they need me in their program."

I don't want to give Reya *too* much credit, but she is doing her little big one with that plan.

"I already know with you helping, I'm as good as in," Reya says. "But what's up? I haven't heard your college plans floating around AHS, and trust me, I've been listening out for the tidbits."

"I'm spending the next four years at Spelman. Then I'm taking over the gaming industry."

"Excuse you? What happened to fashion?"

"Fashion's in the mix, too." I take Reya through my

master plan. "Look at PG County. All kinds of Black people everywhere, right? Blerds. Preps. Intellectuals. Artsy kids. Even ratchet. But in gaming, we get one default face, straight-back cornrows, a baggy hoodie, and a kente cloth scarf to create our characters. I'm tired of the two Afro puffs and curly 'fro hairstyles that come with the base games."

Reya is holding back a smile, but I'm just getting started.

"Black gamers are hungry for more options for their characters. When I build the Black version of *The Sims*, I'm calling it *Pretty Girl County*, and I'm going to drop new outfit options every week."

"*Your* designs?" Reya points out.

I shrug. "Yep."

Reya looks impressed. "That sounds so cool, Sommer. But why didn't you apply to FIT? You can't get better training in the industry anywhere else."

"Spelman has the best of both worlds. Their arts program has a minor in Game Design and Development. Plus, students are coming from all over to the country—all over the world, even—to go to Spelman, which means I get a front-row seat to what Black girls are wearing everywhere. I figured I might get inspired by all the different looks."

Reya smiles. "I'm just picturing you sitting in class, drawing all the students instead of taking lecture notes. That reminds me of the time we—"

Whatever trip Reya's about to take down memory lane is interrupted when my dad's bookstore comes into view. I take one look across the parking lot and let out a blood-curdling scream.

Someone has graffitied three huge letters across the entire front display window.

Before Reya even fully comes to a stop, I get out of the car and rush across the parking lot to stare at the tag up close.

"How could those stupid boys do this to my dad's store?!" I say as Reya comes up behind me, panting slightly. I peel my eyes away from the offending letters to whip open the front door and storm inside.

"Dad!" I call out, darting my eyes everywhere, ignoring Carmen's confused expression. "Dad!"

"I'm right here, Sommer." Dad comes from the back wearing a grim expression—which ticks me off even more, because how dare someone do this to him? After all the work he does in this community?

"Relax, baby. It's going to be fine," Dad says, walking over to me. But a shoulder rub and a pacifying smile aren't going to calm me down. I'm too worked up at this point.

"No, Dad. It's just disrespectful."

"Yeah, I know." My father stares at the huge storefront window, shaking his head. "But there's nothing we can do about it except figure out how to remove it."

I can't even think of how to fix the window right now. But apparently, Reya, who I forgot was even with me, has ideas.

"Maybe you could check the security cameras to see who did it," she suggests.

"First off, we don't have security cameras." I narrow my eyes at her, her presence suddenly becoming extra annoying.

PRETTY GIRL COUNTY

"And you haven't been gone that long, Reya. Look at the window. You know exactly who did this."

The letters SPF continue to sizzle into the grooves of my brain. Someone who isn't from here may not know what those three letters stand for. But *I* do. So does Reya.

Seat Pleasant's Finest.

The immature group of boys from my neighborhood that Octavius hangs out with. The nerve of those clowns to call themselves the finest of anything when I have yet to see them do anything with themselves except hang out on the corner all day and night. All I want to do right now is find Octavius and punch his head off for wrecking my dad's window for no good reason with those bums he runs with.

But instead I'm trapped here for my next shift with Reya, of all people, who is standing there, checking her makeup with her phone camera.

That's the Reya Samuels I know.

Stuck on herself, leaving me to deal with my drama and everything happening in this neighborhood on my own.

8
Reya

THE WAY SOMMER'S looking at me, like I'm some out-of-touch, spoiled little rich girl is unfair. Yes, she agreed to help me with the show, but it's not like I forgot everything I ever knew about my life when I moved to Bowie. Of course, I know what SPF stands for. But everybody from Hill Road to Greig Street calls themselves Seat Pleasant's Finest. *Anybody* could've done this.

I don't say this, though. There's enough tension between us already.

So, I give Sommer some space while she talks to her dad.

I walk over to the display window to get a closer look at the evenly spaced block letters, swirled perfectly and even outlined with a complementary secondary color to really make the let-

PRETTY GIRL COUNTY

ters pop. Spray painting three huge letters on somebody's glass window is disrespectful—there's no disputing that fact.

But the more I look at it . . .

I glance over at Carmen, who's been near the back of the store shelving books this whole time. I'm not about to go over there and throw myself at her feet. But maybe she can back me up—and then we'll see what happens next.

"Um, Carmen? Can you come over here for a second?"

When she comes closer, I point at the window. "Okay, hear me out. What if Mr. Watkins doesn't remove the letters at all?"

Sommer breaks her conversation with her dad to throw me a look. "What are you even talking about right now, Reya?" I look around and my supporters are minimal. Mr. Watkins's face is stony. Even Carmen is raising an eyebrow.

"Hold on a second, just listen." I beckon for everyone to follow me outside. "What if these letters stood for something . . . *book*-related?"

Sommer sucks her teeth immediately. "Reya, please. We don't need any of your quick-fix Disney Channel ideas right now—this is a *serious* situation."

I ignore her negativity, thinking for a second. "Something like 'Suspense. Picture books. Fiction.'"

Sommer doesn't look convinced at all. "Suspense. Picture books. Fiction? You know what, you can just le—"

I think Carmen finally gets it, though. A small smile appears on her lips before she offers, "Some Personal Favorites."

I snap my fingers. "*Yes!* Then you could"—I look at the small

59

round table of books sitting in front of the window—"remove this table to give customers more walking room in the Memoir section. Take the featured books and dangle them from sturdy, colorful string so that they are floating just right in the window. Like, *really* in potential customers' faces, but also really artsy, you know?

Carmen nods. "That's what up."

Even Sommer's frown is starting to shrink.

"Maybe we strategically hang a few inexpensive tapestries here and there . . . not too many—the focal point has to be on the books—until we have an eye-popping, jaw-dropping custom display." I do a grand finale arm flourish. "It'll practically force new customers into the store."

Sommer looks at her dad, who is now staring at me, looking impressed. "I hear what you're saying, young queen," he goes.

Sommer folds her arm. "That sounds cute and all . . . but honestly, Reya, no one has time to redecorate the entire store to accommodate those letters in the window. We already have enough to do, unpacking shipments and ringing up—"

"I'll help out," Carmen says.

Oh, really?! "Me too!" I even raise my hand, like I used to do back in Girl Scouts. "Whatever needs to be done . . . free of charge."

I know I only have a little over a month left to pull off an epic fashion show. Designs need to be tweaked. Fittings need to be squeezed in. There are currently more rehearsal dates in my planner than days left of school.

PRETTY GIRL COUNTY

But now Sommer is helping me . . . even if she doesn't seem very happy about it. And a few guaranteed shifts with Carmen might be nice, too. Plus, I kind of miss Mr. Watkins calling me "young queen" even when I say the most basic stuff.

Mr. Watkins rubs his beard. "That's a nice offer, but I wouldn't ask you to work for free. And to keep it all the way real with you, I don't have room in my budget to pay you to do something like that."

Money is the last thing on my mind right now as I exchange a smile with Carmen. "I actually need to finish up my service hours to graduate. So when you think about it, you're actually doing *me* a favor."

Sommer narrows her eyes.

"You haven't finished all your service hours, Reya? Didn't your mom sign you up for the *very* service-oriented Jack and Jill club the second you two moved to Bowie?"

I cough a little behind my hand. "I mean, I'm sure I completed a *few* hours with Jack and Jill. But, truly, all I need is a week more."

With my busy schedule, I couldn't do more than a few after-school hours anyway. Seven days should be more than enough to get Sommer on my side, and maybe even get Carmen to date me, too. A girl really can have it all.

Sommer follows me. "You should probably go back and recount those hours—"

"*Or* I could move forward, by getting my service hours here." I run my hand along an entire shelf of mysteries.

When Mr. Watkins nods and goes, "Serving the community gets mad respect from me," Sommer comes up behind me and pretends to straighten the same books I just touched, even slamming one back into the upright position.

I can tell Sommer's annoyed with me offering to work in her father's store.

But I just bought myself seven days with Carmen. And if we aren't together by the end of that, then my name's not Reya Samuels.

⑨
Sommer

IT'S CARMEN.

I bet *she's* why Reya's so pressed to hang around the bookstore again. She's still here, by the way, pretending to shelve books.

Diabolical.

I hate to be this person, I really do. But my soul is literally vexed right now. Here I am, busting my butt, giving up all my free time to scrape up every dollar so I can attend the school of my dreams. I actually *agree* to help her.

And here comes Little Miss Service Hours, rolling into our store with promises of charity and goodwill just so she can hit on my co-worker. Gross.

I let out a groan as I slam *Dawn* by Octavia Butler onto the Science Fiction shelf.

Dad looks up from the register. "If I have to discount that book because you've dented the spine, it's coming out of your check, baby girl." He shakes his head. "I love you and all, but you've been warned."

Before I get the opportunity to mention another spine I'd like to dent, the door jingles, and suddenly Dad's attention is on someone else. "Greetings, my good brother! How can we help you today?"

Our newest customer, a tall guy wearing a postal uniform, lingers near the front, flipping through the pages of a book. "I don't know, exactly. My wife wants me to pick up some new book everyone's talking about. By Jasmine McMillan? Terry Guillory?"

"Do you mean Jasmine Guillory?" I ask, knowing exactly which novel he's talking about. I slip the newest rom-com by the powerhouse author into his hand. "But I noticed you mentioned the name McMillan, so your wife must be a fan." I pluck the latest Terry McMillan book from the shelf, too. "And might I suggest a local author? She's local, but trust and believe, her books are read everywhere." I pile a Connie Briscoe novel on top of the other two.

When the husband looks unsure, I smile and go. "Bringing home one book is nice . . . but bringing home three books makes you a hero."

The guy's chest swells a bit as he takes a moment to imagine himself on superhero status. Within seconds, he's whipping his credit card out at the register.

By the time the front door jingles again, Superhero Hubby

PRETTY GIRL COUNTY

is leaving the store satisfied and paying three times the amount he planned—which has Dad smiling so hard, I can count every tooth in his mouth from where I'm standing.

Pointing to the SUV backing out of the bookstore parking space, Dad says, "See that happy customer leaving our store?"

"Yeah."

"*You* made that happen. I sure am going to miss seeing you work your magic."

Dad's eyes are misty and I shake my head. Parents get so sentimental about kids leaving home for college. I bump him with my shoulder. "I'll still be back for breaks and next summer. No doubt you'll be putting me to work then."

Dad just wraps an arm around my shoulder, his expression surprisingly heavy. "I guess we'll see."

Before I can ask him what *that* cryptic remark means, three more customers come in and we get to work.

I play it cool for the rest of my shift for Dad's sake, but the second we close up, I storm off, on a mission to find Octavius.

The playground where SPF hangs out may not have swings, or a lot of grass for the smaller kids to play, but there's a large picnic table under a metal gazebo that the guys sit on top of to chill when they're not at the basketball courts.

Tapping my phone, I check the time and mentally calculate how many minutes I have to deal with this situation before dinner.

Five minutes is all I need. Two minutes to tell these dudes

off. An extra three if anyone has a rebuttal. After that, I'll have to get home before my parents start blowing up my phone.

When I get right up on the picnic table, I hesitate maybe a good fifteen seconds while I ponder whether it's exactly safe to storm the entire crew, yelling and demanding stuff.

Then I toss those worries aside. I went to school with every single one of these clowns before I got transferred to the gifted program.

Santana was too scared to whisper to friends during silent lunch.

I threw sand in Kev's eyes and made him cry the year he decided to steal my shovel at recess.

Foday's parents would send him back to Nigeria for high school if they knew he even *thought* about spray painting somebody else's property.

And then there's Octavius.

None of these fools are gangster for real. But you wouldn't know it by the way they're all sitting on top of the picnic table, smoking weed and freestyling like they're the hottest rappers in the game.

Ugh . . . pathetic.

"Are you kidding me?" I yell directly at Octavius—since he's the one I have the most direct contact with these days.

I'm sure I'm the least-threatening-looking person out here, with my collar polo and cardigan combo, but they could at least look interested. Only a few bored glances acknowledge my arrival.

PRETTY GIRL COUNTY

Octavius takes his time, blowing out a tail of smoke before crushing his blunt against the splintering wood tabletop. Peering over at me through hazy eyes, he goes, "What?"

"You think I wasn't going to say nothing about you doing that to my father's bookstore?!"

Santana immediately looks me up and down. "Man, if you don't get your fake neighborhood-watch-looking—"

But Kev, who now appears slightly more interested, cuts him off. "What bookstore? The one over by the beauty supply?"

I narrow my eyes at him. "You know which one . . . And you know what your ignorant butt did."

Kev turns to Santana. "Ayo, old dude be selling them comic books out of there. Bruh, that new Iron Man had me locked in for a straight hour and a half the other day."

Then he just starts a whole conversation with Santana like I'm not even standing right there, which infuriates me further.

"Is that when you decided to spray paint all over the display window? After you picked up a comic book?"

Santana looks over at me and chuckles. "*Relax*, Lil Bookstore. You out here doing the most right now." He puts his blunt to his lips. "Shouldn't you still be at school, with the rest of the Baldwin nerds, taking notes?"

A few members of SPF laugh, which blows my mind, because who ridicules *note-taking*? Like, be for real right now.

Still chuckling, Foday adds, "I'm not gonna lie, bro. Those Baldwin girls all look good. I keep trying to sneak up in there and get one of their numbers, but security stays pressing me."

"You *too*, bruh?" Kev goes.

Everyone's smoking and having casual conversations about nothing, like I'm not ready to burn their entire picnic table down over the disrespect shown to my father's store.

Except Octavius. He's not laughing or making small talk. He climbs down from his perch and steps toward me, frowning, his six-foot-four height a looming presence all up in my personal space.

So here's the thing. I know these dudes. But we went to school together a long time ago. I can't say I *know* know them, anymore. My heart is beating hard in my chest. But, even nervous, I refuse to back down. Family is everything to me.

"What makes you think it was us?"

"*Really?* The letters were right there. Big as day. SPF. Who else would it be?"

This shouldn't even be taking this long. They are SPF. They hang out on this picnic table, or on the courts, or on the corner doing mostly nothing all day and night. And look at them—who else would do it?

Octavius gives me a long stare-down before shaking his head. "First of all, most people that spray paint SPF *ain't* really SPF. They're just wannabes wishing they was down with the crew. Second of all, you think we really got time to be doing some kiddie stuff like that?"

Octavius playing right in my face enrages me. "You mean to tell me you haven't put SPF on nothing around Seat Pleasant?"

I can tell by the way he looks away that I've got him. "I mean, yeah, in middle school." He stares me in the eye again.

PRETTY GIRL COUNTY

"But I'll tell you one thing, none of us would do nothing *corny* like tag no Black-owned business. Does that even make sense to you?"

Kev shakes his head. "Got the 'Black Lives Matter' sign right in your pops's window, but racially profiling *us* . . . sad . . ."

The rest of SPF shake their heads like *I'm* the one in the wrong. And when I look back into Octavius's eyes, the way he's looking at me, my theory of him and his crew being spray-painting bandits starts to weaken. A weird feeling begins creeping up my chest.

Octavius's face is giving pure disgust. "I suggest you head back home and find somewhere else to be." He shakes his head. "I thought you were cool, Sommer, but you started going to that snooty school and got brand-new."

"He ain't lying, Lil Bookstore." Santana takes another hit of his blunt. "You looking like the opps right now, slim."

What can I say? I messed up big-time, and I have no other choice but to turn and walk home as fast as I can.

69

10
Reya

THE NEXT FEW days, working with Sommer again feels like stepping back through time. We're adding intricate details to existing sketches and erasing overdone looks. Sommer found old books from middle school to pull from. And I bookmarked vintage-style sites online for inspiration.

It's weird, because we haven't said a word to each other in years.

But when it comes to working on this project, Sommer and I are both professional enough—well, mostly—to put our past aside and come together to get the work done.

Trust me, besides Sommer acting a little standoffish, *everything's* going perfectly—until Sommer mentions the color scheme. "Everything's beige," she mentions. "Beige overalls. Beige tops. Beige knee socks."

PRETTY GIRL COUNTY

She holds the matching socks between her thumb and forefinger like someone might hold up a worm.

"*Exactly.*" I take the socks from her to showcase them properly. With reverence and respect for how much thought and design went into creating these identical luxe pieces. "The color scheme is doing its job of highlighting how diverse my models are on the runway."

Sommer's already shaking her head. "But fashion isn't about the models."

"Says who?" I ask, raising a brow.

Sommer sifts through more of my looks like she's browsing the bargain bin at T.J. Maxx. "Models are presenting the clothes to the audience. They aren't starring in this production."

Again, a tad on the disrespectful side given how much love, care, and attention I put into this work.

"People need to be able to *see themselves* in my clothes. So, I wouldn't be so quick to minimize the model's importance." I grab an overall set from her. "If the models don't matter, why not have me model all the clothes. I'd just go down the runway multiple times with quick backstage changes."

"You'd like that, wouldn't you?"

I toss down one of my half-finished pieces. "You say that like you think I'm self-centered. We both know that isn't true."

Sommer raises an eyebrow. "It isn't?"

I put the overalls back down. "Is this why you agreed to help me? So you could act weird toward me?"

Under the tough facial expression, I begin to notice a slight softening. "I'm not being weird . . ."

"Sommer . . ."

"Okay, fine . . . I'll relax," she says, choking slightly on the last word.

I clap my hands together. "Yay! Now you can stop taking shots at my color scheme. Because you have to admit, it's a modern take on—"

Sommer puts up a hand. "Let me just stop you right there . . . Your color scheme? Still terrible."

"*Sommer . . .*"

"Seriously, Reya. There's nothing memorable about an all-beige collection. Didn't you say FIT wait-listed you? You need to do a complete overhaul of this portfolio."

"But I believe in these looks, Sommer. Come to the next rehearsal and witness the clothes in action on the runway. It's the only way you're going to see how it all comes together."

"You asked for my help, so I'm giving it to you, Reya. I *know* you. Your voice doesn't speak in beige."

I can't deny Sommer brings something out of me that even I can't see sometimes. But what I've created isn't a total disaster. She has to see the clothes on the runway so I can prove the color scheme, at least, makes sense. "Just come to the show."

When Sommer still looks unconvinced, I grab her hand. "I've always been the technique. And you've always been the flavor. But I'm right about this color scheme. You have to see everything in action."

Letting out a tired sigh, Sommer finally relents. "Fine. But I'm telling you right now. If these clothes go down the runway

PRETTY GIRL COUNTY

without bringing at least one tear to my eye, we're adding pops of color. Because I can't take—"

I stick my hand out. "Deal."

We shake on it.

The only person who ends up in tears is me. Don't get me wrong, it all starts off fine enough.

As soon as we step into the auditorium, my entire demeanor shifts to business. For some people, fashion is what's trending now. For me? Fashion is my future.

The same classmates who will see this production in a few weeks will someday see my work on a grander scale, at New York Fashion Week, or even Paris. I want everyone who saw my early work to be able to say, "I knew she was going to do it this big someday. You could tell even back in high school that that girl was going places."

I've already moved up once in life. Everything I do now is to make sure I keep moving up, and never go back.

Anyway, everything down to what I'm wearing to rehearsals today matters. (A designer cardigan over a simple white tank and black jeans set, in case you were wondering.) I'm also resting a huge pair of Chanel shades over my hairdo for the afternoon—a pink, blunt, long bob that just barely kisses my shoulders.

Sean comes over to give me a hug as soon as he sees me pushing a huge rack of clothes backstage for the models to change into. When he spots Sommer, his whole energy changes. "So, you agreed to help out with the show?" he goes, smiling all up in her face.

Sommer shrugs. "Something like that . . ." She's smiling, too. O-*kay*.

Normally, I would egg on such a bold display of romantic possibility. But I'm in work mode.

I pull out the miniature bullhorn I had delivered to my doorstep this morning. "Okay, everyone, listen up. We only have a few weeks left until the big show, so I need everyone to focus!"

Putting my hand on my hip, I make sure every word out my mouth feels like bullet points. "When it's time to hit the stage, I need you to *Hit. That. Stage.* No fear. No hesitation. No half stepping. Is that clear?"

I turn my face to stone on purpose—not willing to offer my models even the slightest hint of satisfaction until I see effort on every person's part.

While an array of ninth through twelfth graders mumble their acceptance of the task at hand, I notice something odd about my current lineup of models. Squinting my eyes, I silently count off the number of students standing on the stage.

"Where the heck is Azad—"

A commotion comes from the side door, and suddenly my friend whirls in, looking like she's just performed a round of cheers with the dance squad for a pep rally. Except this isn't basketball season and the cheer squad is on hiatus until next school year. Why the sudden change in punctuality?

PRETTY GIRL COUNTY

"You're late!" I bark into my bullhorn.

Putting my best friend on blast in front of an auditorium full of our classmates might sound cold to you. But right now I am Reya Samuels, director of a highly anticipated school fashion show. I *have* to the set the tone that no one, not even my very best friend, gets special treatment. Rehearsals must start on time, because . . . *professionalism.*

"Sorry, sorry, sorry," Azadeh says, throwing her things into the chair next to me and pulling a pair of black heels out of the tote bag on her shoulder.

I nod toward the stage. "You should probably head up there."

Azadeh scurries toward the stage, and Sean and I follow her. I hand each model the prototype of their outfit, and fifteen minutes later, everyone is ready.

Pointing to the first row of models, I go, "Let me see you walk."

They're off. Back straight. Core tight. Shoulders back and down. Face on expressive. Everybody is giving me what I'm looking for—forcing me to finally crack the smile I've been holding in. And for the record, the color scheme on the runway looks amazing.

I lean over to Sommer. "*Now* you can see how the beige aesthetic really accentuates the mood of the entire production and brings the drama to their unique features, right?" Yes, I'm looking for validation, or at least a little friendliness, from my former friend.

So I'm disappointed when Sommer turns to me and goes, "Reya, we're adding color to this collection."

Arrghh!

Sommer should know more than anybody how much change can ruin things.

But you know what? Fine. While I silently reassure myself that most projects go through a transitionary period, and adding pops of color won't throw off the entire mood of my collection, a commotion breaks out on the stage.

"Hurry up and get off the stage, boy!" Cody Sullivan calls out as he gets ready to walk up. "Parkstar Cody do it better!"

Bryce, who has just reached the end of the runway with his walk partner, takes immediate offense. Making a face, he goes, "Man, shut up! You're always calling out Parkstars like somebody's supposed to care you're from Palmer Park."

Cody makes a face. "What? I know a Bowie *Bandit* isn't talking to me."

Bryce hops down off the stage. "Keep running your mouth, bruh."

That's it. I march over with my bullhorn already at my lips. "Are you two serious right now? Don't bring none of that neighborhood mess to my runway." I clear my throat so they can hear me loud and clear. *"Professionalism."*

Thickness gathers in the air as Bryce and Cody stare each other down a moment. And I assume it'll all dissipate so rehearsals can go on like normal. I *need* this to go right.

But Bryce is all, "What you say?"

So, Cody's all, "Parkstars don't repeat ourselves . . . We get active . . ."

PRETTY GIRL COUNTY

Now they're hitching up their pants and bouncing around on the balls of their feet, like they're in some weird prefight dance number together. Of course, once things get serious, the rest of the models drop focus to gather around to either egg it on or declare, "Come on, y'all. We're better than this."

Now I'm standing outside the fight ring, anxiety surging through my veins, watching all my hard work in serious danger of being ripped apart.

"Everyone, freeze! You two are in my clothes!" I scream into the bullhorn. I charge the stage, push through the crowd, reach for the beige vest Cody's wearing, only to trip on a wire that hasn't been properly taped down and nearly take a nosedive.

"Ooh, she's jumping in!" someone calls out.

"Whose side is she on?" someone else says.

"I don't know. She's just swinging."

Yes, my arms are flailing. I'm trying to save a few items before these two start punching on each other. I reach for the collared button-up Bryce is wearing, and the sash that lies strategically to the side tears off.

A loud rip echoes through the crowd, temporarily freezing the boys' fists, as everyone gawks at the huge hole where the sash used to be attached, now showcasing too much skin from Bryce Powell.

"Look what you made me do!" I no longer need my bullhorn. My shriek can probably be heard in the social studies hall on the other side of the building.

PG County may be known for our big houses, flashy cars,

and parents with good government jobs. But we also see our fair share of scuffles. It all starts out so petty, too. Randomly, one kid will have a problem with someone from another neighborhood, the friends on each side get involved, and then it's chaos that drags on and on, forever.

Cody takes this opportunity to approach me, outfit all rumpled for no good reason. "Look, Reya, I'm not trying to ruin rehearsals or nothing like that—but I'm not about to be disrespected . . ."

I'm too mad to process anyone's excuses right now. "You know who should feel *most* disrespected? The home ec students. Why bother assembling anything if you two are just going to rip it all apart?"

My heart feels like it's trying to beat itself way out of my chest. Everything is wrong. Sommer already thinks my outfits don't look authentic. Now everyone's fighting. I know what I'm capable of—I *know* I can pull this together—but every time I think I'm making progress, another roadblock gets in the way. "Just . . . please. Get into your regular clothes so I can have my stuff back."

Closing my eyes to try and shut out this looming headache, I put my bullhorn to my lips one final time. "I'm shutting down rehearsals for today."

Sommer and Sean come up to me. "Reya, come on."

"I *won't* have that kind of pettiness in my show. Who cares that somebody lives in Bowie, and somebody lives in Palmer Park?"

PRETTY GIRL COUNTY

All the models start mumbling among themselves—even Bryce and Cody.

Sommer smirks. "Oh, I know you're all for the unity. Isn't your new boo Carmen from Palmer Park?"

Okay. I can't front. The mention of Carmen's name almost makes me smile a little. *Almost.* I'm still feeling a way about what just happened. I try to play it off, though. "Don't try to change the subject," I tell Sommer. "I thought you were trying to help me, anyway."

Then I turn to Sean. "You need to talk to Bryce about starting stuff."

Sean looks confused. "How was *Bryce* the one starting it? Nobody told Cody to start yelling in the middle of rehearsal."

I shake my head. "Trust me, that's going to be addressed, too. Because I don't want to hear that on or off the runway."

Sean huffs. "That's not going to happen, Reya. We should've thought about the different neighborhood beefs before choosing the models. You know certain neighborhoods don't get along."

I start throwing my things into my rehearsal duffel bag. "I really hope you're not cosigning any of this, Sean. Because all of it is dumb. None of us choose where our parents live. We go where they go."

I glance over at Sommer. Now that Cody and Bryce are on their way to the bathroom to change, I want to explain all over again that moving to Bowie didn't change me. Despite what anyone else might think.

But Sommer's looking like she agrees with Sean.

"Sauce is right. The different neighborhoods in PG have been fighting since our parents were in school. My dad said homecoming was canceled every year, due to Seat Pleasant beefing with Brightseat Road and Ardmore. It just is what it is at this point."

Not on my watch. Frowning, I pull my glittery bullhorn back out of my duffel. "Attention, fashion show participants. Party at my house Saturday night. Attendance mandatory."

Sommer raises an eyebrow. "Excuse you?"

I lower my bullhorn. "I won't have these weird beefs messing up my show, Sommer. If I have to cut the music and sprinkle a few team-building activities into my next few parties, I will."

Sommer shakes her head. "Welp. Let me know how that goes."

As models begin bringing me back their outfits, I count them to make sure I have them all before I leave. "As special consultant, you're part of this show now, remember? You're coming, too."

Sommer raises her brow. "Why do I need to be there? I have to work Saturday night, anyway."

"Well, call out sick," I insist. "The theme of the party is unity, so we also need to come together and figure out the direction of this collection."

"Oh, like you finally accepting a more color-infused collection?"

"Maybe." With that, I throw my bag over my shoulder and saunter out of the auditorium—with a proper model's walk, to show everyone I know what I'm talking about. But the second

PRETTY GIRL COUNTY

I get in my car, I collapse against the soft leather seats and take deep breaths to calm my racing pulse.

Okay, so now all I have to do is plan a party . . . on top of planning a fashion show . . . and volunteering at the bookstore. No biggie. I can definitely get it all done.

Right?

11
Sommer

OKAY, REYA STORMING out of the auditorium with a fashion-week-worthy walk was a moment.

I might be out of a ride home, though. While I'm trying to remember whether Amara and Reed stayed after school for robotics club today, Sauce taps me on the shoulder.

"Do you need a ride?" he asks me.

"I'll be all right." I've already gotten a free ride in a luxury vehicle once this week. Anything more might be jazzing it.

"Are you sure? It's really not a problem." He glances at me with those cute brown eyes. "It takes like, what, ten minutes to get to Seat Pleasant from here?"

I weigh this against the forty-five-minute bus ride on the C22. Normally, crushes are huge time wasters—but in this sit-

PRETTY GIRL COUNTY

uation I'm actually saving time by accepting the ride. I give myself a pass.

"Sure, why not?" I grab my things.

"It was good to have you there today," Sauce says once we finally make it into his car—a fully loaded six series BMW. "You should think about asking Reya about making a cameo in the show. She might have an extra tank top or something for you to show off."

I laugh at the thought. But also? "I'm just getting Reya to come around about the color scheme. I'm not trying to take up a slot like that. I'm sure Reya has models dying to come off the wait list."

"Yeah, but what if I wanted you to make that cameo so we can chill?" Sauce cracks a smile as he turns out of the parking lot.

I duck down so he doesn't catch me blushing—hard.

My buzzing phone breaks through the tension. I check my text messages and it's a photo from Reed making kissy faces into the camera.

The image quickly unsends, and then he texts, Oops, that one wasn't supposed to go to the group chat.

Side-*eye*.

"Everybody's scrambling to get together right at the end of high school," I say to Sauce. "That doesn't seem weird to you?"

He shrugs. "I don't think people pencil love into their planners like a homework assignment, Sommer."

83

"What? It just pops up unexpectedly like a YouTube ad?"

Sauce smiles at my joke. "Exactly." He glances over at me. "Then it's up to you, to either learn more or press skip."

That makes me laugh. "I've been pressing skip on love all four years of high school."

Dang, everywhere around me, people are pursuing crushes left and right.

Sauce and I make conversation for the rest of the ride to my house. Unlike Reya, he doesn't grip his steering wheel the moment we pass the WELCOME TO SEAT PLEASANT sign, which earns him a few cool points.

I'm not feeling Dad's car pulling up right beside him in our driveway, though. Before I can even get my sneakers on the pavement, Dad is coming over to the driver's side of Sauce's car.

Rolling down his window, Sauce sticks his hand out and goes, "Hello, sir."

Dad squints his eyes for a minute before something registers. "You're Tasha's son, aren't you?"

"Yes, sir."

Dad does a slow nod. "I went to school with your mom. Boy, I practically watched you grow up on Facebook."

Welp. Now I feel like melting into the ground, because telling someone you've been watching their entire life on social media is only the second creepiest thing you can casually mention. But Dad isn't concerned about this at all. Instead, his eyes travel the length of Sauce's car. "Nice ride, son."

"Thanks, sir."

PRETTY GIRL COUNTY

Yep. Time to break this up. "All right, Sauce. Thanks for the ride. Dad?" I say, my eye daggers strongly encouraging him to follow me inside.

Thank goodness Dad throws up the peace sign and follows after me. But as soon as we get inside, he's all, "This is the second luxury car I've watched you get out of this week. You're too good for the bus now?"

I take in my father's words and raise an eyebrow. "Sean offered to give me a ride home from this thing I had to do after school." I toss my backpack on the floor by the front door.

Dad gives me a strange look. "What kind of *thing*?"

"Something Reya wanted me to do." Mentioning her feels so awkward now, after our five-year hiatus.

Instead of letting me be as vague as possible, Dad beckons for me to follow him into the kitchen so he can get more intel on my life.

"So you and Rey-Rey are back now?" Dad goes, kissing Mom hello.

I *knew* he was going to eventually say something. Mom is usually pretty chill about my social life. Dad, on the other hand, wants to know every single detail on what's going on with me.

"Kind of. So?"

"So, where's Amara and Reed? I don't want you getting in good with the rich kids and forgetting your day ones."

"Technically, they're my day twos. And trust me, they're not missing me much these days. They've been busy falling in love. They don't have time for me." I shake my head.

85

"In love?" Mom looks impressed. "You mean those two finally stopped pretending, huh?" She puts her hand to her chest. "I knew those two were in love the moment I met them."

"No, you did not." I swear, my mother thinks she's onto everybody.

"Yes. I. *Did*," Mom insists. "I'm surprised it took you so long to notice."

Dad waves this information off like yesterday's news. "Well, good luck to those two . . . but did you know I just spotted our daughter getting out of a car with one of the Mumbo Sauce boys?"

Mom finally looks surprised by something. "Really . . . Wow, we practically watched those two grow up on Facebook."

I'm seriously going to have to start monitoring my parents' online activity. This being in everybody's business mess is embarrassing.

"Can you call 'the Mumbo Sauce boys' by their name, Dad? The one I go to school with goes by Sean."

"So is Sean who you're dating?" Mom asks.

"I'm not dating anyone," I say quickly, instantly uncomfortable. I've never talked to my parents about dating. Didn't have to. My priorities have always been school, work, and getting out of here after graduation.

Now they have me cornered in the kitchen right after my dad told my secret crush that he's been online-stalking him for eighteen years.

Mom smiles at Dad. "You remember Sean's mom in school, Keith?"

PRETTY GIRL COUNTY

Dad snorts. "Lying to everybody that those blue contact lenses were her real eyes? Please don't remind me."

Mom laughs behind her hand. "Oh, stop. That was her story and she's sticking to it."

Dad smirks. "Tell me something, Naomi. She's at every gala and political fundraiser in the county. Where are those sky-blue eyes now?"

Mom shrugs. "Maybe she's wearing brown contacts now."

They share a momentary laugh as they float on down memory lane. But I need to assure my father of one important thing. "You don't have to worry about me hanging out with them, Dad." I make a face. "I don't need y'all thinking I'm trying to be something I'm not—"

Mom cuts in. "I think you should date whoever treats you with kindness and respect."

My mother can always be counted on for the simple, PC answer. But Dad knows exactly what I'm getting at. I give him a look so he can back me up.

"Why are you looking over here at me?" Dad asks, chuckling. "I'm not going to judge you for liking Lil Moneybags . . . I'm sure he's cool."

"What makes you think that?"

"Because his pops is a real one." Dad looks off a moment like he's trying to remember a moment. "Sauce might have rocked that burgundy blazer and tie set to DeMatha with all the other rich private school kids, but he still showed up at the courts every day after school to hoop."

"Wait. Everybody called his dad Sauce, too?"

Dad shrugs. "That family has been making that sweet and sour blend since before I was born. What else were we going to call him?"

I shake my head at how big this county is, but small at the same time. Everybody truly knows *everybody*.

"Hey." Dad leans in. "You know once you cross that stage next month, life is about to get real, right?"

"I think I might realize that more than anybody else at my school," I mumble.

Dad beckons for Mom to step closer, then pulls her in tight. "Your mom and I, we're going to have an opinion on everything you do. We can't help it . . . We've been infected with Parent-itis since the day you were born."

I roll my eyes at his dad joke.

"But at the end of the day, we've raised our girl to think for herself and trust her own judgment. You want to keep your distance from Reya? We have your back. You want to make up with her, that's cool, too. Same thing with dating."

I hold up my hand again. "I'm *not* dating anyone—"

"I know, I know. My point is, we trust you to do what's best for you, Sommer. I might have my little comments"—he smirks at me rolling my eyes—"but at the end of the day, I'm Team Sommer. I'm going to always support you."

"*Dang*," Mom suddenly says. "Think you can leave a sentimental moment for me?"

They share a laugh right before Dad kisses her forehead. Then Mom grabs my hand.

"Dad and I are going to give you your space to spread your

PRETTY GIRL COUNTY

wings, Sommer," Mom goes. "But just know, no matter what age you are, whenever, wherever, *how*ever you need us, we don't play about our baby. We will always be there for you."

This makes me smile. Because the Watkins family may not have the three-car garage or backyard pool, but we have each other—and on most days, that's enough.

12
Reya

THE DAY AFTER the disastrous fashion show rehearsal, I focus on compartmentalizing. Yes, I'm still working on finding my voice. And I still need to work on building a more positive environment for my models. But I'll get to those issues in a bit. Today is all about Grand Rising.

I breeze through the parking lot, armed with a few spray paint cans of my own, fabric, ribbon, inspo boards pulled up on my phone, and the right attitude to get this job done swiftly and effectively.

I'm dressed the part, too. I roll into the bookstore first-day fresh wearing a pair of bell-bottom jeans, a fitted tee with the Black Power fist front and center, and my curly Afro lace front spritzed with just enough oil sheen and plucked out to full capacity.

PRETTY GIRL COUNTY

Yes, I notice Carmen over there looking as fine as ever. But she still hasn't followed me back on socials yet. So if she wants to play it cool, I can, too. Plus?

Professionalism.

While Mr. Watkins is working in the back, Sommer's on register, and Carmen's working the floor, I use a step stool and sheer willpower to transform the window into a work of art.

I'm looping and cutting and gluing and performing magic on this window. During a quick water break, I tiptoe around Sommer, who's been quietly sketching behind the counter.

Grabbing a paper cup, I pour myself a little water. "You think Carmen likes what she sees?"

Because come on? What good is having a crush if you can't deliberate with a friend about it?

But Sommer's giving me nothing to work with. With her sketching stylus in hand, she scrunches her nose at me. "Girl, what did I tell you before? I'm not getting involved in y'all's business."

I smirk. "But is she looking? We can worry about the other details later."

Sommer deadpans me, then goes back to her sketching.

I end up finishing five days of work in two hours—which leaves me just one hour of my shift to mingle.

I head straight to Carmen, who's arranging a special cubby display of Toni Morrison books. Now, I've never been the thirsty type—ask anyone—but I do like to get the ball rolling. So, I throw a sneaky question out there to get the answers I'm looking for.

91

"Your girlfriend must miss you while you're at work . . ."

Carmen turns toward me, still holding a book in her hand. I silently pat myself on the back when I catch her checking out my baby tee. "What makes you think I have a girlfriend?"

Hmm, so she wants to play *this* game, huh?

I want to get the scoop on Carmen, for sure. But I also like the way she's choosing to make me work for it.

While I'm thinking of a good comeback, the front door jingles. A lady walks in wearing Jimmy Choos and an authentic beige Chanel handbag. Best of all, she's wearing a silk turban. One of the fancy kind with a faux jewel sewn onto the front. Now, if there's one thing I know, it's that a woman luxurious enough to wear Chanel and silk turbans for simple bookstore runs will go all out come Sunday morning, when it's time to show out in the church pews.

Like I said: I know people.

Despite the woman's flawless toffee-colored skin, I can tell she's older by the distinguished way she carries herself. If my personality radar's on and working properly, this is the sort of woman who demands respect, writes thank-you notes after every major and minor event, but loves a little church gossip.

Carmen gets ready to introduce herself to the woman, but I block her path. "I'll take this one," I whisper to her.

"Hi, I'm Reya," I say, sticking out my hand while Carmen watches me with a questioning expression.

Elizabeth Taylor's White Diamonds perfume wafts from the woman's neck as she grips my hand. "Ms. Johnson."

PRETTY GIRL COUNTY

"Are you looking for anything in particular, Ms. Johnson?" I ask her.

The woman's pink-stained lips curve into a smile. "I've just finished Victoria Christopher Murray's Seven Deadly Sins series."

What did I tell you? I know a woman who loves a little church gossip when I see one.

Now, I may not have read most of the books in this store, but I have used my time wisely by reading the book summaries on the inside jackets of the hardbacks. So I instantly think of another author she might like.

"Have you heard of the Reverend Curtis Black series?" I ask, walking her toward the R section in Fiction.

Ms. Johnson frowns as she follows me. "Sounds familiar, but . . ."

I pluck a book off the shelf. "It's about a shady pastor with a wandering eye. He causes all sorts of scandals in the church he leads. It's by Kimberla Lawson Roby."

Ms. Johnson's eyes light up as she takes the first book in the series from my hands. While we're on this winning streak, I add a ReShonda Tate Billingsley novel and another from Mary Monroe to her stack before helping her to the register.

My efforts do not go unnoticed. Sommer's dad mouths *good job* to me and even Sommer gives me a begrudging smile as she's ringing up the books. The moment Ms. Johnson leaves the store, Carmen goes, "That was pretty good work for a newbie."

I use this compliment as an invitation to get back in the

93

game. Walking over to where Carmen's working, I nod toward the book in her hands. Her thumb is covering, like, half the cover. But I would know that novel anywhere.

Oh yeah. "*My Eyes Were Watching God*? By Toni Morrison?"

Carmen raises an eyebrow before sliding her hand away from the book so I can get a better look at the cover. "This is *Sula* by Toni Morrison."

Before I can say anything, she smirks, walks to the Must-Reads shelf, plucks a book from the stacks, and hands it to me. "And don't you mean *Their Eyes Were Watching God*? By Zora Neale Hurston?"

I could literarily melt into the floor right now. Except I can't because my pride refuses to allow Carmen to think I'm not well read. "I don't even know how I said that. I read *Their Eyes Were Watching God* in AP English junior year."

I can't read Carmen's expression well enough to tell whether she believes me or not, but she does give me this intense stare before holding out her palm. "Okay, hand it over."

"Hand over what?" I'm not holding anything at the moment.

"Your Black card." She wiggles her fingers in my direction. "There's no way anybody should butcher a title and attach the wrong author to a literal classic inside of a Black-owned bookstore. Come on, hand it over. Pull out your cookout tickets, too. You're no longer invited."

I crack a smile, because now I know for sure she's flirting. "First of all, Carmen, I'm not handing over a thing. My tickets to the cookout are nonrefundable. And my Black card *never* declines."

PRETTY GIRL COUNTY

That gets a light laugh out of her—which is all the in I need to keep going.

Taking a step closer into her personal space, I stare into Carmen's growing smile.

"Second of all, if I *hadn't* read it, you should be helping me, not judging me. Toni Morrison herself didn't read Zora's work until *after* she won the National Book Critics Circle Award for her third book, *Song of Solomon*." I throw in that last bit of info to let Carmen know she's in the presence of a biblio baddie. I might start out a little slow, but I'm a literal page-turner once I have you hooked.

By the way Carmen's eyes are fixated on mine, I can tell she's hanging on to my every word.

"So, you're a Toni Morrison fan, huh?" she throws out there.

I make this next part easy for her. I've given her enough of a hard time for one day. "Yeah." I shrug. "But probably not in the way you're thinking. I'm a fan of Toni Morrison because, like, she's this really smart lady, known for writing all of these really iconic books, and there's tons of pictures all over the internet of her partying at Studio 54 every night."

Carmen squints at me. "So, you're a fan of an author because they like to club hop?"

"No." I run my fingers through my curly 'fro. "I'm a fan of what that *represents* . . ."

As a person who's already made it her life's mission to dip her toe in more than one lane, I have a lot to say on this subject. Carmen doesn't even know she's opened a whole can of worms with this one.

95

"Think about the author aesthetic when Toni began publishing. Old. White. Cis male. Tweed jacket. Confined to a dusty office, or among the tomes at an old library."

I move a little closer to Carmen. "Toni was everything publishing said she wasn't supposed to be. Black. A woman. And she wore spaghetti straps to the club on a random Tuesday night if she felt like it. That's bold. I admire people who don't subscribe to everyone else's expectations."

Now Carmen looks impressed. "Okay, I've never, *ever* heard Toni Morrison described that way."

Suddenly, I hear a loud cough behind me. I turn around, and Sommer's standing behind the register with her arms folded. "Uh, Reya, can you come here a minute?"

"Sure!" When I get to the register, Sommer leans over and whispers, "Can you get out of that poor girl's face? She is over there trying to shelve books and you're over there—"

"I know what I'm doing, Sommer."

"Do you, Reya?"

I feel like I've just spent enough energy proving to Carmen that I actually know my stuff when it comes to books. But I have a little more left in me to show Sommer, too—if that's what I need to do.

"I wouldn't be over there talking to her if I didn't think she liked me."

"She's being friendly, which is all you should be doing, too. You chose to volunteer here, so try to be at least a little professional."

PRETTY GIRL COUNTY

Okay, she has a point there. Still, I'm not wrong on this. I can prove it.

"Fine, Sommer. I will go back to business-as-usual after I do this one little thing."

Sommer folds her arms. "What's that?"

"Get her to go out with me."

Sommer can shake her head all she wants. I know what I know.

Thinking of a great way to inject Carmen into my world a bit, I saunter back across the bookstore. "So, Carmen, do you have a little Toni Morrison in you?"

Carmen considers my question. "I do a little writing—mostly poetry."

I shake my head. "No, I mean, do you have her party spirit?"

I sneak a glance back at Sommer, who rolls her eyes dramatically.

I turn back around just as Carmen is finishing a shrug. "I mean, I go to parties here and there."

"Good." I pull out my phone. "Then, I'm formally inviting you to a party I'm having Saturday night." I hand over my phone. "Add your number to my contacts, and I'll text you the details."

While Carmen's putting in her info, I shoot Sommer the most satisfying smirk.

Now that I have Carmen's number, the text-flirting can officially begin.

13
Sommer

HOURS LATER, I'M trying to remember if Reya was ever as into reading as she made it seem in front of Carmen, while I work on new designs for my *Sims* collection. Now that I think about it, we did start our own two-person book club the year we discovered that middle grade book about those kids starting their own fashion club. We would probably still be doing stuff like that if things didn't change so drastically.

But that was a long time ago. And that book wasn't a Toni Morrison novel.

Anyway, I'm elbows deep in my sketching when a few pebbles hit my window.

At first, I think it's the roof caving in, because we did have that annoying leak last April.

But when it happens again, I lift the window and poke

PRETTY GIRL COUNTY

my head out. Confusion slaps me across the jawline.

Sitting on his bike, in a sliver of grass between my house and Reya's old house, Octavius shakes his head.

"What are you doing here?" I ask. Still embarrassed by my accusations from the other day, I start rambling. "Look, I'm really sorry . . . I—"

"I didn't come for all that," he says quickly. "I came to see who's been messing with your dad's store." He points to his handlebars. "Roll with me."

I hesitate. "It's already dark out."

It's only nine, but it's way too late for me to be joyriding around Seat Pleasant on the front of anybody's handlebars.

Octavius looks unfazed. "Girl, this is my hood. Nobody's going to mess with you while you're with me. Hop up here."

I grab my shoes, go outside, and scooch up onto the front of Octavius's bike because I want to find out who's been messing with Dad's store, too.

While I grip his wrists for dear life, Octavius pedals off down the street and into the night. We ride up the hill and through the gas station, where I can literally feel Octavius's head bob behind me as he yells out, "What's up, Darryl?"

He stops on the corner of MLK, mashing the white cross-walk button a thousand times, even though we both know it won't help the light change any faster.

When the little white guy finally blinks, Octavius taps my shoulder. "Hold tight, because I don't want you slipping off and busting your head open on this road."

"If I start falling, I'm taking you down with me," I joke. But

I grip his wrists tighter when he takes off across MLK.

When we reach the empty parking lot where Dad's bookstore sits, Octavius nudges the kickstand with his foot and sets his feet down on the pavement.

Together we stare into the darkness for at least a good twenty minutes at literally nothing going on outside the store.

Finally the sound of giggling and rubber sneakers slapping on pavement slices through the night air.

A group of middle school–looking kids dart from around the back of the abandoned buildings. One boy is shaking a metal canister in his hands.

"Hey—all of y'all!" Octavius shouts. "Get in the house!"

Most of the boys scatter. But the one holding the spray paint recognizes Octavius.

Smiling, he moves toward us with his hand extended. "Oh, what's up, Tate? What you doing out here?"

Octavius allows the boy to dap him up. Then he snatches the spray paint can. "Trying to catch whoever's been messing with my friend's bookstore window, Noah."

Noah finally acknowledges me, still balancing awkwardly on Octavius' handlebars. "That's your store?" He tilts his chin like he doesn't believe it. "Yeah, right."

"It's her pops's store." Octavius says. "But it don't matter whose store it is. Stop spray painting all over everything we got." Octavius mean mugs him. "Why are you out here anyway? Don't you have school in the morning?"

Noah shrugs. "If I feel like it."

Octavius grabs Noah firmly by the shoulders, spins him

PRETTY GIRL COUNTY

around, and gently shoves him back in the direction of the apartment buildings where he lives. "You *better* feel like it. Take yourself in the house."

Sucking his teeth, Noah starts walking. Octavius nudges his kickstand back and pedals slowly behind him until Noah reaches the corner of Greig Street.

I want to thank Octavius for helping me tonight. I also want to tell him I think it's sweet the way he cares about the kids around here. The wrong person would've snitched on Noah and been obsessed with getting him in trouble to prove a point instead of guiding him in a better direction.

But I'm so weird about initiating nice moments. And I'm practically in Octavius's arms, riding on his handlebars like this, making things ten times more awkward.

So I keep my mouth shut.

When Noah disappears into his building, Octavius shakes his head, turns his bike around, and starts pedaling back toward where I live. "They out here making their own fun because there's nothing to do around here."

The playgrounds in Seat Pleasant have been falling apart for years. The nearest library is twenty minutes away in Fairmont Heights. The courts are so full of teens playing ball—which isn't *their* fault, they need things to do, too—that the younger kids have to wait hours, sometimes days, to get a game in down at Goodwin Park.

He's not lying. It's the truth.

When we finally make it back to my house, I hop off Octavius's bike and smooth down my clothes. Under the streetlights, he actually looks kind of cute—not that I would tell *him* that or anything. But something about this lighting is working for him.

"Hey, um, sorry for approaching you like that, the other day."

Octavius shrugs. "I mean, I know that new bougie school has you acting all soft now. Just don't start clutching your purse when we walk by each other."

I roll my eyes at that. Because, yeah right, I am *not* Reya Samuels. "*Anyway*, thanks for helping me check on my dad's store," I tell him. "For real, I really appreciate it."

Octavius nods, and I can't lie, his smile is kind of cute or whatever. "It wasn't nothing . . . Aye yo, Sommer."

When I turn around, he's pointing down at something on my legs. "Glad to see you finally grew out of them skinny knee-caps you used to have."

Side-*eye*.

"First of all, my kneecaps were never too skinny. *Second of all*"—and I mean this next part most of all—"this might be your way of flirting, but I am not interested."

Most of the boys around here will *still* be here next year. I've spent my entire life in Seat Pleasant. I love my hometown, but I want to see what else the world has to offer. When I do decide to date seriously, I want to be with a guy who wants the same things.

Someone like Sauce, I catch myself thinking.

Now Octavius looks offended. "Girl, don't nobody want you.

PRETTY GIRL COUNTY

I got eyes. I saw your lil Bowie Bandit drop you off the other day."

I chuckle at his reference to all the dudes from Bowie who pretend they're from the hood, when they most *definitely* live behind the gates. "Don't call him that."

Octavius peers over at me. "So, what . . . that's your man?"

"No," I say quickly.

Octavius twists his lips. "Yeah, right . . ."

"He's not. We're just doing a school thing together." I don't know why I steer away from revealing my feelings for Sauce. Maybe because, technically, he's *not* my man. And maybe, I don't know, I just don't want Octavius in my personal business like that. I just accepted the fact that he didn't vandalize my father's store. Let's not do too much now.

Octavius raises his chin and looks down at me for a second. "Aight, I believe you." Then he waves me toward my porch. "Now get in the house. You have school in the morning, too."

He waits for me to make it safely inside before taking off down the street on his ten speed. And you know what? This wasn't a bad way to spend my evening.

14
Reya

WHEN THE LITTLE blue notification pops up that Carmen's finally accepted my request and followed me back, a rush of dopamine hits my system, sending me straight through the fluffy white clouds.

We've been texting, but this digital access is a new level. I sit in my parking space a few blocks away from Grand Rising looking through each photo on her page, paying close attention to my fingers so I don't accidentally like something from four years ago.

I check out pics of her family and birthday captions. I dig into the comments to smile over the way she jokes back and forth with her friends.

Maybe I even visit her stories.

PRETTY GIRL COUNTY

Now, trust me. I feel a little weird about coming to the bookstore so soon after officially connecting on social media, too. But how was I supposed to know she would be hitting the follow button today?

I mean, I could have just driven home and gone to the store another day. But Sommer and I need to touch base on some fashion show things, and I have an idea I want to tell Mr. Watkins about. And if Carmen just so happens to be there for another in-person flirting session, so be it.

I wait in my car an additional fifteen minutes after pulling into the bookstore parking lot to avoid looking thirsty—just in case. I clean up a few gum wrappers off the floor. Then I reapply my lip gloss. Then I listen to that new song that just came out.

Finally, when I have successfully bypassed the road to Thirstville, I unbuckle my seat belt and slip out of the car.

I breeze into the store, just as casual as a freshly washed pair of distressed denim jeans. "Hey, everybody . . ."

I try to ignore the nose wrinkle from Sommer. "What are you doing here?"

"Oh, just browsing . . ." I make my way to the least thrilling section of the store—the How-To/Manuals section. I pick up one of those map foldout booklets, frown, and bring it up to the register.

"Why is this here? GPS has been around since before we were born."

Sommer slips the book of maps from my hand. "Aren't you

supposed to be looking at new fabric options today? Priorities, Reya. *Priorities.*" She folds the book back together and takes it to its place on the shelf.

"Well, I came to see if you've made any progress on that digital book you're supposed to be putting together."

This brightens Sommer's mood some. "Oh yeah. I actually have a few you can check out." She slides her tablet across the glass counter, then waits as I swipe my finger through.

"Oh yes. Cute, *cute*. Okay . . ."

I sneak a glance back at Carmen.

"Reya, get out."

"Okay, *okay*, I'm really looking now." This time I keep my eyes glued to the screen, and you know what? "The digital version of these looks *are* super cute," I tell Sommer. "So, when you color these in, they're going to match the new fabric I pick out?"

"Yup!" She strikes a pose. "This is my first paid side gig, so I've been making sure everything's extra on point."

I nod. "It shows. But, Sommer, I wanted to talk to you, too. The lookbook's not actually the only reason I'm here. I have an idea for the bookstore."

"The bookstore?" Sommer repeats, looking skeptical.

Her dad shoots her a look. "I'd like to hear it, Rey-Rey."

"So I was texting with Ms. Johnson earlier and—"

"You're texting with a customer?" Sommer interjects.

"Well, yeah . . . you know, just in case she needed more book recs and I wasn't here. Anyway, she said at least four of her friends are reading the same book, so I was thinking,

PRETTY GIRL COUNTY

if we painted a few folding chairs and arranged them in this underutilized space over *here—*"

Sommer drops her stylus on the counter and raises her eyebrows. "What are you adding to your plate now, Reya Samuels? And it better not include me, because I'm still saving for Spelman."

"Hear me out, hear me out."

Mr. Watkins nods for me to continue as I launch into my master plan. I outline a forty-five-minute gathering each month featuring a book. I half expect some resistance on their part—like, maybe it'll cost too much to host a gathering every month. Or maybe it'll be too much work. But when I'm done, Sommer looks impressed, but her dad hesitates.

"We actually had something similar a few years back. But it didn't really take off like I expected."

"Was the book club specifically for seniors—and during the day? From what I remember, there's not a lot of meetup activities for seniors around here. And plenty stop in during the day, because they hate shopping when things get super busy in the evenings. There are at least six regular customers who would definitely join something like this."

"You know what?" Mr. Watkins says. "Let's try it."

"Yeah?" I say, grinning.

"Yeah." He nods. "Are you sure you don't want to open your own bookstore one day? You've got the chops."

I shake my head. "Nope. I'm going to be too busy taking over the runways in Milan. Speaking of, Sommer, I would love for you to send me a copy of those digital sketches." With that,

I put my sunglasses back down on my nose and sail out of the store, pretending I'm not extra pumped about Sommer smiling at me on my way out.

Every busy girl needs a little downtime to recharge her batteries. In my case, I'm using my quiet time to go over a few sketches Sommer sent. She's included a hot-pink baseball jacket dripping in plastic jewel-toned appliques for streetwear, a floor-length gown with built-in cargo pockets for evening wear, a bathing suit with fluorescent chain-stitched seams, and the cutest baby doll dress with Chantilly lace resting over a scalloped collar.

"Hey, Reya, hon!" Mom comes walking in with a handful of shopping bags from her impromptu trip to the mall this morning. She dumps the bags on the floor, near our shoe basket, then comes over to give me a kiss on my cheek.

"What are you working on?" she asks, glancing down at the designs I've printed out for a closer look.

"Sommer's helping to fine-tune my designs for the FIT panel, and I'm looking over some of her ideas."

Mom picks up one of the sketches and nods. "Good for you—doing what it takes to prove to the Fashion Institute you belong there." She glances down at my printouts again. "Many people would've assumed that wait list was the end of the road—but not my baby. You're just like your mama, willing to do what it takes to achieve your dreams." She sits down beside me on the living room floor. "I'm proud of you, you know."

PRETTY GIRL COUNTY

When she wraps an arm around my shoulder and pulls me in close, a warm feeling overtakes me. My mom didn't have to say the actual words. We're so close that our love for each other shines through. Still, it's nice hearing them.

While Mom's busy giving me kudos, I ruminate over something that's been bugging me a little.

"You don't think this is a little unethical, though?" I ask my mom. "I keep looking at these designs, and they look great. But the panel wants more from *me*, and I didn't create these looks alone."

Mom thinks on this a moment. "Well, fashion design is all about finding inspiration to create a piece your way." She smiles. "Maybe Sommer is your muse."

I chew on this a moment. Maybe she's right. I have been feeling more creative since Sommer's been around.

Mom shrugs. "I'm just grateful she's able to email these to you, so you don't have to go all the way to Seat Pleasant to get them."

While I'm wondering what *that* statement is supposed to mean, Mom picks up the bathing suit sketch. "This is a fire look, but if you were wearing this down a runway, what would you add to really make this piece say something?"

I take the sketch from my mother and turn it around in my hand a bit. "I like the fluorescent stitching, but I would probably use a sturdier material to really make it stand out. I might not use as many colors, and—"

I run to my room to grab my sketchbook. "I'd probably

add something complementary to the front to tie everything together."

Mom smiles. "See, there's a way to get a little help, but use your ideas, too." She draws me close again. "As long as you still see yourself in your work, it's fine."

I breathe a sigh of relief, happy to have one less worry to think about.

Mom's hand suddenly flies to her mouth. "Oh, before I forget . . ."

She grabs her phone and pulls up an email. "You know I've been working behind the scenes doing my best to convince the producers to film your fashion show."

I sit up so fast my sketchbook slides off my lap onto the floor. "And?" A slow smile appears on her face.

"And . . . they finally agreed."

"WHAT?!" I waste no time jumping into my mother's arms and squealing loud enough to rattle the artwork over the couch.

I've been on her since getting wait-listed about drumming up a little clout by having my work featured on the show. Now my mother just gifted me the biggest possible boost to my fashion career.

"You really made it happen, Mom," I say, my voice thick with emotion. I brush a few tears from my eyes, completely in awe of my mother's ability to do the impossible.

Joking, she does a little hair flip with her hands. "Um, *hello*? Don't I always? I am a Samuels woman, you know."

Yeah, I get it. But I don't think my mother understands how much of an inspiration she is to me. I mean, I wouldn't even be a Samuels woman without her. But being around her and watching how she moves is setting me up to win just like her. Her tenacity, her stubbornness, her refusal to settle for less have all been traits that have helped her be great. It may take me some time to get on her level, but trust and believe, I'm going to be just like her someday.

15
Sommer

"DO YOU REALLY think this kickback at Reya's house is going to have all the neighborhoods peacing it up poolside?" I ask Amara and Reed in the Uber on Saturday afternoon.

Reed chuckles. "You saw the evite. The Reya Samuels First Annual Stop the Beef Soiree is the first step toward world peace. What could go wrong?"

"My feelings exactly." I laugh as we turn into Woodmore, Bowie's nicest and most prestigious neighborhood.

Yes, I'm on my way to a Reya Samuels party. No, we aren't friends again. She just thinks she's slick adding Amara and Reed to the invite list to make ghosting this event impossible.

"I've never been inside those gates." Amara practically swooned when she got the invite.

"I just want to stand around and daydream about what

PRETTY GIRL COUNTY

mansion life is going to be like for me in ten, fifteen years," Reed said, smiling.

No questions about how Reya got their numbers.

No thoughts on why they've never been invited to a Samuels soiree before.

Just one sketchy reason to get inside the Woodmore gates and here we are.

Against my better judgment, I gave up my Saturday evening shift to come here. The missing money in my paycheck already burns my soul.

As we head down the main road of the development, I shake my head at all the random cars parked along the curb. Our Uber driver turns off on the next street, and now the sight of cars double-parked and blocking driveways makes me doubt I'll be able to find Reya in her own backyard.

"Did she invite the whole PG County?" I wonder aloud.

As our driver pulls up to Reya's house, I notice Sauce used his Brat Pack privilege to park behind Azadeh's jeep in the driveway next door.

As we get out of our Uber, it hits me that I've never seen Reya's house. Even in the months after she moved when we were still pretending to be best friends, before our daily texting tapered off to nothing, she never invited me over—not once. This sad fact burns me up a little, but I try to tuck away my personal feelings.

Starting drama is probably a faux pas at a Stop the Beef party.

Amara, Reed, and I walk up a long driveway and bypass

six huge stone lions standing next to their own porch column. The house is a simple white color, but I count at least three half-moon-shaped balconies on the front of the house and two on the sides.

So, basically, Reya and her mom live in a White House dupe? Okay, got it.

We don't bother walking up the porch steps. Per Reya's invite instructions, my friends and I go around the side of the house and through a white picket gate, until we are knee-deep in the festivities. The backyard is huge and perfectly land-scaped. Box-cut hedges line the property, and a pool sparkles in the sunlight. Everything gives off major country club vibes, even though as far as I know, only two people live here.

Scanning the party, I recognize a few models from the fash-ion show and . . . literally no one else. I'm so busy scoping the scene, I don't realize my friends have broken away from our agreed-upon buddy system until they're already on the way back to me.

"Oh my gawwwwd," Amara says, speed-walking across the expansive yard. "They're handing out chilled shrimp with little paper cups of cocktail sauce!"

Reed can't even make eye contact with me. He's too busy craning his neck for another view of the buffet table set up in the back corner. "There's no limit on the amount you can eat, either. I've had at least four already. I might go back for another."

"Reed," I go, making a face. "Please stop acting like you

PRETTY GIRL COUNTY

haven't been anywhere before. It's shrimp. You can get a whole box of them at Popeyes."

Reed glances back at the table again. "Are they free, though?" He doesn't bother waiting for an answer. "Let me go grab a few more before they run out."

I shake my head as Amara and Reed disappear into the crowd again. I'm already planning to cut them off before the night is over.

At least half the kids in here are sitting on lounge chairs next to the pool, talking and hanging out.

A commotion on the deck makes me look up just as Reya's mom walks out. My heart quickens. The last time Angelica Samuels saw me was before freshman year, the day she and Reya were moving out and she came over to gift an armchair Mom had always liked. But the last time I saw Ms. Angelica was when she went viral for splashing champagne in her castmate's face.

New cast members always bear the weight of proving to the rest of the cast that they belong. In Reya's mom's case, she had the literal boat to prove it. On her first season she took her castmates out on the water, for a nice day at sea, and what does one of the OG Housewives do? Immediately ask if the boat seats are made of pleather "because they appear to be two seconds away from peeling."

"I guess this is what new money gets you," the opulent octogenarian said, shooting the rest of her minions haughty looks.

Now, Reya's mom could've stayed quiet. But this was an

opportunity for her to make a splash and keep her spot on the show. So she stood up and smiled brightly before saying, "Yes, new money *did* buy this boat, Heather. New money also bought this champagne. Why don't you have a *taste!*"

Before Heather had time to duck, eight ounces of the finest champagne new money could buy was dripping from her mink eyelashes, 4-carat diamond stud earrings, and silk Roberto Cavalli blouse. That champagne toss had the rest of the cast in total disarray—screaming, scrambling, and scolding, "Violence is so not *Potomac!*"

Ms. Angelica might be (in)famous now, but for a long time, she was a "play mom" to me who let me stay at her house when my parents were working late, and played hide-and-seek with me and Reya. Once she popped out of the middle of nowhere after almost an hour of us searching for her.

"See, girls, winning's always about paying attention to the littlest opportunities," she said then, pointing to a barely there crawl space, "and wiggling your way in."

But, when I think back on it, Reya's mom didn't have a lot of time to be a play mom back then—she was always in school, taking classes or studying for some big test.

Still, when she could hang out with us, she was awesome.

Now I'm staring up at the two-story deck in the fanciest house I've ever been to. She might as well be miles away. I watch her hold up another drink that I pray she isn't planning to hurl. But instead, she proposes a toast.

"Cheers to the end of high school," she coos at a crowd of my half-listening peers. "But no eating or drinking in the

PRETTY GIRL COUNTY

pool, and no one better step *foot* on the black-eyed Susans I've just planted." Reya's mom holds up her glass flute. "Cheers, kiddos!"

Then the woman whose tagline is "I put the cute in prosecute" walks back inside without even noticing me.

This backyard is too crowded for me to feel this alone. Amara and Reed are busy getting cozy with the buffet table. Sauce is holding court near a group of guys. I can't find Reya. And Carmen hasn't responded to my text about whether she's here or not. The only other person I know here is . . . well, Reya's mom.

I look up at the deck again, an idea forming.

This is the Stop the Beef party, right?

I should go inside and ask Ms. Samuels why she never brought Reya back to visit. Why she never offered to pick me up and bring me out here while my parents were working. Why they both just up and moved to Bowie and forgot the Watkins family ever existed.

All the feelings I've had over our friendship breakup suddenly rise to the surface, prompting me to march up the deck stairs and storm into Reya's house.

I'm thinking I'll catch Reya's mom alone, and I'll air my grievances in private, without the cameras or fan reactions.

Instead, I find Reya's mom huddled around her large kitchen island with a group of her own friends—not her fellow Housewives, at least—but still, they're a group of Woodmore moms who look like they wear diamond necklaces to breakfast and are definitely tuned into my arrival.

So much for my one-on-one opportunity.

When Ms. Angelica spots me, her face lights up brighter than the sun. "*Little* Sommer Watkins. Look at you all grown up!" She squeals as she comes over to swoop me up into the tightest hug I've ever experienced in my life.

"Ladies," she says, presenting me to the group. "Meet my baby girl, Sommer. I practically raised this sweetie pie."

Umm?! That's not exactly true. If anything, my parents were babysitting Reya while Ms. Angelica took all those night classes. But I accept the kiss she plants on my cheek anyway.

After the kiss, Ms. Angelica takes a long, drawn-out moment to lean me at arm's length so she can get a good look at me.

"You have grown into a beautiful young woman!" she says with tears in her eyes. "How long has it been, baby?"

"You tell me," I want to say. But, you know what? Not the time. Not the place. Instead, I let her fawn all over me like a doll she's just opened on Christmas morning.

Instead I give her a short but honest answer. "A long time."

Things are going better than I expected, I guess. But I'm still unwilling to erase the years of resentment I felt over this woman taking my best friend away.

Until she leans in my ear and whispers, "I'm so sorry we haven't been back to see you and your mom and dad." She stares at me with sincerity in her eyes. "But between all these cases and the TV show, and trying to pick up a brand deal or two, I've been working like a dog to keep up with these Mc-Mansion payments . . . ya know?"

PRETTY GIRL COUNTY

Now, *that* I can understand. But we both know it's more than that. Even if her mom was super busy, Reya could've caught the bus back around the way. *She* was my best friend. *We* promised to have each other's back forever—not the grown-ups.

"It's okay, Auntie," I tell her instead, planting a return kiss on her cheek.

"So how *are* your mom and dad?" she asks.

"They're doing okay," I tell her.

"Good, good." Ms. Angelica finally releases my shoulders, but she holds up her pointer finger to let me know she's not quite done with me yet.

"Now, while I have you," she says, walking back into the kitchen area, "tell me something, sweetie. If you were filming a scene exposing someone for tax fraud, would you reveal what you know by the stove?" She walks over to the six-burner oven range and turns one of the knobs. "So they'll feel the heat? Or . . ."

She cuts the stove off and scurries over to her stainless-steel fridge. "Would you expose them near the freezer to send the message that revenge is best served cold?"

Her mom friends giggle and drink more wine from their glasses.

"Umm . . ." I force an awkward smile. "I probably wouldn't expose someone's tax problems on TV. That seems kind of—"

But before I can even finish my statement, disappointment crosses her face. "You would if you wanted to return for another season." Her eyes find their way to my feet.

"And, baby girl? I know I used to let you and Reya track dirt all over my cheap vinyl floors back in Seat Pleasant. But here in Woodmore? We don't *do* shoes in the house."

"Oh, um, I'll just head back outside," I say while I slowly die of embarrassment. I turn quickly on my heel and head back down the hallway I entered from. I open the door I swear I came in through, but instead of the yard, a darkened garage with a few boxes and a gigantic boat (?!) stares back at me. The same boat Ms. Angelica was brunching on when she splashed champagne in Heather's face.

"Why aren't you outside with us?" a deep voice asks.

Now, I don't know about you, but whenever I'm in someone's home that's much nicer than mine, I'm always spending all my time either trying to prove I won't break anything or reassuring the host I don't steal.

In this case, I blurt out, "Don't worry, I don't steal. I was just looking for the door."

Sauce laughs, stepping into sight. And I feel silly for what I said.

To play off that embarrassing moment, I point into the darkened garage. "I wonder if that's the boat from the show."

"I think it is," Sauce says.

"The champagne toss," we both say at once. We lock eyes and laugh.

Then I shake my head, because, like, I'm staring at an honest-to-goodness boat in Reya's garage. So I can't stop myself from saying, "I still can't believe Reya lives like this. I mean, who even has a boat?"

PRETTY GIRL COUNTY

Now Sauce looks embarrassed. "Well, actually, my family has one."

"Does it just sit there, or do you guys ever take it out on the water?"

I've heard people talking about owning a boat. And I've seen other people's boats sitting under carports. But I don't know if I've ever actually witnessed someone take said boat out for a spin. I guess I just always thought they were status symbols or something. Like a "Hey, here's proof that I am rich—*very rich*."

Sauce shrugs. "Every now and then." He side-glances me. "Why? You want me to take you out on it sometime?"

Now, if I were a lovergirl, I'd be pulling on a sailor's cap and heading for the Chesapeake Bay right now. But since I'm me, I immediately question his motives.

Is Sauce being serious or sarcastic? Will his dad write this boat ride off on their taxes as giving a charity boat ride to a disadvantaged youth? Yes, Sean gave me a ride home the other day, and we've chatted a few times, but making actual plans to hang out? That's a different story.

While I'm mulling on this, Sauce reaches over and grabs my phone. "How about this? I'll put my number in your phone. You can text me if you ever want to take the boat for a ride on the water."

Sauce hands me back my phone with the name Sean written in the contacts, with a tiny little yacht emoji next to his name.

I stare for a second at the name of the hottest guy in our school, whose number is now in my phone.

He points to my phone. "Send me a text with your name so I can lock you in . . . Cool?"

I barely eke out "Cool" before he turns and disappears down the hall, leaving me wondering if Sean "Sauce" Levi just asked me out on a date.

16
Reya

"HEY, BRYCE AND Marlon!" I wave to my friends as I work the party. "Having a good time?"

"Yep!" they reply between football throws.

Dressed in a lacy white Michael Kors dress paired with strappy white lace-up sandals, I am a walking white flag. I *dare* someone to try and start something while I'm working the party carrying my sparkly peace-symbol clutch.

I scan the party, hoping another important guest is in attendance. Finally, I see him. "Cody?" I call across the yard. "Everything cool?"

"Yeah, these grilled kabobs are *on point*," he goes, bobbing his head to the music a few feet away from where Bryce is playing football.

Look at that. *Unity.*

Out of the corner of my eye, I see Sean walking over to me. The funny look on his face tells me something's bothering him.

"What's wrong with you?" I ask him.

"*Cocktail* Sauce?" he says, pointing to the buffet table. "When we just released a line of jalapeño-flavored Mumbo Sauce. It's the disrespect for me . . ." He shakes his head.

"Boy, not everything is about you." I make a face. "Who puts Mumbo Sauce on shrimp, anyway?"

Sauce looks over my head at the buffet table. "You could've at least put a few bottles on the table."

"Well, run back to your house and grab a few. Problem solved. Everything doesn't have to be a prime-time drama."

*Any*way.

It's time to find one of *my* personal favorites.

I scan the yard several times as fear creeps up my spine that maybe Carmen found somewhere more interesting to be tonight.

Then I see her, lying back in a lounge chair by the pool.

I head across the yard.

"You're here? Why didn't you come find me?" I ask as soon as I get up close.

Throwing her hands back behind her head, Carmen is giving cool and unbothered. "I haven't been here long. Plus, all your friends are here. I didn't want to hog all your time."

My smile widens. "Take all the time you want." Then, feeling like I'm hovering, I put my hands on my hips. "It feels ridiculous trying to talk to you while you're laid out like that!"

Carmen flashes me that easygoing smile. "This was the only

PRETTY GIRL COUNTY

place to sit. But if you have somewhere better we can chill, I'll definitely follow."

Well, *okay*!

While I'm briefly considering the chairs over by the firepit, a football comes flying toward me, crashing directly into the peace symbol my mother painstakingly cornrowed into the side of my head before the party.

"My bad!" Bryce yells. "Come on, Reya, toss it back!"

I'm mad enough to stomp a hole in this football with the heel of my shoe. But that wouldn't be modeling peaceful comradery, would it?

Controlling my temper, I shout back, "You're the one who threw it over here. Get it yourself!"

I hold out my hand, inviting Carmen to lace her fingers through mine. Then I part the sea of seniors hanging in my backyard, to lead my bookstore bae to one very special place inside the house.

I walk Carmen upstairs and into my bedroom.

"Ta-da . . . you have now entered Reya's Romantic Resort . . ."

I plop down on my bed to give Carmen time to take it all in. The posters on the wall. The pink-painted furniture. The soft, comfortable rug Mom had shipped back here when she and the cast took a girls' trip to Greece last summer.

I'm expecting a little admiration that my room is so tidy and color coordinated. But Carmen has a confused look on her face.

125

"Whose room is this again?"

"Mine."

"What happened to the hanging chandelier and the bay window made of pure crystal?"

It takes a moment for what she's talking about to register.

"Ohhhh, you're talking about the house from the show." I fan away the thought. "That's my room at the Potomac House. All fake. Basically a rented Airbnb. I don't even know who could feel comfortable snuggled up at a bay window made of crystal anyway."

"Wait, so the bedroom where you and your mom had 'the birds and the bees' talk isn't your bedroom?"

I raise an eyebrow. "You watch the show?"

A bashful look appears on Carmen's face. "I might have watched a few episodes to check you and your home life out a bit."

Ahh, so she *is* super into me. Feeling like I've just completed a victory lap, I walk over and slip my arms around Carmen's waist. "No, that isn't my bedroom. That talk wasn't real, either. My mom talked to me about sex before I even hit middle school."

Carmen takes a few steps back from my embrace. "But why? The house, I mean. Not the sex talk, obviously."

A little put off by her snuggle rejection and already tired of this conversation, I shrug. "Who knows? Showbiz, I guess. Curated content to capture the right fanbase . . . blah, blah, blah."

She frowns. "But that's fake."

"I know . . . I said that." I go in for another snuggle moment, but Carmen sideswipes me again.

PRETTY GIRL COUNTY

"You're cool with that?"

Uggghhhh! Why is she ruining a perfectly good romantic moment? "Carmen, I don't really have much to do with the show. I do what my mom tells me and then move on with my everyday life. Trust me," I say, giving Carmen my flirtiest look, "I'd much rather hang out with you than shoot scenes."

For the next several minutes, I lead Carmen by the hand around my bedroom, pointing out all the things I've created to make the room feel like me.

"I don't get it," Carmen says, "Why don't you all film here? This actually looks better than that extra fancy Potomac bedroom. It looks more you."

Are we on this again? "I don't know. It's easier to compartmentalize, I guess. Show stuff goes on in Potomac. Family life is here at home. School and fashion stuff is at Baldwin."

"Book stuff is at the bookstore," Carmen finishes for me.

I give her a sharp look. "What's that supposed to mean?"

Carmen shrugs. "It just seems like you should be you, no matter who you're around or where you are."

I raise an eyebrow. "So, twerking . . . that's acceptable at church?" I dare her to try to make her point stick.

Carmen smiles at where I'm taking this. "I don't twerk at all. It's not me." She moves a little figurine on my desk. "But I do have a mean two-step, and I would do that at church if the mood hit me." She glances out the door. "Or in your backyard if you ever get around to getting the music started."

I laugh. Fine, she got me. "Want to head down?"

127

She meets my gaze. "Yes, but first, can I tell you something?"

I feel it coming . . . the big "I've loved you from the moment I laid eyes on your hand-painted jeans. You are the apple of my eye, the key to my soul, and I just"—

Carmen clears her throat. "I really love . . ."

My heart soars.

". . . your window display at Grand Rising. But there's just one thing that's been bugging me."

My bubble is popped harder than a firecracker on the Fourth of July. "What?"

Carmen draws her knees up to her chest. "The storefront window looks dope—you really did a good job with it."

"But?" Because come on, let's get to the point.

"But I'm not really feeling your book choices."

Well, now I'm offended. "What's wrong with my book choices? Some of those books are huge bestsellers."

"And that's cool and all, but they're all romance."

My hand immediately goes to my hip. "And what's wrong with romance?" I swear, if Carmen ends up being one of those "romance isn't literary" snobs, I'm pushing her into the pool.

"Nothing's wrong with romance. I'm a huge Beverly Jenkins fan myself."

Oh, *okay*. Because I thought—

"But you can't have a display window full of *just* romance at the store."

My hand flies back to my hip. "And why not?"

"Because Grand Rising is so much more than romance. To

PRETTY GIRL COUNTY

catch every type of customer, you want to include a sampling of all the kinds of books a reader can find inside."

Fine. Carmen did her little big one with that. Her point is turning out to be pretty valid.

"So, what do you suggest, Bookstore Bae?"

The minute my secret nickname for her slides out, I'm a little embarrassed. That nickname is for private group chat use only, not to ever be used in public.

But Carmen just smiles and shoves her hands into her pockets. "I suggest we get together another time and talk about it more. I know how you like to compartmentalize, and a party isn't time for work."

Beaming, I ask, "Is this your way of asking me on a date? If so, I'd like to throw out a few dream date aesthetics. Jet-setting. Private islands. Crystal-blue waters. Sun and heat."

Carmen grins. "Trust me, when it's time for our first official date, I'm going to take you somewhere you'll never forget."

17
Sommer

NEXT SATURDAY, I'M pulling an early shift at the bookstore so later on I can sail away with Sauce. I pull up our text chain for what feels like the hundredth time, trying to discern whether this is a friend-hang or a date.

Sauce: Hey Sommer, was thinking of taking
the boat out Saturday. You in?

Sommer: Sure. Sounds fun.

Sauce: Make sure you bring sunscreen.
It gets pretty hot on the boat deck.

Sommer: No problem. Anything else I should bring?

PRETTY GIRL COUNTY

Sauce: Nope, that's it.

As long as you're on the boat, I'm good.

Like, what's that text about? Is it flirting? A friendly gesture?

It's hard for me to read between the lines when there are so few of them. I text back a few heart emojis and leave it to him to decipher. But just in case that *was* flirting, I hit up Wigs Beauty Supply and purchase an extra-long drawstring faux ponytail so I can cosplay my own Little Mermaid look.

I'm wearing it to work. The customers will just have to deal, since I don't have much time after my shift before I have to be on the boat. Maybe I'll use this new look to hand sell a few copies of *Storm: Dawn of a Goddess* by Tiffany D. Jackson.

Since it's still early at the store there's not a lot of foot traffic yet, so I work on my *Sims* designs while Dad chats quietly on the phone with someone.

"Are you sure you don't need me to stay longer?" I ask Dad. "Carmen's never taken a shift by herself before. She might need my help."

Dad sets his phone on the counter, looking distracted. "Nah, that won't be necessary."

A part of me is hoping Dad will tell me to stay and get me out of having to end up face-to-face with whatever comes from this boat ride with Sauce.

It's not just the maybe-possibly-dating stuff, either. Even with Reya's money in hand, it's hard to relax about my finances. Every moment I'm not here is a dollar I'm not earning. And in this case, I'm *spending* money just to go on this excursion.

As nice as he seems, I wonder if Sauce is worth the risk of an entire Uber ride over to the waterfront.

Once I'm actually out there, though, I realize I might have been thinking too far into all of this. Sauce isn't by himself. Marlon, Bryce, Azadeh, a few fashion club girlies, and Sauce's *dad* are standing on the dock with him.

Is this what the friend zone looks like?

"I hope you don't mind," Sauce says, looking embarrassed. "Once I mentioned I was taking the boat out, my friends sort of invited themselves. And my parents don't let me take the boat out by myself, so . . ."

I mean, *that's* understandable. Recalling the moment weeks ago when Sauce crashed into me in the cafeteria, I don't know if I would trust him sailing my expensive boat on his own, either.

"It's cool," I tell him. Because what else can I say? It's not like I'm chartering fancy yachts every day. But, dang, if I knew all these people would be joining us, I would've told my own friends to come along. Amara and Reed would love a boat ride.

I'm almost wishing Reya were here. I haven't turned into one of her little underclassman fans or anything. It just would be nice to have someone here slightly more familiar than a casual acquaintance.

I can forget about any last-minute pink cars pulling into the parking lot, though. Everyone saw the epic rant she posted on socials this morning.

PRETTY GIRL COUNTY

> Don't text! Don't call! Don't send over morse code! If I don't
> spend today locked in my room finishing up fashion show stuff,
> my life is ruined!!!!!

Anyway, after Sauce's dad—a balding, stern-faced older version of Sauce in a captain's hat—goes over safety instructions with everyone, he gets behind the wheel of the boat.

"Sail-away party!" Azadeh yells, holding her Beats speaker in the air. A few of the other girls shimmy out of their sundresses and start dancing, revealing an array of fluorescent bikinis. Even Bryce gets a little sturdy once the beat drops.

Sauce remains seated next to me, where I'm more comfortable watching what's going on.

I mean, my dancing skills are on point, okay? But my moves are usually reserved for family gatherings and the occasional wedding. I don't know these kids like that. Plus, I'm currently enjoying the wind whipping past my face as the boat picks up speed.

After a few moments, Sauce leans over. "You look nice," he says quietly in my ear. The way his lips tickle my ear makes up for all the extras currently dropping it low all over the deck. "Did you do something different to your hair?"

Self-consciously, I check for the million and one bobby pins I stuck into the base of my ponytail to secure everything in place. Cool, nothing's sliding around and blowing in the breeze, yet. "Nothing too special," I tell Sauce coyly. "I just pinned my hair up."

"Sauce, come show us that dance you were doing in study hall the other day!" Azadeh shouts.

From behind the wheel of the boat, Sauce's dad turns around and frowns.

Ducking a little under his dad's gaze, Sauce yells over his shoulder, "Nah, I'm going to chill out here for a while." He pauses. "Y'all were there. Have Bryce give everybody a re-enactment."

But his dad still looks a way. "Your mom and I don't send you to school to clown around, son."

Embarrassing.

I'll tell you one thing, my parents may not own a boat, but they do have enough self-awareness to refrain from chastising me in front of my friends like I'm still a toddler.

Sauce shrinks further under the weight of his father's deep voice. His vulnerability is relatable. So I grab his hand for support.

I cringe for a second, hoping I'm not looking extra thirsty out here in the middle of the Potomac River, and all. But it's not like Sauce is pulling any fingers away, so I settle down and quit overthinking things.

Once the Brat Pack and Sauce's dad are back focusing on their own activities, it's just Sauce and me, in our own little world, which feels great—until the clouds start fading and the sun comes out in full force.

Already sweating, I lean into Sauce's ear. "Is there somewhere I can change?"

He nods toward the stairs. "Downstairs in the bathroom next to the captain's quarters," he says.

Fanning myself from the sudden heat, I head downstairs, squeeze myself into the bathroom that turns out to be smaller than a broom closet, slip out of my clothes, and shimmy into my simple one-piece suit.

When I'm done changing, I step out of the bathroom and Azadeh is standing there.

"I'm all done if you need to use it," I tell her.

But she just stands there, staring at me, making me so uncomfortable, I start to wonder if she thinks I'm stealing captain hats or life vests down here on this fancy boat. I *almost* start my "Don't worry, I don't steal" monologue.

But look, I'm not a thief, and quite frankly? I don't owe this girl an explanation—this isn't even her boat.

While I'm attempting to walk around her, she blurts out, "So, are you and Reya best friends again?"

Ohhh, so this is what all the staring is about. "No. We're just working together. *Trust me*, you still have your best friend position."

She looks relieved. "Oh, okay, cool. I know—well, I know what your friendship meant to her back in the day. So I just wasn't sure or whatever."

"She said that?" I'm shocked Azadeh even knows my name. According to Sauce, Reya didn't really talk about me. "I didn't think Reya talked about life before high school." Specifically me and her Seat Pleasant roots.

"We *are* best friends, Sommer. We talk about more than Chanel purses, you know." She shrugs. "It's cool how you're helping her, especially if you're not friends."

I shift uncomfortably in a way that has nothing to do with the hot weather. I don't know how "cool" it is to be price gouging Reya for my opinions on her fashion collection. But, if Azadeh isn't judging me, I guess I won't be too hard on myself, either.

"Yeah, Reya's always been talented," I admit. "I hope she gets into FIT."

Suddenly, Azadeh wraps her arms around me, squeezing so tight. "Me too."

Okay now, not too much. I'm already getting in too deep with one, possibly two Brat Pack members. I need some time before letting my guard down with the rest of the crew.

I shoot Azadeh an awkward smile and together we walk back up to the deck, where Sauce has joined his friends on the other side of the boat. "Come dance with me, Sommer," he yells.

A small part of me cringes over my simple navy blue one-piece suit, while all the other girls are decked out in black-and-gold Versace bikinis and lavish, colorful Dolce & Gabbana sets. But I force myself to go join them.

Now, for me to explain to you how to get to the other end of the boat, you have to picture how the whole thing works. There's plenty of space to relax and snack and dance with the friends on the front and back of the boat. But that little transition area? On the side of the boat? That's where things get

PRETTY GIRL COUNTY

sketch. You can't get to either side of the boat without shimmying yourself across a very narrow "breezeway," stepping one foot in front of the other, body pressed against the plexiglass.

Let's just say someone should have warned me.

I do my part by carefully gripping the shiny metal handrail and sliding, very carefully, across the custom, imported wood planks.

But suddenly my foot slips and I'm stumbling back, arms flailing. Azadeh reaches for me and Sauce rushes over, but they're both too late. I'm falling off the boat, backward, into the cold, *brown* Potomac waters.

I'm an okay swimmer, so I immediately bobble back up, kicking and splashing. Now, at this point, I'm doing okay. My nose and my mouth are above water. All I have to do is wait to be saved.

Except.

A cool breeze is currently massaging my scalp—and not at the front of my head where I braided in a few cornrows. I'm talking about the *top middle*. Where the ponytail used to be.

Bobby pins are falling like rain and all I can do is flail my arms and scream "Arrggh! Help!" which means my hair piece is somewhere under the sea.

"Sommer, grab hold of this!" Azadeh screams, dangling one of the life preservers from the edge of the boat. She thinks I can't tread water—that I'm struggling to survive out here in this murky water.

She doesn't know my real struggle—that my ponytail is somewhere under the sea with Sebastian the crab.

I hold off on grabbing that life preserver until I spot a glimpsing of my little pony floating on top of the water a few feet away.

"Sommer, please! Try harder! Use your arms!"

The last thing I want is to scare Azadeh and cause her to send distress signals out to the Coast Guard, but some things can't be helped. I duck down under the water again, to hide my ponyless look. Holding my breath, I paddle around trying to connect with the soggy bundle of hair, but I can't see in the murky waters, and I'm basically clamping air like a Maryland snow crab at this point.

Another loud splash distracts me, and this time when I come up for air, Sauce is in the water, looking like Black Michael Phelps, gliding across the water toward my bobbling pony. He grabs it in one hand, treads over to me, and grabs me with his other hand, then he paddles back to the boat.

After we're both back on board, Sauce spits a mouthful of water out, then holds my limp hair up like a prize trophy. Everyone starts to clap, and I run to find a forgotten beach shirt to sling over my head.

Everyone on board makes a big show clapping and whooping it up for Sauce's rescue. But Sauce's dad is pissed. "I told you kids that boat safety is nothing to play with. We're turning around!"

This time, Sauce ignores his father's annoyance and focuses on me as he ushers us to the back of the boat.

"Sit right here a second." He disappears for a moment, and when he reemerges, he has white towels in his hands.

PRETTY GIRL COUNTY

Sauce sits down next to me and wraps a fluffy white towel around my body.

Feeling the heat sizzling from our closeness, I scooch over some and attempt a little joke to cool the mood. "Is this how you get girls to fall for you? Rescuing them when they fall off your boat?"

This makes Sauce chuckle. "Something like that." He watches patiently while I try and fail to reattach my ponytail. "Need help?"

"I think it might be a lost cause," I say, laying my limp hair down next to me. "I might as well take my hair out now. I'm not going to be sitting on this boat rocking straight-backs while everyone else is all glammed out."

"Okay, so let me help you with that, then," Sauce says, cracking his knuckles. "I've helped my mom take her hair out plenty of times before her hair appointments."

I side-eye him. "Are you being serious right now?"

"Why not?"

My heart continues skipping beats after I *explicitly* told it to act normal. But I can't help it. I like him. There. Happy now? I like Sauce.

"Fine, you start on the left. I'll work on the right."

Together, while the rest of the Brat Pack cuts the music and sits quietly—under strict orders from Sauce's dad—Sauce and I work on unbraiding my hair until it's a wet, curly Afro.

I immediately dig my fingers into my scalp and scratch—the most luxurious feeling in the world after finally being released from a protective style.

"Your hair looks so cute like that," Sauce says, admiring my curls.

"Tuh, it won't be so cute once it air-dries before I've had a chance to untangle it."

"I think you look cute, whatever hairstyle you have," Sauce goes.

I try to hide my growing smile.

"I'll bet you say that to all the girls," I deflect.

He nudges my leg with his. "Nope. Why can't it be that I just like you?"

I swallow hard and ask a question that's been on my mind. "Why now?"

"What do you mean?"

"Sauce, we've passed each other in the halls for the last four years, we've had at least two classes together, and you've never come at me like this." I try to breathe through all the thumping in my chest. "So why now?"

Sauce looks down a moment. "I guess it's just easier to shoot my shot now. We're graduating in a few weeks and won't see each other if you turn me down. Especially with you going to school in the ATL in the fall."

I glance in his direction. "You know about Spelman?"

He smiles. "Anybody who pays attention knows how much you love Spelman." He goes quiet again. "Long story short, rejection sucks—and I was trying to avoid it."

I wave him off. "Like that matters. Girls at our school are all over you . . . It's not possible to feel rejected when you have your choice of—"

PRETTY GIRL COUNTY

"They aren't you."

We lock eyes a moment. Suddenly, he's not Sauce—the rich kid who lives behind the gates and spends his weekends on luxury boats. For the first time, I see . . . Sean.

My lips are so close to his, I could taste them if I wanted to.

I glance up to make sure his dad isn't paying attention to us. Then I grab Sauce's hand, and lead him back down to the bottom deck—where we snuggle up in the tiniest little sitting area to kiss. Again. And again. And again.

I feel like every cliché out there as I float into my house hours later. I'm so busy experiencing tiny bursts of happiness, I almost don't notice my dad sitting silently in the living room until he lets out a sigh. I start to tell him how great the boat ride was, how scenic everything looked on the water, how the river wasn't so brown up close.

But the look on his face stops me.

"Is everything all right?" I ask him.

Dad's hands are now steepled and covering his face. When he finally reveals his face again, his expression looks pained. "Nothing you need to be worried about" is all he says.

But I know that look. It's the same one he had when the layoffs happened all those years ago. Before he opened the bookstore. Something is wrong, and I need to know what it is. "Tell me what's going on, Dad."

Dad looks at me for a long moment, like he's trying to figure out whether he can trust me with whatever info he's

141

holding in. "Promise you won't worry?" he asks.

Great. Now I'm extra nervous. "I'll try . . ."

Dad's shoulders droop. "I've been having conversations with the county about all these boarded-up buildings around here."

"Okay . . ."

"And it looks like they're finally going to do something with the street where the bookstore sits."

My heart leaps. "Dad, that's amazing. What are they talking about building?"

But Dad's shoulders are still sunken. He doesn't look as overjoyed as I would expect.

He looks down at his wedding ring—twisting it around his finger a few times before speaking again. "The truth is, in order to build all of these great things they're planning, they're going to have to make other changes."

He finally looks over at me again. "In a few months, the entire space in our shopping center will be gutted—including Grand Rising."

My heart drops to the floor. "What?"

For a second, I can't even talk. But finally I manage to give voice to my worst fear. "Will you lose the store?"

"I don't know, Sommer. I just don't know if we can afford to move," my dad says with another heavy sigh.

I immediately go into action mode. "What can I do to help? Do I need to work more shifts? I will if you need me."

Sadness lurks in my dad's eyes. "Your mother and I agreed that working in the store was a good way to teach you responsibility and contributing to your dream. But you're still a child,

PRETTY GIRL COUNTY

Sommer. And honestly, we both think you've been working too hard lately." Dad sighs. "You have your whole life to work. But being a kid is over before you can blink. I work too hard for my kid not to understand what it means to truly be a kid."

"But, Dad."

"I'm serious, Sommer. This store problem is something for your mother and me to handle. I don't want you taking this on. If I have to fire you, I will . . ."

But we both know that in a couple of months, there may not be a store to fire me from.

18
Reya

I WOULD'VE *LOVED* being a witness to the Sean/Sommer boat link up.

Unfortunately, I have work to do. While my friends are out sailing, I'm in my zone, adding strategic cutouts to pants and bedazzling hemlines.

The doorbell ringing is the only thing capable of cutting through my workflow. For a second I expect my mom to get it, but then I remember that she's also working, logging extra hours at her law office, making up for the dent that filming a boozy lunch with the other Housewives put in her week.

I put down the scarf I'm working on and head downstairs.

When I open the front door, Carmen's standing there, looking fine AF in a red bathing suit under a pair of red swimming trunks. She's holding a swim bag in her hand.

PRETTY GIRL COUNTY

"What are you doing here?" I ask her.

"I can't tell you everything just yet. But are you ready for your dream date?" she asks.

I look at all the work I'm leaving behind if I don't focus on priorities. But this is *Carmen* we're talking about. "I can't go anywhere with you right now, unless you've planned some once-in-a-lifetime jet-setting, can't-miss private-island excursion or something."

There's a twinkle in her eyes when she says, "You would be surprised at what I've managed to throw together."

This intrigues me. "What do you have planned?"

"You have to pop out to find out."

That's it. She's got me. I snatch a pair of sunglasses and a swimsuit from my room as she instructed and return to the door with my car keys in my hand. "I'll drive. Just tell me where we're headed."

Carmen nods slowly. "I want this to be a full surprise, so I'll be the GPS."

I try to hold a conversation while we're riding, but my brain is going a mile a minute, trying to suss out clues on where we're going.

So far, we've gone down Route 202, passing PG Community College, Jasper's, and Woodmore Towne Center. When we stop at the light next to FedEx Stadium, and Carmen tells me to turn left, I raise an eyebrow. "Where are we going?" I ask.

"I told you . . . It's a *surprise*," Carmen insists.

"Yeah, but nothing that way gives island energy."

She puts her hand on my knee. "Will you trust me, please?"

I do my best.

But once we pass the stadium and start slowing down at the next light, I get extremely suspicious. "Hold up . . . I know we're not—"

"Make a quick left at the next light," Carmen cuts in, and my heart sinks.

"The Sports and *Learning* Complex?"

Listen. I know Carmen just moved here from Baltimore City, but she had to know the Sports and Learning Complex is the furthest thing possible from a private island. It's basically a giant recreation center—which is fine, as far as community centers go. But the furthest thing possible from all the "pop out and find out" energy Carmen was dishing.

I try not to look disappointed, but my face has never been able to play off a moment. I frown all the way inside to the front desk, where Carmen shows her rec card, and we head over to the aquatic area.

Finally, I can't take it anymore. "This is a pool—not a private island."

"Hold on, you don't know that yet."

Is this girl playing with me?!

I follow her down into the locker room, where we turn away from each other so I can change out of my street clothes and into my bathing suit. I slip into a pair of pink slides and follow her out to the pool area.

The second we hit the pool deck, the pungent smell of chlorine stings my nostrils and the sound of kids splashing around in the pool rattles my eardrums.

PRETTY GIRL COUNTY

Carmen's smiling, though, like she's presenting me with a new car. "You mentioned islands, crystal-blue waters, and waves." She nods toward a fake mushroom sprouting up out of the splash pool, with water running over the top and down its sides. "We even have a waterfall, if your imagination is hitting."

A kid screams out "Marco," a bunch of other kids call back "Polo!" and then scatter off in every direction imaginable to get away from the first kid. Water splashes everywhere.

"So, what are we supposed to do, dodge all these kids or stand around and get splashed?"

I feel like plugging my ears with my fingers when a random kid screams on their way down the slide. When she slams into the water, ice-cold water splashes my legs.

I jump out of the way, frowning. "Sorry," I quickly mutter when Carmen's smile starts fading. "But it's just too noisy, and there's too much splashing everywhere. The front of my lace front wig is going to lift the second some kid splashes water on me . . . Then what? I'd be forced to look busted on our date?"

Carmen grabs my hand. "We're not getting into the splash pool . . ." She guides me over to a corner near the back. "You said you wanted to feel the heat, so here we are."

I look down at the circular jacuzzi next to us. "What about the crashing waves?" I ask.

Carmen walks over to the wall, pushes a button, and the still waters start bubbling. Slipping out of her flip-flops, she leads me into the water.

The ninety-two-degree bubbling water feels instantly

luxurious on my skin, and I sink down low, letting the water reach the bottom of my neck.

Okay, I have to admit, *this* feels amazing.

Carmen sits down next to me and grabs my hand. "Obviously, this isn't a private island, but I wanted to do something bigger than the typical movie-and-a-restaurant date. I'm an out-of-the-box kind of person." She scoots closer to me. "Maybe later, if we're still hanging tight in college or something, and my financial-aid refund money is giving, we can go somewhere fancy."

I smile.

"But, hey, we're seventeen, this is the best I can do with what I've got."

Suddenly, Carmen's best is good enough for me. I can tell she put her entire heart into planning this date. "You're right," I tell her softly. "This *is* perfect."

And it is. The water's bubbling just right. This cute, thoughtful girl is right next to me, and the chlorine scent in the air is starting to give tropical breeze.

Carmen pulls up the Notes app on her phone.

"Okay, but we still gotta workshop your personal favorites for the bookstore, though."

"Now?" I laugh.

"Why not?"

I shrug and scoot closer.

Together we add Toni Morrison, Gloria Naylor, and Kimberla Lawson Roby. From time to time, I grab the phone to type in some books and authors I love myself, like J. California

PRETTY GIRL COUNTY

Cooper and Dolen Perkins-Valdez. When our fingers touch, the electricity is palpable.

When Carmen adds an unfamiliar name, I make a face. "Iceberg *Slim*?"

Carmen smiles at my forehead crinkles. "Yeah. Toni Morrison may be your favorite author, but Iceberg Slim is mine."

Once again, hearing that name makes me cringe hard. "Your picks have been top tier so far . . . but I can't approve the addition of Mr. Slim."

Carmen shakes her head. "No, see. You have to read at least one of his books. People love bragging about how much they love Toni Morrison's writing, because it sounds classy to mention her name. And it makes them look smart around other people. But Iceberg Slim deserves just as much respect. Both writers wrote the world as they saw it—authentically. They both had the ability to make some readers feel seen and open a window for other readers to peek into a different perspective, *without* watering down the delivery for those outside the culture."

Carmen shrugs. "Just because one talks like this." She tilts her chin and starts talking in an exaggerated British accent. "And one talks like this," she goes, purposely letting her words drag, "doesn't mean one is any more and or less legit than the other."

"The name Iceberg Slim sounds like it belongs on the front of a pack of cigarettes," I insist, frowning.

Carmen gives me a disappointed look. "Is this the same person who claims they like Toni Morrison because she writes all this great work by day and parties with the best of them by night?"

"Yeah, but that's different."

"Shoot, Toni and Iceberg Slim were probably at Studio 54 together a time or two. Check this line: 'Moon-drenched branches of a wind-mauled tree outside the bedroom window cavorted spectral shadows about the suite.'"

I sit up. "Iceberg Slim wrote that?!"

"Yes! The gothic imagery and metaphors in that one sentence rival Toni Morrison's symbolism in *A Mercy*. Slim was a literary baddie, too. You can't argue with me on this."

"I *could* . . ." I warn. "But I don't want to." I lean back into her chest. "You made your point perfectly with that one sentence."

"That's the thing about working in a bookstore." Carmen tucks a lock of hair behind my ear. "On your own time, read what you like—and that's cool—no judgment. But at *Grand Rising*? You have to be up on everything we have to offer. We can't have customers walking in looking for vintage street lit, and you've never heard of Iceberg Slim or Donald Goines."

"I hear you." I grab her phone to type in Sister Souljah. When our list nears thirty solid picks, I slide Carmen's phone out of her hand to scroll back over it. "I think it's really cool that you did this for me." I look up into her soft brown eyes, and warmth takes over me.

Carmen smiles again. "I mean, it's mostly for Grand Rising . . ."

I go to play hit her, but she pulls me in for a kiss. *Finally.*

PRETTY GIRL COUNTY

After a moment, though, a shadow drops over us, and a whistle, as loud and shrill as a train thundering through the backroads of Upper Marlboro, blasts in my ear.

"There are kids around." The lifeguard gestures to the splash pool.

Okay, *and*? "What's the big deal? Kids literally see kissing in fairy tales." I force down an eye roll.

The lifeguard frowns. "Well, this isn't some enchanted castle. This is a *family pool*. You can either keep it PG or leave."

We roll our eyes, but for the rest of the date we keep our hands to ourselves and get to know each other better over the bubbling water.

We discuss where we're going to school next year . . .

"Bowie State?" I exclaim. "Why not somewhere out of state?"

"I'm from Baltimore, remember? Bowie *is* practically out of state," she says, laughing.

Our hopes . . .

"I just hope I figure out my major by the time school starts. I don't really know what I want to study yet."

"It's okay, Carmen. Not everyone knows freshman year."

"Yeah, that's easy for *you* to say. I don't have the money to keep switching up and taking extra classes."

And our dreams . . .

"You already know I want to be a famous fashion designer someday," I tell Carmen with conviction.

She looks off a moment. "Yeah, but what are you trying to do with that dream, though?"

"What do you mean?" I ask, wrinkling my forehead.

"I mean, like, whenever someone talks about dreams, it's always material things, like a bunch of money. Or a fancy car. You know, always focused on *stuff*."

"You don't have those dreams?" I ask her.

She shakes her head. "I mean, those things would be nice. *My* dreams are linked to things money can't always buy, like bringing my entire family together under one roof, or one gigantic compound, one day. Like, grabbing up my aunts and uncles from Philly. My grandma back in Baltimore, my brother that stays down South with my cousins. Just having everyone together and doing well, you know?"

I raise an eyebrow. "You think I don't have those same dreams? I'm just not the kind of person that pretends you don't need money to get what you want out of life. A *compound*, Carmen? That takes real money."

She shrugs. "Depends on where you buy the land."

"Maybe." I reach over and twist the tiny diamond stud in her ear. "Fashion design is a dream that's linked to my heart, because it's something I love. But it's also linked to money. If I'm successful, I can do almost anything." I stare at Carmen a moment. "You don't think I care about my family being good, too? *Money* is what put my family in a better place."

She holds her hands up in defeat. "Okay, okay. Just promise you won't forget all the little people like me when you make it big."

"Like I could forget you," I say with a grin.

She laughs. "I'd kiss you, if it weren't for . . ." She nods in the direction of the scowling lifeguard.

PRETTY GIRL COUNTY

"Someone should kiss *him*. Maybe he'd lighten up if he had a little more love in his life." We both laugh.

By now, I feel like I've known Carmen my entire life. This date, I must say, is going in my top ten.

After we change back into our clothes, we head back outside. The lot is completely packed. But my car is nowhere to be found.

"Where are you going, Reya?" Carmen asks, following behind me as I dash out into the lot.

I barely hear her. At this point, I'm in panic mode.

"Somebody stole my car." I start walking faster through the parking lanes, desperately searching for a sign of pink. But all I see are a bunch of Hondas.

"*This* is why I don't come down this way!" I snap. The Sports and Learning Complex is cool and all, but this area is *definitely* not Bowie. Glenarden's to the left. Seat Pleasant's to the right. Kentland is right down the street. And right outside the parking lot is Palmer Park.

"Reya, what's wrong with you?" Carmen finally gets up on me and she's frowning, like I shouldn't be having a problem with my car mysteriously missing from the parking lot.

"Somebody stole my car!"

Carmen folds her arms and stares at me. "Nobody stole your car, Reya."

I raise an eyebrow. "Listen, Carmen, I know your mail probably says Hyattsville now. But let me tell you . . . *This?*" I point to the area surrounding us. "This is still Palmer Park, and around here—"

153

"I don't need your opinion about where I live," Carmen says quickly.

"Oh yes, you do, because the thing about Palmer Park is—"

"Okay, first off, I just *told* you, I don't want to hear nothing you're about to say about where I live. I had to deal with that enough living in Baltimore," she says, fuming. "Second of all, your car is right there, behind that minivan."

Wait, what?

Suddenly my whole body goes cold even though it's over eighty outside. Feeling ridiculous, I walk over to my car, which is indeed hiding behind a poorly parked minivan. It's not until I click the unlock button that I realize Carmen isn't beside me.

I turn back to find her making her way to the curb.

"What are you doing? I was planning to take you home."

"I'll walk." She nods toward the traffic lights at the end of the hill. "My house is only a few blocks away."

"Come on, Carmen. Don't be like that."

But she just stands there with her arms crossed, a hard look on her face. I give her my brightest smile, trying my hardest to smooth things over. "Look, sometimes I get a little overwhelmed."

She refuses to even look at me. "You can leave now. I don't need an escort back to the *hood*."

And with a shake of her head, she turns on her heel, leaving me staring after her, wondering how my dream date just turned into a nightmare.

19
Sommer

SUNDAYS ARE MADE for rest and rejuvenation. Unfortunately, I'm not only spending every second worrying about how to save Grand Rising while I restock books at the store, I'm also losing steam listening to Reya choke and wheeze over being verbally throat-chopped by Carmen yesterday.

"I must say, it was a bold move coming here after running your mouth in such a reckless manner," I tell her as I turn a book around to its rightful spine-out position. "How did you know Carmen had the day off?"

"She told me she was off before the date went downhill yesterday," she says, sniffling. "I'm telling you, Sommer, I didn't even mean it to come out like that!"

Sigh.

Reya should've paid Azadeh a visit instead. Or even called

Sauce if she wanted a sympathetic shoulder to cry on. Because she knows I'm not the one, or the two—especially when it comes to this subject.

Part of me wonders why she *did* come to me. We're barely friends, much less confidants. It's not like I'm going to talk to her about the bookstore—I'm still processing my feelings about it, I don't need to take on hers, too.

But then I think about what Azadeh said, how our friendship meant something to Reya. Is this her way of showing it? It gives me a strange, satisfied feeling, like deep down, despite all her new money, she's here leaning on *me*. Or maybe this weird energy isn't satisfaction at all, but impending doom from news of the store closing. Or maybe I ate something weird for breakfast. Who knows?

"Soooo, you basically called Carmen's neighborhood a war zone and expected her to thank you for your TED Talk?" I shake my head. "It doesn't work like that, Reya. You can't judge where somebody lives without expecting them to feel a way about it. You must remember what that feels like. You lived here not *that* long ago."

Reya cocks her head, and for a second I think she's going to give in. But then she recovers enough to prove why she was named president of the debate club last year. "Okay, so you're telling me the news is lying? That Palmer Park never has any crime?"

I mull over what she's saying. "I think most of the time, when you walk down the street, nothing's happening. Moms are going to work. Kids are going to school and playing outside,

PRETTY GIRL COUNTY

and people are generally just trying to live their lives." I shrug. "I'm not saying Palmer Park doesn't have its issues. But who are you to talk down on a whole entire city? Especially from your three-car garage? No one wants to hear all that."

Reya folds her arms. "So, no one in Bowie can say anything about Palmer Park?"

"Not when you're doing nothing to fix all the so-called problems. Don't just talk about the issues. Do something about it or keep your opinions to yourself."

Watching Reya with her nose in the air makes me wonder how I would react to a sudden case of the monies. Would I still be me? *Could* I stay the same?

Suddenly, as quickly as Reya threw on her imaginary debate club blazer, it fades away. A glimmer of little Rey-Rey pops back out. The one who stuck her middle finger up at the ice cream truck guy and skated past trouble by claiming she was simply ordering a Ring Pop. The one who crashed into the neighbor's car with her bike, then fixed the dent with a toilet plunger before he woke up from his afternoon nap.

Maybe I'm not so worried about Reya getting herself into things, because I've seen her get herself out of jams just as fast.

Sigh. Maybe this time I should help her without a paycheck attached. So I don't let money take me down the same cold, heartless path it took her years ago.

I shake my head. "You really like Carmen, right?"

Reya nods.

"Okay, so you need to make things right." I pause a moment. "And not with any empty apologies, either. You have to really think about what you said to her. Because it's not right."

Just then, an incoming text vibrates my phone.

Sauce: Since you like swimming so much,
maybe we should link up at Six Flags next.
Maybe hit up the wave pool or something.
Senior skip day is coming up.

Tuh. Not *Six Flaaaags*. Of *all* places.

Every year, it's the same mess. Somebody has a problem with someone else, and they use water slides and funnel cakes as a backdrop to their brawl.

Still, I fight back a smile at getting a next-day follow-up text after our time together on the boat. That's what's up.

"What has you over there smiling?" Reya pauses her impromptu volunteer book-stocking session to raise an eyebrow. "Ooh, Sean." She sighs. "At least someone's love life is on track."

I roll my eyes. "Love life is kind of an overstatement. We had one hang. With his *dad*."

"You can't downplay a yacht party, babe. I know you like him." She purses her lips and hefts her bag on her shoulder. "Now, thanks for the advice, but I'm going to head out. I need to get a head start on planning the Reya/Carmen reboot."

"Good luck," I say.

Reya nods, a determined look on her face. "Thanks."

I watch as she leaves the store, half wondering if I should warn Carmen about some grand Reya scheme coming her way. But you know what?

PRETTY GIRL COUNTY

I'm actually sort of warming up to the two of them being a thing. If Reya can make things right with Carmen and get her newly discovered fear of the hood under control, those two could work. I'll admit, I didn't see it at first. But they did look cute together at the Stop the Beef party.

I think I might actually tune into the Reya/Carmen reboot—if it ever makes it on air.

Two days later, it's here.

Senior Skip Day.

Four years of English. Three years of math. Too much gym. Not enough snow days. Finally, Senior Skip Day has descended upon the entire DMV. Freshmen? Sophomores? Stay out of this one. This year, all the seniors from every high school in the county are going to—you guessed it—Six Flags for the day.

"Does everyone have a season pass?" Sauce asks on our car ride over to Largo.

Amara pipes up from the back seat. "Reed and I are getting ours when we get there."

But I shake my head. "I'm still saving up to get one." Between the rising prices of school lunch, senior fees, and having to get a dress for graduation soon, my season pass probably won't be in my hand until July at this point.

"I've got you," Sauce says as he leans over me to reach into his glove compartment.

"Really?" My spirits are instantly lifted—

Until I look down at the card he hands me. "Sauce . . ."

He turns to me with a goofy look on his face. "What?"

"Is this your *mom's* pass?" I hold the card up to my face so he can get a side-by-side view of how ridiculous I will look trying to sneak into the park with this.

"What's the problem?" he asks slowly.

I turn to Amara and Reed in the back. "Do I look like the lady on this card?"

Amara slaps her hand over her mouth to hold back a laugh. Reed pretends to be really into the music playing through his AirPods.

I turn back to Sauce. "I mean, she's pretty and all, but come on now, Sauce. You're jazzin' it. I do not look thirty-five!"

Sauce shrugs. "Actually she's forty, but she looks young for her age."

I roll my eyes as Sauce lets down his window to pay the parking attendant. "I swear, if you get us thrown out of here."

To Sauce's credit, we make it through with no problems, fraudulent ID and all.

While Amara and Reed go to the season pass office to take their photos, Sauce and I head over to the wave pool. We don't stay long. Everybody and their mother are squeezed together in the water, and we look more like a crowd doing the wave than swimmers enjoying the actual waves. I get sick of knocking into people and dodging inner tubes, so we get out. While I sit on a beach chair, shivering under my towel, Sauce gets us a bucket of Boardwalk fries.

"Where do you want to go next?" he asks.

By the time we change back into our clothes and head for

PRETTY GIRL COUNTY

the rides, Amara and Reed have met up with us. Together, the four of us get on the Batwing first. Then the Joker's Jinx. Finally, we head for the Superman.

"Whoaaa . . . Nah," Sauce goes, shaking his head.

Amara raises an eyebrow. "I know you're not scared of a kiddie roller coaster . . . ?"

Sauce points to the red-and-blue coaster that looks like the top might reach the clouds. "*That* is not a kiddie ride."

Reed swoops in to push us closer together. "Come on, Sommer. Didn't your man have your back with the season pass? It's your turn to return the favor. Support your man, girl!"

Sauce grabs my hand. "You heard him. Support your *man*."

The look he's giving me dips me harder than the drop we just experienced on the Joker's Jinx. "Who said you're my man, yet?" I ask, flirting hard.

"Trust me, it's coming," Sauce says.

Liking his response, I sling an arm around his waist, and together, the four of us get in the ridiculously long line to ride the Superman.

But Sauce goes pale again the second he gets locked in the seat.

"Come on," I tell him. "It's going to be fine . . ."

"Nah . . . nah," he says, shaking his head. "I don't really do heights like that."

"I'll hold your hand," I tell him softly.

I lock my fingers through his while my free hand grips the lap bar. Then the ride takes off, cranking up the steepest hill.

Being extra, kids start screaming on the way up the long,

sharp incline. I'm not fazed in the least. But Sauce's eyes dart around excessively the closer we get to the top.

"You're really scared, huh?" I ask him.

He low whistles. "These rides have been breaking down since before we were born. My mom got stuck on the Iron Eagle for like an hour when she was our age. Man, I'm not trying to get— *Ahhhhhh!!!*"

Our coaster dips over the peak, and we're off, sailing down the sharp hill so fast it literally feels like we're flying.

I'm in love with roller coasters—I have been going on them with my parents ever since I was little. I do a little screaming on the first dip, but mostly I'm enjoying the rush of wind on my face.

The weightless feeling of flying on the first dip makes me think of college next year. That no matter how scary all the new changes will be, I'm going to be out of here . . . fluttering my wings toward a new life, new dreams, new possibilities. The sky won't be the limit for me. Yeah, the bookstore closing feels a little on the hopeless side, but my cute little drawstring ponytail staying in place this time, down one of the biggest roller-coaster drops in the park, lets me know that anything's possible.

So, yeah, I'm all peace, love, and prosperity on the first dip.

Sauce, on the other hand, screams his lungs out the entire way down. He yanks his hand away and clutches his lap bar like a backpack strap the rest of the way.

Another few seconds of him high-pitched screaming in my ear, and the coaster jolts, then eases back into the holding bay.

PRETTY GIRL COUNTY

We all hold our breath until we hear the familiar clicking sound of the lap bars unlocking and lifting. Then we head to the right, while the next riders hop quickly into our spots.

"That wasn't that bad," Sauce goes, rubbing the back of his neck as we head for the exit.

I stop dead in my tracks on the platform. "I *know* you're lying."

"What?" A slow smile breaks out across his face. "All that screaming was coming from someone in the back." Then he pulls me under his arm, and we exit the ramp together.

After the Superman, Sauce is mysteriously "tired of roller coasters" for now. So we ride the bumper cars, the swerving cows, and sit for the cowboy show. Sauce uses his baseball arm to try and knock down a pyramid of milk jugs. When he fails after three tries, he offers to CashApp the worker forty dollars in exchange for the biggest stuffed animal he has. The worker doesn't hesitate to accept Sauce's offer.

Ten seconds later, I'm dragging a giant yellow Tweety Bird around the park.

"You want me to carry it?" Sauce asks, after poor Tweety has been dropped on her head several times.

I hand over the bird.

Everything is going perfectly. I can't ask for a better day with the most perfect guy.

Until the trouble starts.

We haven't run into a single member of the Brat Pack since arriving. But after the cowboy show lets out, Sauce spots Bryce, Marlon, and a few other guys from Bowie near a cotton candy station near the front of the park.

"Yeah, boy. I told you it was up Senior Skip Day, right?" Bryce is saying, confronting Cody. "Well? What's up?"

Cody doesn't hesitate to step forward.

"Wait," Sauce says, squinting. "He has, like, the whole Palmer Park standing behind him."

"Please don't go over there." I reach for Sauce's arm, but it's too late. He's already making his way to the group.

But before a punch is thrown, park security comes running. Bryce, Cody, and their respective crews are all ejected from the park. We watch as half of the Brat Pack is ushered away.

"I can't believe them," I tell Sauce.

Sauce huffs. "Cody's the one who brought all those Parkstars with him."

"And Bryce was the one who started it," I point out. "And I can't believe *you* for running over there."

Sauce sighs, taking a hold of Tweety and putting his other arm around my shoulders.

"Nothing even happened," he says. "Don't stress. Let's just snag some Dippin' Dots and ride the teacups, cool?"

I don't want to ruin our perfect day together, so I try to let the incident fade from my memory as we get ice cream cups and slide into each other on the teacup ride. Despite the almost fight, the rest of the day finishes strong, and I'm still feeling Sauce more than ever.

However, when it's time to leave, and we go back through the turnstiles, red and blue lights are flashing from police cars in the parking lot. I'm reminded all over again what could've gone down—and how Sauce could've been a part of it.

PRETTY GIRL COUNTY

"See what I mean?" I tell Sauce. "You could've been arrested."

Sauce scrunches up his nose. "Will you chill? They're always here when the park lets out."

I can't just chill, though. He's not getting it. Fights aren't just simple arguments. They escalate. And the more people involved, the more it leads to jumps and guns. And don't let the police get involved. The more people involved in these petty beefs, the more unpredictable everything gets.

Me? I like to know *exactly* what's happening next. I don't have time for any unexpected mishaps throwing me off my goals.

Almost like it's been listening to my thoughts, my phone buzzes. I look down and it's a text from my dad.

Dad: Hey Sommer, on second thought, I might need you to pull some extra shifts after all. Your mom thinks we should get an early start on packing up all these books.

What did I *just* say about unexpected stuff? Just like that, reality intrudes on my almost perfect day. My chest starts closing up, and I have to sit down on one of the benches near the pickup lot to catch my breath.

Sauce immediately clocks this and comes over to sit down with me. "Hey, I didn't know all the drama had you *this* worried. Are you okay?"

I want to explain to Sauce that this has nothing to do with the drama in the park. But I'm still struggling to catch my breath. So I let him put his arm around me and hold me close, while I slowly count to ten in my head and try to get my breathing back under control.

Sauce's patience more than makes up for his impulsive sprint toward that fight earlier. So much so that I trust that I can tell him what's really going on.

"My dad's bookstore is closing down and I'm just . . ." I squeeze my eyes together a second to stop the tears. "That's what really has me in my feelings. Tuition for Spelman is coming up. Not to mention that without the bookstore, my dad is also out of a job for a while. I just—I don't know what my parents are going to do and I'm feeling really guilty about still wanting to go to my dream school."

A part of me feels funny spilling all my family business to a kid like Sauce, whose parents probably already paid his tuition bill in full for Howard next year.

But the other side of me feels like he should be able to handle listening to my problems if he's claiming to really like me.

To his credit, Sauce doesn't seem put off by my big family secret. He sits and thinks a moment before pulling out his phone. "Why don't I text my dad right quick and see if he knows of any available commercial space around the county?"

"Yeah, that sounds cool . . . Thanks," I say, because at least he's trying to come up with a solution.

"Aight," Sauce says, dropping his phone back down into his lap. "Dad says we can talk about it more when I get home." He smiles. "See, I don't only jump in stuff for my bros, it's like that

PRETTY GIRL COUNTY

with everybody I care about." Then he leans over to kiss me.

If you would have told me, even three months ago, I would be embroiled in a sizzling lip lock with the cutest member of the Brat Pack, I would have checked your forehead for fever. But, for like ten long seconds, we share something amazing.

When we finally come up for air, the problems are still there. The beef between Cody and Bryce isn't showing any signs of cooling off. The bookstore hasn't been saved yet.

But this thing between me and Sauce has me feeling like I'm floating on air.

So, hey. Maybe there is something to this dating thing after all.

20
Reya

I DIDN'T *WANT* to miss Senior Skip Day. But focusing on fashion stuff and my college goals comes first. Besides, is a roller coaster even fun without leaning into your bae and pretending to be extra scared going down that first dip?

I *have* to fix things between Carmen and me.

But Sommer's right—handing out flimsy "my bad" apologies will never work. Not for someone like Carmen.

If I want my future girlfriend to really know I'm a good person, I have to show her not only that I've changed my judgmental ways but that I actually care about her. Her likes, dislikes. Her hopes and dreams.

Carmen's dream is family and togetherness, right?

Okay, so boom. Here's the plan—stay with me on this one. Since I'm nice with the googling skills, I found her mom's

PRETTY GIRL COUNTY

work number. I even put $12.99 on my debit card to dig up the phone number and address of her aunt and uncle in Philly.

I may not be moving them all in together, but your girl Reya Samuels is bringing all of Carmen's day ones together for a good old-fashioned family dinner.

Maryland style of course—where we pull out bushels of crabs instead of plates of mac 'n' cheese, and sprinkle in a little Old Bay seasoning for a little razzle-dazzle instead of Lawry's or paprika.

First things first. My mother has already gone to DC to pick up the live crabs from the trucks down at the wharf. She's supposedly throwing an upscale crab boil at the Potomac house today to announce her upcoming dance single, "Don't Be Crabby, Let's Get Classy," which she secretly produced with a local DJ last month.

Now all I need to do is convince Mom to donate a small pile of those crabs she's steaming in the kitchen for *my* special event and my plan will be complete.

"Mommy?"

"Down here, sweetie!"

I try on a few new sympathetic faces as I follow her voice to the kitchen.

"So, remember how I said I might have a few, um, *friends* over . . . ?" My voice trails off as the barrel of crabs resting on the floor moves a little.

My mother's turned around, pulling out the tall pot and grabbing the stirring spoon, so she doesn't notice what I see.

But, um . . . Do I hear snapping claws coming from the

inside of that barrel? Is the freaking top lifting itself?!

Suddenly, one of the crabs breaks free from the others, climbs over the edge of the barrel, and drops to the kitchen floor.

"Aaaaagh!!! Get him, Mommy! Get him, get him!"

Mom turns around just in time to witness me pole vault myself onto the kitchen island.

"Girl! Get your toes off my quartz countertops! We have to eat there!" Mom shouts, clicking a pair of metal tongs in my direction.

If my mother thinks I'm putting my feet back on the floor while that crab is down there doing the Electric Slide across our kitchen, she doesn't know me as well as I thought she did.

I peek out from behind my hands, make eye contact with a very angry-looking crab, and squeeze my lids shut again. "Ewww, it's looking at me."

"Reya! That crab isn't thinking about you. You are doing too much right now!"

I open my eyes again. "Or is that crab doing the most by being alive right now?!" The sound of snapping claws as the other crabs climb over each other inside the barrel gives me the heebie-jeebies.

Mom laughs as she pulls out butter from the fridge and Old Bay from the cabinet. "Girl, you have to steam them this way—that way they're good and fresh!"

I hear one of the kitchen drawers open and then slam shut. Then Mom appears holding the peeping crab in her oven mitt.

PRETTY GIRL COUNTY

"You are ridiculous," she tells me, shaking her head. "Now, what's this about you having people over?"

I don't climb down from the kitchen island until Mr. Krabs himself is back in the barrel. "I'm trying to do something special for Carmen and her family," I try to say quickly under my breath.

Mom clocks my tea, though. "Excuse me? I know you're not about to have a house full of strangers up in here—you barely cleaned up after the last party I let you throw."

"Mommy, I told you that was a mistake. Know better, *do* better."

"Uh-huh."

"I know what you *can* help me with, though . . ."

"Mm-hmm, I knew it." Mom checks the time on the oven. "What do you need, Reya?"

I slide up on my mother and wrap an arm around her waist. "Just a few of your crabs. No more than about, I don't know, fifty or so . . ."

"Reya!"

"Mom, please. I have a lot going on with the fashion show and not getting into FIT yet, and . . ."

Mom puts a hand on her hip. "Now, you know I don't mind sharing what I have with you, Reya. What's mine is yours, and it's always going to be like that." She takes a breath. "But I can't look like I'm skimping on the crabs on national TV . . . You know how that Tabitha Pigford likes to downplay everything I do as it is."

171

"I only need enough for about four . . . five . . . maybe *six* people, Mommy. I promise, I won't take one crab over what I need." I point to one of the barrels on the floor. "Especially Mr. Crawly Crab over there."

Mom raises an eyebrow in my direction. But she walks over to the barrels to start counting up her inventory. "You'd better be glad I'm known as one of the best party hosts on the show. I can't have strangers showing up at my house with nothing to snack on." She strikes a pose holding her silver tongs and wearing her best Potomac pout. "*Image*, Reya, is everything."

Carmen and her family are arriving any minute, and I'm so nervous my stomach feels like it's *full* of angry crabs. I'm dressed for the occasion of course, in a red two-piece matching set and red soft leather slides. My nails are painted pure white with little crab decals I ordered online.

My attention to detail—like my jeans when we first met—is what caught Carmen's attention. If I stick to my strengths, I'll win her back. The only thing is, I'm still a little worried Carmen won't be able to get over my impulsiveness.

When the doorbell rings, I nearly jump out of my skin, but I play it cute and put on a dazzling, welcoming smile to greet my guests.

But when I open the door, it's just Carmen with her arms folded across her chest as she levels me with the glare of a lifetime.

"Uh, where's the fam?" I ask, peering behind her.

PRETTY GIRL COUNTY

Why are her eyes twitching like that escaping crab an hour ago?

"First of all, inviting my family over when they don't even know you? Not okay. Asking them to keep their arrival a secret from me? *Unhinged.*"

Really?! "A girl can't surprise her one and only love interest?" I step out on the porch. "What time are they getting here? Dinner's starting promptly at four."

Now both of Carmen's eyebrows are raised. "You can*not* be serious right now. I told them not to come."

My heart flops faster than Mom's crabby/classy pop number. "Why not, Carmen? I was trying to do something special for you."

"Because they are my family." Carmen points to her chest. "And I get to decide if I even want you around them."

Oof. Okay, that hurt.

Carmen catches me wince and immediately softens her tone. "I don't mean it like that, Reya. But come on. You haven't even apologized to me about what happened. You have to make things right before we start adding in extra people."

The word *we* offers me a glimmer of hope.

"Do you mean that?"

Carmen tries to keep up her tough-girl persona, but it's not working. "I mean, it depends," she says slowly. "How do you season your crabs?"

"Heavy."

Carmen tries to hide her forming smile. "Hmm, okay, we'll see."

173

I usher Carmen into the dining room where I have newspaper spread out over the table, silver nutcrackers, trays, and plastic "pickers" set up at each place setting. Since my guest list just dropped from six to two, I sit down next to Carmen and scooch my chair closer.

"So, are we going to talk before, during, or after crabs?"

Carmen grabs the plastic bib in front of her. "You think I'm going to wait to dig into this? *Tuh*." She slides a few of the Potomac River's finest crustaceans onto her plate and gets to work cracking shells and digging out juicy white crabmeat.

"I like you, Reya, I really do, but I don't know how much more I can take of your classist nonsense."

"I'm sorry," I tell her, not sure what else to say. "But I was freaked out about my car. What was I supposed to do?"

"You're supposed to *know* better," Carmen says. "I've been trying to tell myself you're like the one uncle at Thanksgiving who says things for laughs and attention. That your mouth is a little reckless, but your heart is genuine. But I'm starting to think you actually believe the elitist and self-centered stuff you say."

My eye starts twitching. "Elitist and self-centered? I have won *awards* for my volunteer work, Carmen."

Am I expecting a little applause? Maybe.

It never materializes, though.

"Whoop-de-freaking-do, Reya. Helping somebody means nothing when you think you're above them."

"That's not fair," I tell her, stung.

"*Life's* not fair, Reya. If it were, we'd all be sunbathing in our backyard pool after school." She stops a moment. "I'm not

PRETTY GIRL COUNTY

even hating on your come up, Reya. I think it's amazing. *My* problem is how quick you are to turn your nose up at a place that looks a lot like the place you grew up." Carmen pushes her chair from the table and looks around.

"Look, I'm sorry. I just . . ." I let out a big breath. "Mom is always on me about driving my car around Seat Pleasant, and I'm always pushing back—because that's where I grew up. I know every sidewalk, swing, and crosswalk over there. But I guess I let her get in my head." I wince at the unimpressed expression on Carmen's face. "What I'm trying to say is I hear you, and I was wrong."

I'm not sure what Carmen's thinking, but I'm not satisfied with my apology. I feel like I'm holding too much in. Me? I have to say what's on my heart, it's the only way I know how to be.

"I'm *not* turning my nose up, Carmen. I just call things like I see them."

I take a moment to dig out a chunk of crab meat, and dip it in my tub of butter. "I'm not calling Palmer Park *bad*. In my opinion, every place has a downside." I shrug my shoulders. "I guess I just got used to not having to worry about my car getting jacked over here in Bowie—that's all."

I hear it, too. I know. But I don't know how else to explain it.

Carmen's back to shaking her head. "It's not even just about neighborhoods, though, Reya. You make *everything* about money and image. Like, you won't even consider Bowie State because you think FIT is some sort of brand name."

I try to hear what she's saying, but I can't say I agree. "You're not in the fashion world, Carmen," I tell her carefully. "You can't tell me how to choose the right school."

Carmen shakes her head. "Reya, I don't have to be in the fashion world to know you are smart and talented. You could walk into fashion rooms with a degree from anywhere if your work is undeniable. Since when do you need anyone to cosign your greatness?"

I open my mouth, then close it again. I haven't thought about it like that before. Of course I deserve the best of the best, but . . .

"You act like I'm just the worst," I tell her. Like, is that how I come off? Or is that just how *Carmen* sees me?

Carmen softens again. "I don't think you're the worst, Reya. I wouldn't even be here if I thought that." She grabs my hand. "It's just . . . you've got to stop looking down on things you don't consider good enough. *We* create the world around us. Beautiful spirits create beauty wherever they step foot." She gives me a piercing stare. "When you get into FIT, you're going to set that place on fire. But the way *I* see you?" she goes, tapping her chest. "I know those flames would burn just as bright at Bowie State. *You* are the special thing, not the place."

She leans back in her seat. "And anybody can come up, but everyone has the potential to slide back down. You have to be able to see the beauty in both to push through sometimes."

I find my way into the nook between her arm and torso. "Well, I know that part. Why do you think I work so hard at everything?"

Carmen smiles as she wipes her hands off with a little wet

napkin. "I see that, Reya—and that's one of the things I admire about you. But, come on, can you promise me one thing?"

I stare up into her gorgeous eyes. "Anything."

Carmen chuckles. "Can you promise me you'll think about how you might make someone feel before you just say things?"

I consider her request. "Of course."

When Carmen grabs my hand, I give it a squeeze to let her know I'm a girl of my word. If I say I'm going to try harder, I will.

I look around at the empty seats at the table. Even though everything didn't go exactly as planned, somehow it all ended up perfectly satisfying.

Suddenly, I remember the crown jewel of my plan.

"I actually have something for you," I tell Carmen. "Be right back."

I dash upstairs to my room and grab two of the tops I worked on, then head back to the dining room.

"Ta-da!" I say, dumping the outfits on Carmen's lap.

She looks down. "What's this?"

"Hold it up, and see for yourself," I say, beaming.

As Carmen's unfolding the shirts, I explain everything. "I skipped Senior Skip Day to finish up fashion show stuff. But I still thought of you the entire time. See?"

I hold up a pair of matching shirts. "I know I may not get everything right, but I trust my heart. You're my person, Carmen."

Carmen holds out her tee, trying hard not to let her smile give away her feelings. But I peep those pearly white teeth.

"You're my girl," I tell her. "And before I messed up, I was yours, too. I'll try to think about what I'm saying before I just blurt stuff out moving forward, I promise."

I know I have her when her face melts into a smile. She gives the shirts one final glance. "You made these, Reya? You are getting *too* nice with the needle and thread."

"Tuh! Didn't I say I was busy finishing up my collection?" I grab one of the shirts and flip it inside out to show the tag. "I just sprinkled a little glitter on the back to razzle-dazzle the look. These tees are Fendi!" I brace myself. "Look, I know the designer brand doesn't help me beat my elitism case. If you want me to take them back, maybe I can try scrubbing the glitter off or something—"

I go to grab Carmen's shirt from her hand, but she yanks it away at the last second.

"I said stop calling Palmer Park ghetto. I didn't say anything about turning down a Fendi top." She leans over to give me a quick peck on the lips. "Thanks for the gift, babe. And the food. And for trying to host a get-together for my family. You did the most, *again*—but I'm glad you put so much thought into all of this."

Carmen's sweet words finally restore my aching heart. When I lean over to kiss her, her lips taste like the perfect mix of Old Bay and forgiveness.

21
Sommer

THE NEXT DAY, I'm at the bookstore, flipping over the brochure Bowie State sent in the mail, feeling like I'm torn in two between my heart, which wants to be in Atlanta, and my head, which knows that Bowie is the more practical decision.

I try it on for size. What if the key to the rest of my life *isn't* buried at Spelman? I mean, Bowie State has a good game design program, too. I could still chase after my dreams right here at home—for a lot cheaper. Not every bright idea goes the way you plan. I know that more than anybody.

I look down again at the brochure, at all the Black kids in the picture.

They look so happy. They look like how I felt when I visited Spelman.

The front door jingles, taking me away from my thoughts.

Octavius is walking in, wearing black sweatpants, Nike boots, and a black Nike Tech hoodie. Behind him is a girl with long cornrows down her back, a hoodie dress, and black-and-white Pandas on her feet.

"Um, welcome," I say, tucking my brochure under the register. I haven't seen Octavius in a few weeks, not since he put me on his bike handles, and for some reason, his sudden presence now has me feeling like I'm sailing down the biggest drop on the Superman ride.

He spots me behind the counter, walks over, and leans on the glass counter. Tapping a little beat on the countertop with his knuckles, he gives me the once-over, then bobs his head. "Don't worry, I didn't come to spray paint no books." He points to the girl with him. "We just want to see if you have that new Iron Man that just came out."

Octavius's friend plays with the thick wooden beads on the ends of her cornrows. "I also wanted to go see if y'all still have this book I love. My little sister asked to borrow it and I haven't seen it since." She pokes her lip out. "That's why I don't lend my books out to people now."

I take a closer look at her. She's *so* pretty. "We live down the street from each other, right?" I ask her.

She nods and goes, "Yeah, I'm Jada."

I give her a smile and say "Hey." For a brief second, I wonder if she's Octavius's girlfriend. A second later, I decide that's none of my business.

I point Octavius to the rack where we keep all the comic books.

PRETTY GIRL COUNTY

"You'd better grab your copy quick. I'm not sure how long you'll be able to get it from here."

Octavius walks to the back and plucks a fresh copy from the rack. "Why, they're going quick?"

"No," I say slowly. "The bookstore may be closing in a few weeks."

Octavius freezes. "What? Why?"

I point toward the door. "The county is about to have a recreation space built up around here—with a new park, new basketball court and everything."

Octavius nods his head. "That's what's up." Then his eyebrows scrunch. "But I don't get it, what's the problem?"

Dad sighs. "Tuh, where do I start?" When he starts pretending to get really busy with paperwork, I can tell he doesn't want to talk about it.

"In order to build the space, the county is going to tear down my dad's bookstore," I offer from behind the counter.

"Why can't both exist?" Octavius asks, looking confused.

Even having to repeat the plans makes me feel weepy. But I hold it together. "Dad says that he can't afford to rent one of the spaces they're building."

Jada shakes her head. "That's messed up, I'm sorry," she says before disappearing into the Fiction section.

Octavius looks over at Dad. "Man, I'm so sorry." He rubs his palm through his hair. "If you need any help this summer, you got it. I'll be around until I go off to school in the fall."

Despite his offer to help, there's only part of his sentence I latch on to.

181

"You're going to college?" Right away, I hear how I sound, like one of those people who act like it's a Christmas miracle when they catch a Black person reading for fun. I try to clean up my words. "Not that I'm doubting you or anything, but I just never heard you speak on your future plans."

Jada peeks her head around one of the bookshelves. "Yeah, you didn't know? You gotta start popping your ish more, O," she calls before disappearing back into the stacks. "Getting into Morgan State is a big deal."

I nod, because she's right. "Congratulations," I tell him.

But Octavius is looking down and sheepish. "I don't have to go around bragging on myself all the time. What's understood don't need to be explained. Plus"—he looks at me—"I honestly wasn't sure if I even wanted to go to college for the longest."

Glad to sway the conversation away from the bookstore closing, I make a face. "Why not?"

He shrugs. "I couldn't figure out what I wanted to do. I'm not about to take out a bunch of student loans without having everything figured out yet. I can't afford to spend extra years trying to figure everything out."

Facts.

But Dad is shaking his head. "College is all *about* figuring stuff out—I think you would've been fine either way."

Octavius looks around the store. "Did you always know you wanted to open up a bookstore?"

Dad nods. "Yeah, pretty much . . . I knew I wanted to do something to help my community."

PRETTY GIRL COUNTY

Octavius's smile fades. "So, how can you let the county shut you down like this?"

Watching my father's eyes dim makes my heart hurt. "Things don't always go the way we plan them, son. Sometimes you do your best, things don't work out, so you pivot to plan B to make your dreams happen anyway."

"So, what's *your* backup plan?" Octavius asks.

Dad shakes his head. "You know why I'm stressing y'all about backup plans?"

Octavius shakes his head. "Nah."

"Because I don't have one."

Dad peeps the look of horror on my face and tries to clean up his admission. "Trust me, I'm going to make a plan . . . It just might take me a little longer since I didn't see the closing coming."

Octavius nods, then walks over to extend his fist to Dad. "You've made this store thing happen for the longest, Mr. Watkins," he says. "I know something's going to work out for you."

Dad daps him back up. "Thanks for the support, king."

Octavius moves closer to me. "But seriously, you can't let your dad go out like that."

"What am *I* supposed to do? If my dad couldn't convince the county to keep the store open, what makes you think I can do anything?"

You could take away some of these money worries by going to Bowie State next year, the voice in my head says. I try not to look at the hidden brochure under the register.

"I see people make something out of nothing every day around here. I wouldn't just give up because some people behind a *desk* made a decision." Octavius goes quiet a moment. "Let me think on all this." He holds out his comic book for me to ring up.

Jada reappears holding a small purple paperback in her hands. "Here it is." She holds the book out to Octavius. "*The Coldest Winter Ever.* I'm telling you, read this one time, and you'll be hooked on books for life."

But Octavius shakes his head. "I'm not that big on thick novels." He grabs his receipt from me. "But give me a good comic book or graphic novel and I'm locked in."

Jada shakes her head as she steps in front of him to place her book on the counter. "*Okayyy,*" she goes. "But you don't know what you're missing."

She looks at me. "You have a marker?"

I grab one from a little canister on the counter and take a hard look at her face. She's a baddie for sure. Okay, O . . . I see you.

"Thanks." Resting the book on its spine, she takes the marker and writes *JADA* in big block letters on the paper edges. "I dare someone to walk off with *this* copy."

My heart twists watching them walk out the door together, and I wonder how many more books I'll be able to ring up for readers once the county closes us up for good.

22
Reya

I AM IN the best relationship of my life—and I feel super guilty about it. How can I toss Carmen flirty looks across the store when my oldest friend is behind the register looking like she's slowly dying inside? Sneaking off for a quick kiss while Sommer's scribbling possible college solutions on register tape is out of the question. Winking at Carmen while the county's putting orange demolition stickers on the window? Insensitive. Crass. Off with my head, immediately!

But it feels so *good* to be in love! Someone mic me up because it's confessional time.

Being with Carmen is like having a bestie who *also* lets you pick the pepperoni off her pizza at your leisure and who never tires of kissing you. Are you getting this? This is Dating 101, people. If you lock in with a crush, and you're not in a constant state of exhaustion from staying up until dawn FaceTiming? You're doing it all wrong. Abort mission. Get you a new boo stat.

Because being in love isn't worth it if you aren't at least a *little* seasick from all the butterflies flapping around your insides at top speed.

I look at Carmen, over there shelving Octavia Butler novels like a goddess, and an imaginary heart emoji appears directly in the pupils of her eyes.

Then I look over at Sommer. Nothing but storm cloud emojis.

And as happy as I am, it makes me feel awful to see her like this—to see her whole family like this. I wish I could help, but this isn't some spray-painted window that I can just make over. But I can try to cheer her up.

I make my way over to the register. "I'm so glad we decided to go through with the book club thing. It's always best to end things on a high note, you know?"

Right on cue, Ms. Johnson strolls into the bookstore with a smile on her face and a dog-eared book in her hand. "Are we all set?" she asks.

Thank goodness I'm the only one who can hear Sommer's mumbling "What's the point?" behind me.

"Of *course*, we're ready," I tell my favorite customer with a bright smile on my face. I go in the back and return quickly, carrying a pair of brightly painted chairs in both hands. "If I told you my girlfriend and I barely slept the last two days making these chairs especially for the first meeting of the Seniors on the Move Book Club, would you judge me?"

PRETTY GIRL COUNTY

Ms. Johnson grins. "Are you still making the grades?"

"Straight A's."

Ms. Johnson slaps me on the back. "Then, losing a little sleep never hurt anybody—especially for a good cause."

I literally feel Sommer's eyebrow slide up a centimeter. *"Actually . . ."*

I cover up the rest of her statement with a charismatic laugh. "Now, Ms. Johnson. With that flawless skin, I know you're not sacrificing any beauty sleep. But I know what you mean."

We share a laugh while Sommer's mood continues to curdle behind me.

When Ms. Johnson wanders away to check out a collection of Nikki Giovanni poetry, I turn to Sommer. "Come on, friend. We worked too hard to pull this together for our readers. Hold it together just until we get through the book club, and I swear, I'll buy you comfort food and let you cry on my shoulder until the sleeves wrinkle. Deal?"

Sommer sighs. "Deal."

I feel bad watching her force her mouth into what should be a smile but actually looks like the beginnings of a bellyache. But hey, the book club must go on.

When all the ladies in the newly formed Seniors on the Move Book Club arrive, they fight over the chair Carmen and I stayed up all night painting in Toni Morrison's likeness. Until Sommer pulls out the Angela Davis chair. Then the Octavia Butler chair.

"All right, are we ready to get this party started?" I ask, taking my own seat in the Connie Briscoe chair. The members of her new book club don't know it, but I personally witnessed Carmen earmarking pages of this month's book selection and carefully writing out a few insightful questions—even penciling in a few book-related jokes.

"In case the conversation suddenly runs dry," she confessed while I yawned and continued painting James Baldwin onto a fresh black chair.

Today our hard work doesn't go in vain. For the next hour, the ladies talk, laugh, and shove pages in each other's faces to really drive their various points home, and with each passing moment, I see my old friend come back to life until there's a real, actual non-bellyache kind of smile on her face.

After purchasing a totally unrelated book, a customer spots the club chatting in the back and wanders over. "What book are you discussing?" she asks.

"*The Vanishing Half* by Brit Bennett." I show her the cover.

The woman's face lights up.

"*I* read that book—oh my goodness! Can I join the group?"

"Of course!" I run to the back and bring out the Maya Angelou chair for the woman before grabbing a copy of the book off the shelf. "Now, be careful with this one," I warn her. "I don't want a customer leaving here with wrinkled pages."

The woman sits down and makes herself comfortable. "Don't worry. I will treat this book like the precious jewel that it is."

After our first official book club meeting comes to a close, Mr. Watkins nearly trips over himself to be the first to ring up all the books being brought to the counter by new book club members.

PRETTY GIRL COUNTY

While he and Carmen are bagging tall stacks of books and running credit cards, I help Sommer put the chairs away in the back.

"This was an amazing idea, Reya," Sommer says. "I don't know how long we're going to be able to continue doing this, but for now, I just wanted you to know that I appreciate you coming up with the idea, and honestly? It took my mind off the bookstore issues for a little bit."

For the second time today, she flashes me a real smile.

I look down, feeling suddenly shy. "Usually when I do something, it's all about me—something to further my fashion career, or that will look good on college applications. This time, I wanted to do something that was a hundred percent for someone else. I'm just glad it all turned out okay."

"This is more than okay, Reya," Mr. Watkins goes. "I'm proud of you. I know you're juggling a lot right now."

"I am." I shake my head. "On that note, Sommer, I want to show you something out in my car."

After we check in with Mr. Watkins about taking this impromptu break, we go outside and climb into the back seat of my car.

There's barely any room, with all the fabric, spools of thread, and sketchbooks thrown all over the back seat.

"I swear, Reya. If I get randomly poked by a needle . . ." Sommer warns.

"I've been a little disorganized trying to get everything together for the show, Sommer, you know that." I shove some outfits to the side to make room for Sommer to sit comfortably

189

without tangling myself up in a pair of sparkly jeans. Then I dig around until I find what I'm looking for.

"Found it!" I say, holding up a small vest covered in feathers. "Remember this?"

Sommer gives a small smile. "I *do!*" She reaches out and takes the garment from my hands. "You actually saved this?" she asks me.

I nod. "You think I would lose contact with this beauty?" I stroke the vest. "Remember when we made this?"

She nods slowly. "Yeah, it was our first piece together."

"Remember when my mom said we were going to catch bird flu from all the goose feathers?" I say, laughing.

Sommer shakes her head, laughing. "Then *my* mom immediately took her side, so we had to show them we were making responsible choices by washing each feather one by one by hand."

"It took us hours!" I say.

"But it was worth it," she says softly.

We look at each other. "Because if so many feathers were just laying around in our neighborhood, all unattended, the geese were obviously donating to our fashion enterprise."

We both crack up laughing. Then Sommer takes a closer look at the craftsmanship of the piece.

"You know what, Reya? This is actually really good for a couple of eight-year-olds."

"I know," I say. "It was the first time I realized we could actually take an idea from our heads and make it a thing."

She looks at me. "We made the best stuff together."

PRETTY GIRL COUNTY

I nod. "Yeah, we really did. And we're doing it again. I think this fashion show is going to be our best work yet."

We sit together, not saying much of anything for a while, but then I work up the nerve to say what's been on my heart.

"Things are going to work themselves out, Sommer. I know it." I grab her hand. "Even when things looked bleak with us, we found our way back to each other . . . and things are looking up again, right?"

Sommer shakes her head. "That's different."

I stare through the windshield at Carmen laughing at something with Mr. Watkins. "You know what my girlfriend told me?"

Sommer looks over at me.

"Hold on, I'm trying to remember it all. It was something like things don't have to be the best to be okay. And we still have the right to exist and create beauty, even when things don't always appear perfect around us."

I slide our feathery design onto her lap. "No matter where you go, or what life throws at you, Sommer, you're going to keep creating beautiful stuff. Beauty lives in you. Anyone with eyes can see that."

Without warning, Sommer leans over and wraps her arms around me, hugging me tight. When she finally lets me go, she's smirking—which surprises me, because I thought we were having a touching moment.

"Your girlfriend, huh?"

"Yup." I point in the direction of the store. "That girlfriend of mine is a wise, wise woman. You should get you one."

"So that's how it's going to be?" Sommer's smile fades.

"Huh?" Uh-oh. "What did I do now?"

"You're going to be one of those 'my man, my man, my man' girlfriends?"

I stick out my tongue and create a heart with my hands. "That's right!" I exclaim. "When I know I have a winner, I'm going to make sure everybody knows my girl, my girl, my girl!"

23
Sommer

THE FASHION SHOW is officially one week out, and to say the first official run-through has been a disaster is a massive understatement.

Think of it as a dress rehearsal for a play, where everyone's costumes are supposed to fit perfectly, everyone knows their lines, and it's basically opening night, just with 100 percent less pressure.

Then picture the opposite.

So far, somebody got dressed behind the stage instead of in the bathroom and crashed through one of the backdrops. Marlon randomly lost some weight and now his evening wear look is practically falling off him. A freshman has to wear a mask through all of her runway looks, because she thinks she's coming down with something. And now, after the intense face-off at Six Flags, and taking several shots at each other on social media, Bryce is circling Cody like a lion prepared to pounce on its prey.

"What's up with round two, Park*star*?"

Before I can remind these two that there was never actually a round one, Reya comes busting through the models with a sewing needle and random fabric in her hands. "We're not *doing* this right now," she says through her teeth.

Even Sauce, to his credit, backs her up by telling his friend, "Come on. Not today."

But Bryce ignores their warnings and continues staring down Cody. "Nah, I'm standing right here. What was all that you were talking in your IG stories earlier today?"

Cody shakes his head. "Man, if you want to do this, we can schedule something for later on in the week, but I'm supposed to be walking in the show with my girl, and I'm not messing up my evening wear look stomping out a Bowie Bandit."

Bryce rolls up his sleeves. "Then let's change into our swimwear looks and get down to business—"

"Stop!" Reya shouts.

I think I might be witnessing the impossible: a full-on panic attack from the most confident person I've ever met.

She comes over to me, looking like she's seconds away from losing it. "They're going to ruin the show," she hisses. "I know it. We're already down a backdrop, and now they're about to tear up the outfits I spent weeks making over a stupid fight."

Since I'm still feeling sentimental about her pep talk the

PRETTY GIRL COUNTY

other night, I do my best to help ease some of her stress. And there's only one solution I see here.

"Bryce!" I yell. "You're out of the show."

Bryce takes his time looking me up and down. Then he brushes me off. "*You* are not in charge of nothing, so you can turn around and go back to where you came from." He squints his eyes at me a second. "What city are you from, anyway?"

While I'm raising an eyebrow, Reya steps in front of me. "I am in charge of this show, Bryce," she goes. "And Sommer's right . . . you're done."

Now Bryce looks like a wounded cat. "*Me?* What did *I* do?"

"You're ruining my show!"

"What about him?" Bryce jerks a thumb toward Cody.

Reya shakes her head. "Look, I don't care what Cody posted on IG earlier today. He was minding his business when it matters." She points her sewing needle at Bryce. "*You* walked up to him trying to reignite the beef. At this point, you're a loose thread in the fabric of this show."

Bryce's face is extra tight as he stalks off. But Reya's back in director mode, so I assume everything's about to settle down.

Sauce, though, still looks worried. "You think she might need me to take her outside for a second to get some fresh air or something?"

I look over at Reya and shake my head. "I'm not sure. On one hand, I see what you mean." She's back in the swing of things, straightening someone's lapel while giving stage directions to another model. Basically doing a hundred things at once without stopping for a breather. "But if we stop rehearsals again, she might kick us out of the show."

Sauce nods. "Where are her car keys? I'm going to run to her car and get her Stanley cup. She should at least be hydrated through all this."

I give him a thumbs-up. "I'll keep her distracted so she doesn't notice you gone."

As Sauce runs out one of the side doors and Reya repositions models, I'm standing in the thick of things, genuinely surprised I've gotten so invested in this event. A few weeks ago, I would've checked the temperature of any person who predicted this. But I've just finished the digital lookbook, and I'm proud of the looks. Even though I gave my two cents, these designs are 100 percent Reya. It's pretty exciting watching them come alive on the runway.

The moment Sauce runs back over with chilled water for Reya, she thanks him and takes a sip.

"Okay, Azadeh!" she calls out. "Let me see you walk like it's graduation day and you're valedictorian!"

Azadeh smiles. "Sure thing." She struts across the stage in an exaggerated way that shows off her walking skills. But right before she gets to the stairs, her heel gets lodged in a crack in the stage's wood grain and she wobbles a second. Then falls to the floor.

"My ankle!" she cries out.

I gasp and run over immediately, with Reya following right behind me. By the time we reach the edge of the stage, Sauce

PRETTY GIRL COUNTY

is already stooped down, holding Azadeh's foot—which is beginning to swell.

"Are you okay?" he asks.

"Look at my ankle! Does it look like I'm okay?"

I can see from here that her ankle is already the size of a tennis ball. This doesn't look good already. For Azadeh. Or for Reya's show.

"Can you carry her to the nurse?" Reya asks Sauce.

He looks off toward the hall. "Is the nurse even still here?"

A freshman pipes up. "I saw her leave with the buses right after dismissal."

"It hurts so bad!" Azadeh moans.

"Well, I know first aid," Sauce goes. "The custodian can probably let me into the nurse's office to grab an ice pack and an ACE bandage."

You know, this whole first-responder thing is a *really* good look on Sauce. I make a note to ask him what he plans to major in at school next year.

Immediately, Sauce jumps into action, carrying Azadeh out of the cafeteria. I wonder if he's ever considered becoming an EMT, or a firefighter. Four years of college isn't the *only* path to a rewarding career.

Anyway, Reya is left standing with her bullhorn, clearly trying to figure out the professional thing to do in this matter. "My friend is hurt. But the show is only in a few days," she mutters to me.

I get it. "The show must go on" is a phrase for a reason, but it feels wildly awkward to say that right now. I do appreciate Reya thinking of her friend first in the midst of all this show stuff.

Almost like he can read our thoughts, Sauce turns just before he carries Azadeh into the hall. "Keep going," he tells us. He nods to Reya. "We've got this."

So that's what we do. While Sauce is working on Azadeh's ankle, Reya and I help the rest of the models perfect their walk, turns, and overall stage presence.

Fifteen minutes go by before Sauce and a hobbling Azadeh return to the cafeteria. "Are you feeling better?" Reya asks her friend.

Azadeh slumps down into the nearest chair. "No."

Reya hesitates. She looks at me before looking back at Sauce. "So, um, everyone's been down the runway at least a dozen times. Sean? Do you think you could hop back up there? I'd like to see your turn again."

Sauce nods and heads to the stage.

Reya turns back to Azadeh, and a sinking feeling hits my belly. *No, Reya, you were doing so good.* But I already know when she bites down on her lip like that, she's on the brink of asking something wildly inappropriate.

"Um, Deh? Do you think you could . . . maybe . . . go up there with him? I know your walk won't be perfect, given what just happened to your ankle and all . . ."

Azadeh looks at Reya like she's grown two heads. "Are you kidding me right now? I won't be walking anywhere for weeks."

PRETTY GIRL COUNTY

"Of course, of course," Reya says quickly. "I just had to ask."

Reya grabs her Stanley cup and takes a few massive gulps as she watches Sauce walk down the runway.

"Not so fast," I tell her, prepared to whack her on the back if she starts choking. "Azadeh already knows the routine, and Sauce can walk alone until her ankle feels better."

"That could take forever," Reya moans. "We have, like, zero time for this. The entire show's aesthetic is counting on a certain number of models and we just lost two. I don't even have time to remake costumes in new sizes. Not to mention, I have to fix the backdrop."

Just then the freshman with a mask comes coughing over.

"Hold it in," Reya shrieks. "I can't lose another model."

This gets a side-eye from me. "I'm not getting sick this close to graduation so you can send a model down a runway with a miniskirt and a fever," I tell my friend.

Reya stands up. I can tell she's finally come to terms with this being over—not for good, but at least for the day.

She puts her bullhorn to her mouth. "That's it. Shut it down. Seriously, everybody. Cut the stage lights. Show's off. Canceled. Done. I'll just take a gap year and try again next year."

Wait. *Gap year?*

All strutting has ceased. The remaining members of the show are all frozen in place like JCPenney catalogue models. No one knows what to do—or what to say. Including me.

Since when are we taking things this far after one failed rehearsal?

Reya holds up her glittery bullhorn and stares at it a moment. Then walks over to the trash cans and dumps it in before storming out of the cafeteria.

Sauce walks over to grab her forgotten Stanley cup. "You think she's serious?"

I'm wondering the same thing. "She'd better not be. Not after I spent all that time working on that digital lookbook she just *had* to have." I shake my head in disbelief. "Plus, with the bookstore already closing, I don't think I can take another thing in my life shuttering to a close."

Sauce wraps an arm around my waist. "That reminds me," he goes. "I went to my parents to see if there was something they could do. Maybe donate money, or talk to someone at the city. They said they would look into it."

I look up at him. "Why didn't you say something?"

"I mean, nothing is for sure yet, so I didn't want to get your hopes up." He looks down. "But I wouldn't just leave you down bad. I care about you, Sommer—a lot. I can't be good unless you're good."

Okay. It's that part for me. Just knowing he tried is enough. I'm *this close* to calling for an all-school ban on the use of the name Brat Pack.

Then he blows it.

"Yeah, my dad suggested moving the bookstore altogether. He thinks Grand Rising will do more sales in an area like Bowie or in a prime spot down at the National Harbor, anyway."

PRETTY GIRL COUNTY

I frown and slide out from under his arm. Grand Rising is a part of *Seat Pleasant's* community. The readers in our own neighborhood kept the store afloat, even growing, all these years. Taking the bookstore out of its home doesn't feel right.

"Why *there*?" Would Grand Rising even have the same flavor in a place like Bowie? What about all our current customers who don't have cars? Would they have to take several buses out to Bowie or the National Harbor to pick up books?

Sauce tries to slide his arm back around my waist. "They're better areas, where there's more demand for books."

Pushing his arm away, I don't even try to hide the edge to my voice. "There's a demand for books in Seat Pleasant."

Sauce finally gives up on his wannabe warm embrace. "I mean, I *guess*. I'm just saying if you have to move the store anyway, maybe do it where your dad will have a better shot at success."

Something about that "I guess" itches my nerves. What is that supposed to mean? People in Seat Pleasant don't read? You know what? Let me just go ahead and grab my stuff before I pull a Bryce near this runway.

The truth is, I already know Grand Rising is basically over. But moving it somewhere else? And trying to turn it into something it's not? That will not happen.

24
Reya

WHAT DOES A gap year baddie do when she's just announced she has no post–high school plans days before graduation?

Lie in bed all weekend and keep the trend going through Monday—taking a much-needed break from bell schedules, hallway gossip, and most importantly, after-school clubs.

Look, don't judge me, okay? Everybody else got to have their Senior Skip Day. I just delayed mine for a few days is all.

Instead of riding roller coasters, I'm going to stay right here and pretend that all my plans aren't crumbling around me.

But then that plan crumbles, too, with the ring of my phone.

"Where are you?" Sommer demands. "And what are you doing today?"

"I'm taking my own personal Senior Skip Day."

PRETTY GIRL COUNTY

"No, you're not."

I sit up in bed. "Oh *yes*, I am. Everybody else got to have their—"

"Reya . . ."

"What?"

"You do know Friday was the last day for seniors, right? At this point, you would probably get in trouble for *showing up* to school."

That's it. I throw my head back and let out the biggest silent scream. Because at this point, I'm even failing at skipping school. Where does the injustice end?!

"So, um, since seniors have a free week from now until graduation, you can do me a tiny favor and drive me to Bowie State, right?"

"For what?"

"I want to tour the campus again . . . you know, in case I decide to go there."

Before I can say a word, Sommer launches into a detailed itinerary of her plans for the day. "We'll even be back in enough time for final rehearsals for the fashion show."

I glare at my phone. "I thought I made it perfectly clear last Friday that the show was off."

"What about FIT?"

I let out a long, exaggerated yawn. "Not a good fit, evidently." I'm still going to turn in the final portfolio to FIT in a few days, but I doubt I even check back in.

A few awkward pauses later.

"Well, it won't be if you just give up."

"Already given up, Sommer, darling," I sing into the phone.

A sigh comes through the line. "Well, now you really should come tour Bowie State with me."

Aggravating. "What part of 'I don't feel like going to college anymore' don't you get, Sommer?"

Sommer doesn't acknowledge this. Instead she goes, "Please just be here to get me within the hour. I want to get there early enough to see everything and ask lots of questions."

"Whatever." I end the call and pull the covers up to my chin. Less than a minute later, I throw the covers off and head to the shower.

I pick up Sommer thirty minutes later and we head up the road toward the university nestled deep in the heart of Bowie.

"I still can't believe I agreed to do this." I sigh.

"Well, you did, so try to perk up some," Sommer says.

"Fine, I'll try."

"And please don't walk around the campus with your nose stuck up in the air." She gives me a look. "I mean it, Reya. We might have to live on this campus next year. I don't need people thinking I share your biases and judgments."

"When have I ever?"

"Reya . . ."

"Fine. My nose will remain at a reasonable altitude."

Sommer leans back in her seat. "I know this isn't your

PRETTY GIRL COUNTY

precious FIT, but it's still a really good school. I've been on Reddit checking out student reviews for days now."

I'll be the judge of this.

The first thing I notice when I pull into the entrance of Bowie State University are the trees. "Wow, I could sit almost anywhere out here and design," I tell Sommer as I drive through the roundabout and closer to the academic buildings. "When I come to visit, of course."

Sommer nods, taking it all in.

I find a space in visitor parking, and together Sommer and I take our time touring the campus. We check out the residential halls, but that adventure is short-lived. No one in Tubman Hall looks down to let a couple of strangers snoop around their dorm room. So, we backtrack out to the quad and head for Banneker Hall to see where the students graduate when they've finally completed their degrees.

Right before we reach the doors of Thurgood Marshall Library, I read the plaque stationed out front.

"Bowie State University, the oldest HBCU in the state of Maryland. Around since 1864." I give Sommer a funny look, and she gives me one back.

"What? You thought Howard University was our only option back then?" Sommer asks.

"Well, yeah."

"Well, you have a lot to learn about HBCUs."

You can totally tell it's finals season because it's packed inside the library. Students are filtering in and out the stacks, bent over textbooks and using the quiet rooms to study together.

205

Since Bowie State is an HBCU, I already expect to see Black students everywhere. Still, seeing everyone looking like a college brochure brought to life feels nice.

"This school is prettier than I thought," I tell Sommer.

She raises an eyebrow. "What did you expect?"

I shrug. "I don't know . . . I guess, I always see the school sign when I pass it on Laurel-Bowie Road, but I never knew all of this was back here."

When we finally make it back outside, I cup my hand over my brow and look off in the distance.

"What are you looking for?" Sommer asks.

"The School of Fashion."

She gives me a look. "Oh yeah? Rethinking that gap year? You starting to get serious?"

I shrug. "No. I'm still planning to backpack through some distant country for a year or so. That doesn't mean I don't want to see what Bowie's fashion program is like."

Sommer walks me over to a large plastic board showcasing a map of the campus. She trails her finger along the diagram, stopping on a small blue rectangle.

"I think it's on the other side of the quad," she says.

"Let's go."

The fashion students don't need to get on bullhorns and introduce themselves. Their outfits do all the announcing. Summer scarves. Bespoke 'fits. Stilettos in all colors. They are the epitome of fashion, and I am all the way here for it.

A little spark of something tingles inside, but I chalk it up

PRETTY GIRL COUNTY

to simple nostalgia—from the days I actually believed fashion would take me somewhere.

I may have given up hope on myself, but I'm still friendly.

I finger wave to a small group of fashion students lounging on the steps of the academic building. Only one waves back. The rest are engrossed in a fan of sketches and lightly debating over which look will be cut from their final project.

"Nice outfit," a member of the group calls out.

"Thank you." Secretly, I'm blushing. An actual student of the craft recognized something in *me*.

We walk through the heavy double doors and down the hall, stopping at one of the studios to watch another student adjust the hem of a dress draped over a mannequin, her fingers performing a perfectly synced two-step with her needle.

"May I help you?"

Sommer and I turn toward the tall woman standing a few feet away. Her hair is cropped into a short Afro. A colorfully beaded strap hangs from her cat-eye frames. Her expression is curious.

"We're just looking." I walk over to the woman and extend my hand. "I actually applied to FIT next year, but I didn't get in." Discomfort starts to swell inside me. "I was also planning to throw one of the biggest fashion shows of the year at AHS . . . but that isn't happening, either," I say quietly.

The woman ignores my obvious discomfort. "So, you're a student of fashion?"

"Not yet." I shrug. "Maybe one day."

The woman raises a brow. "One doesn't *become* a student of fashion. One must be born with a certain level of curiosity for the art form." She opens a door marked DR. APOLONIA WILLOW-BEE, DEAN OF FASHION.

Her office is a sanctuary of fashion sketches, a dress dummy in the corner, and an archive of lookbook albums, arranged by semester and year, shelved behind her desk.

When we move inside, she sits and folds her hands. "Let's see some of your work."

Huh?

"Oh, we don't have to worry about that, Dean Willowbee," I tell her. "I've already been accepted into Bowie State. But a lot of stuff happened . . . and I'm probably not going anywhere."

She raises an eyebrow. "What does school have to do with sharing your work with a fellow fashion colleague?"

Hmm. I like this woman's style.

Quickly, I dig my phone out of my purse and pull up an album in my photos. "These were some of my pieces for the show I canceled." I hand over my phone.

Dean Willowbee spends no more than fifteen seconds frowning at my screen before handing my phone back. "I guess it's good you're not coming here."

Um, excuse me? "Why's that?" I ask, fighting to keep my voice respectful.

"We don't like quitters at Bowie." She shrugs. "Not to mention, this collection is incomplete."

My right eye twitches. "Well, I know that. They weren't done yet. I still have zippers to install."

PRETTY GIRL COUNTY

"No," she states matter-of-factly. "*Those* pieces are still in concept development."

Her slander annoys me, and even though I've called off the show, suddenly a deep-seated need to stick up for myself emerges. "Dean Willowbee, no offense, but if certain things didn't transpire, my collection would be hitting the runway in days. These pieces were practically done."

Dean Willowbee sighs, then reaches into a glass jar on her desk for a piece of peppermint candy. She leans forward. "Have you ever eaten a piece of chicken without seasoning?" She shudders for affect. "Sure, it's edible. But digestion becomes harder without the flavor. If you just added a *few* signature additions to these looks, they would soar."

She enlarges the screen of my phone with her fingers. "It's too bad. With a little more commitment on the part of the designer, these pieces could have been great."

I narrow my eyes. But before I can say anything, she opens the door for us. "Have a good day, girls. Unlike you, I have to get back to work."

I bet you think I left Dean Willowbee's office fuming. You probably think my ballerina flats are practically racing toward an unsuspecting mannequin to kick, right? *Wrong.*

I politely thank the dean for her time and critique and swipe a card from her desk before walking back into the hall.

"Please don't tell me you're going to call her later in the week to continue your debate?" Sommer asks.

"No," I say quickly. The truth is, I do plan on debating Dean Willowbee, but not in the way you might think. Something about the way she called me and my collection out offends me.

I look back at the sign on the dean's door and sniff. "I won't have anyone compare *my* collection to unseasoned chicken." I swallow hard. "I'm going to send the dean a few photos of the collection once it's a hundred percent complete and see what she has to say then."

Sommer frowns. "Doesn't she have actual students to focus on? How can you be sure your email won't end up in her junk folder?"

I turn to Sommer, eyes blazing. "Because I don't create *junk*!"

I only make it a few steps across the quad before I pull out my phone and check the time. "Grab your phone," I tell Sommer.

"Okay, why?"

I look around me. "Let's AirDrop a few show flyers around campus on our way back to my car." I check the time again. "We should probably hurry, too, if we're going to gather up everyone and make it to fashion show rehearsal on time."

Sommer looks at me, her eyes suddenly sparkling. "Oh, so the show's back on just like that?"

"Haven't you been paying attention?" I ask, rushing back to my car. "Of course it is, and we only have six days to make it amazing."

25
Sommer

EVERYTHING ABOUT BOWIE State was beautiful. The layout of the campus. The buildings named after important Black historical figures. All the Black students walking around making progress on their dreams.

I think about this throughout the entire "fashion show's back on" emergency rehearsal. And yet, I can't bring myself to get as excited about attending Bowie as I am about Spelman.

"Am I being a snob for not appreciating the whole Bowie State experience?" I ask Reya. She's without her glittery bullhorn this afternoon, but with less than six days left until the show, she still commands the entire room.

"Priorities, Sommer," she says without taking her eyes off a sophomore strutting down the runway.

"Also, Bowie State can be the most amazing school in the

world," she throws in. "But if going there next year isn't in your heart, then it's not for you."

I realize she's right. I'm not choosing Spelman because every other Black girl wants to go there. I'm choosing it because *this* Black girl has never been close to anywhere like it.

I want to see something brand new—that isn't in Maryland. A whole new world, even if I'm only traveling to a different state. No shade to Bowie State, but Mom and Dad have driven me by there so many times on the way to the hair salon, or the mall, or to a friend's house, that it feels like I've been there before. If I'm ever going to branch out and spread my wings, I *have* to see something different.

But I can't *afford* Spelman, especially with the bookstore closing. So, I try to throw my heart into Bowie State anyway—through the end of rehearsals, and even on the long bus ride back home.

I'm still trying and failing to come up with a way to fall in love with a school that isn't a part of my dream, so I'm not paying attention to my surroundings as I walk up my front steps.

I don't even feel his presence until I hear his voice.

"What's up, Lil Bookstore."

I turn around and there's Octavius, wearing a simple white tank and a pair of royal-blue gym shorts. A little thrown off guard, I let the first thought to pop in my head slip out of my mouth. "You're not with your girlfriend, Jada, today?"

I'm instantly embarrassed. Because what am I doing?

Octavius's forehead wrinkles. "What? Jada is not my girl. Don't play with her like that. That's been my play cousin since

PRETTY GIRL COUNTY

we were in diapers. We're really just friends . . . unlike you and your Bowie boyfriend."

Now I'm in denial mode. "I told you, Octavius . . . that is *not* my man." I'm not trying to downplay my situation with Sauce. I like him and everything. But we've never made anything official. And frankly, our last conversation has me feeling a little off-balance about the whole thing.

Octavius doesn't seem bothered by the logistics of my love life, though.

"Anyway," he says, still straddling his bike. "I pulled up on you to show you something that might help your dad's store."

This gets my attention immediately. "Oh yeah, what's that?"

Octavius nods toward his handlebars. "Hop on the whip and I'll show you."

I walk over and take my usual front row seat. But I literally could've walked. We ride four houses down to Octavius's house on the corner.

He stashes his bike in the bushes and digs his key out of his sock.

We've lived on this block our entire lives, and I'm realizing this is the first time he's ever invited me in.

Octavius sticks his key in the door and we walk into a house that's laid out very similar to mine. Steps right by the door that immediately walk up into a living room / dining room combo with a kitchen off the side. Instead of having a BLESS THIS MESS sign near the door, though, there's a giant oil painting of Black Jesus making prayer hands over a sign that says THE FAMILY THAT PRAYS TOGETHER STAYS TOGETHER.

When Octavius catches me staring at the painting, he goes, "Oh yeah. My mama don't play about church, Bible study, or my schoolwork." He gives me a look. "You ever been threatened with the Bible?"

"What, like, 'Thou shalt not sin'?"

Octavius chuckles. "Nah. Like, 'Boy, Imma go upside your head with this thick Bible if you roll in here with one more missing assignment.'"

I fake gasp. "Did she make good on her threat?"

Octavius chuckles. "Heck no. I made sure I got all my work in. The Bible my mama carries around is thick. I'm not taking any chances."

As we're heading up the stairs, Octavius puts me on notice. "Aight, so Imma let you in on one little thing. We're not one of those bougie one-kid households like your family."

"Being an only child doesn't make me bougie," I protest.

"You have your own room, don't you?"

"Yeah, so?"

"Well, I don't. I've been sharing a room with my two brothers my entire life. But this is my senior year. I couldn't go another year with one brother kicking me in the face in his sleep and having to get dressed in the closet for a crumb of privacy."

He puffs out his chest. "I'll be eighteen this month—and a man needs his own space."

We stop in front of a white rectangle cut into the ceiling. A thick frayed string hangs from its center. Octavius pulls on the string, and after a lot of creaking and groaning, the white rectangle pulls down, revealing a hidden ladder.

PRETTY GIRL COUNTY

Octavius unfolds the ladder, then beckons me to follow him up into the attic. "I'm not going to lie," he says, hoisting himself up. "It's hot as hell up here. But nothing a good box fan from Family Dollar can't fix." He pats the whirring metal box. "Plus, once I save up for one of those air-conditioning units that sit in the window, you're going to be looking at the Seat Pleasant Drive penthouse."

I take a look around me, amazed at what Octavius has done with the spot. Faux wood planks have been installed across the floor. Walls have been put up with drywall and painted a baby blue. Posters of Che and Malcolm X adorn his walls over a queen-size blow-up mattress in the center of the room. A tiny desk sits in the corner with one of those old-school desktop computers.

"This is amazing, Tate," I tell him. "But what does it have to do with Grand Rising?"

"Everything," Octavius say. "Okay, check this. So, like, I've been thinking about building my own space since forever. But we're connected to another house, so it's not like I can build out. The only real option I had was to build up."

I look at the stars glowing green on his ceiling. "I still can't believe you did all this yourself."

Octavius looks proud of his accomplishment. "It doesn't take as much as you think to create something big," Octavius goes. "This room gave me more than just a private place to lay my head at night, though."

"It gave you a study place, too."

Octavius shakes his head. "That, too," he goes. "But working on this project also showed me what I want to do after high school. I think I could make a good architect."

I look around the room again. "The best."

Octavius smiles at this. Then he gets serious again. "What if the county left your father's store where it is and build a community center on top of it." He shrugs. "Everybody would be getting what they want."

I'm not sure when the county plans to knock down the store or if it's too late to throw out new ideas for the space. But the fact that Octavius thought enough about my dad's store to try to save it presses on my heart.

"You care that much about my dad's store, huh?"

"Yeah." Octavius walks close enough to me that I can now smell the light scent of his bodywash. "Grand Rising is like a hood legend."

He gets it—why the bookstore is more than just a few shelves lined with books. It's a landmark, a hangout, an important part of our community.

"That's what's up," I say softly. I smile at him, and as he smiles back, his eyes locking with mine, I realize that I may have gotten this boy all wrong.

26
Reya

I'VE SPENT EVERY waking second since leaving Bowie State working on the collection—fixing the torn pieces and backdrop, sewing zippers, and adding "seasoning" to the chicken, thank you very much. We're five days out from showtime when Sommer video calls with a problem. This time *not* related to the bookstore.

"So, Amara and Reed are judging you for maybe liking Octavius?" I prop my phone up on my desk so I can use both hands to get these last-minute touches to my outfits done.

"Yeah, I talked to them a few minutes before I called you," Sommer says. "They feel like I can't betray Sauce by even thinking of Octavius in that way, especially since Sauce and I have been building toward something. But, like, Amara and Reed are already a couple. Their situation is different than mine. I know I've been building things with Sauce, but I never said I was his girl. We're just figuring things out."

"Yeah, but," I say, playing devil's advocate, "how do you think Sauce would feel if he knew you were having feelings for Octavius?"

"He would be crushed." She looks up at me. "I'm not some heartless person, Reya. Sauce is amazing. He's not perfect, but his heart is genuine, and he's been applying pressure for weeks." She goes quiet. "But Octavius, he knows me, knows where I come from. Understands parts about me that would take years to try and get Sauce to understand. I never even thought about Octavius like that before. But now that I have, I can't stop thinking about him."

A part of me wants to pledge immediate allegiance to my friend Sean. But I've known Tate forever, too. "It's like you're caught between two worlds, huh?" I ask.

Sommer deadpans me. "This is nothing like what happened between us," she says quietly.

I put my fabric down. "How is it different? You're caught between two good things. And choosing is impossible."

Sommer makes a face. "So, I guess according to Reya logic, I should choose Sauce. He's rich and handsome, with an expensive whip. That's the more exciting option, right?"

I think about my mother and her hangups on image.

"I'm not saying that at all. I'm saying that regardless of what he has or doesn't have, Sean is a good guy. If you were on him for his car, you would've been in his passenger seat years ago."

Sommer looks down. "True."

PRETTY GIRL COUNTY

"You like Sean because he's a good guy. The problem is you're just now finding out Octavius is bae material, too."

"Please stop saying 'bae,' Reya. I know you want that word to still be a thing, but—"

"It's true, though, right? You're caught between two good situations and there's only one of you." I drive in my point. "Choose Sean, you've been dating him longer."

"Yeah, but Octavius gets me . . ."

"So, choose Tate . . . You've known him longer."

"Yeah, but . . ."

"You see what I mean, Sommer?"

I don't mean to make this situation about me, but I think it's long overdue I say something about our friendship and my role in its demise.

"Sommer, I've been wanting to say something. Explain myself. I don't know . . . I didn't leave you . . . I just had trouble splitting myself between an amazing new experience and a situation I've loved forever." I bite down on my bottom lip. "I'm sorry I didn't know how to juggle both worlds, Sommer."

On the other end of the screen, Sommer's eyes soften. "When you left, I was really hurt. I mean, how far apart were we, really? But . . . I guess everyone makes mistakes. At the end of the day, you're not perfect, but you're not a bad person. I might have been mad over how you carried things, but you've been my day one, too. Honestly? It's been really nice having you back."

I smile into the phone screen. "Also, while we're having a moment, I realize I never properly thanked you for helping

219

me save the show—and my collection." I run my finger over a zipper that took me forever to install. "I just wish there was something I could do to help save the bookstore."

Sommer shakes her head. "At this point, unless a bunch of people stage a sit-in or make the store go viral, there's basically nothing that can be done." She ticks off her list on her fingers. "Protestors or influencers, that's it."

"Or Housewives . . ." I say, already feeling a good plan forming.

Sommer makes a face. "Yeah, right. *Housewives* cameras are not coming to Seat Pleasant."

Come on, plan. Do your thing. "What if we went to the cameras?" I blurt out.

"Reya? Enough with the schemes."

I ignore Sommer's lack of enthusiasm. Now that the plan is materializing in my head, I can't be stopped.

When my mother yells up the stairs, "Reya, you know we have to leave soon. Are you riding with me?" I know now is my only chance.

Quickly I yell back, "Uhhh, I'll drive myself, Mommy!"

"But that's wasting gas, we're going to the same place . . ."

"Yeah, but . . . um . . . um . . ." I'm not a superhero. I can't come up with two plans at once. "I'll just drive myself, okay?"

From one floor below, Mom sighs. "Fine, whatever. Just be at the Potomac house on time. You are supporting cast. No one's going to hold up production for you."

PRETTY GIRL COUNTY

I turn back to my phone. "Come to Potomac with me, Sommer."

"For what?"

"To film."

Sommer raises an eyebrow. "You want me to suddenly appear on TV, to the entire world, and you haven't even given me time to get my hair and nails done? Are you trying to get me picked apart by social media?"

"Listen, Sommer. Trust me. We want social media to pay attention." I dive into my plan.

"Come to Potomac with me. We're shooting a sketchy dinner scene that's going to be fake boots, but that's not our concern." My scheming grin grows larger. "We're going to sit side by side at dinner and mention 'Grand Rising' and 'an important Black-owned bookstore' every other sentence."

Sommer raises her eyebrow. "And production is going to edit that right on out—come on, Reya. This isn't your mom's first season."

I won't let Sommer's lack of confidence deter me. "You're underestimating how many times I can work 'Grand Rising' and 'I just love a good Angie Thomas novel' into a conversation."

Sommer shakes. "Okay, I still don't think you're going to get away with that. But honestly, I'd try anything if it could help."

I watch her walk over to her closet. "So who am I supposed to be? A family friend?" she calls back to me.

I shrug. "Since we're having dinner at a house we don't even live in anyway, we might as well pretend you're my long-lost sister."

Sommer giggles while throwing up the peace sign. "Smile, it's a photo shoot!"

"*Exactly.* Get dressed in your most luxurious finery. If you need to borrow a faux leather vest, I got you."

"In *this* heat? Girl, I'm wearing jeans and a tee."

"Whatever. Just be ready by the time I get over there to scoop you."

Her expression suddenly gets serious. "Seriously, though, Reya. Thank you."

I smile as we hang up. If we're lucky, we may save more than just the bookstore.

27
Sommer

"AMARA AND REED would chuck their laptops to be in a *Housewives* scene," I slide my simple plastic Target sunnies down over my eyes, feeling like I've snuck my way onto "it girl" status for the first time in my life. "So what am I supposed to do while you eat lobster and drink Fiji water at the dinner table?"

Reya squeezes my hand. "Look cute eating lobster and drinking Fiji water with us."

We giggle as we continue riding up 495 northbound toward Potomac, Maryland.

"So, will the other Housewives be there?" Now that we're nearing the exit, I'm getting a little nervous. What if the Octo Housewife showed up looking for a rematch? I don't exactly meet the emerald brooch and diamond tennis bracelet requirement.

"Not that I know of. This is supposed to be, like, a family scene."

I quietly let out a sigh of relief.

My lack of Gucci and Fendi aside, I'm still pretty excited about filming. It goes right along with my plans of new worlds and new experiences.

Reya drives into the exclusive Potomac Round Hill community. In PG County, the houses look nice, but are pretty much the same. Colonial. Two- and three-car garages and nice-size front and back lawns clustered pretty close together.

In Potomac, the mansions are palatial and spread out over acres of rolling hills and backed up to glistening lakes and streams. Each is uniquely sculpted to impress. A French chateau–inspired estate with elaborate window boxes and fancy shutters sits on a hilltop, overlooking the Potomac River. A historic-looking Tuscan-style country estate sits behind a circular cobblestone driveway. Two breezeways connect the main house to two other structures. A sprawling patio sits to the left. Horse stables sit to the right. A hidden enclave reveals the most grandiose estate yet with two tennis courts and a golf cart sitting directly outside a garage that looks bigger than my entire house.

When Reya drives through the entrance of this home, my jaw drops over how vast everything looks. There is more manicured lawn than I can take in on one look and a quietness to the space that somehow appears warm and inviting.

Reya parks on the corner of the circular driveway, but be-

PRETTY GIRL COUNTY

fore she gets out of the car, she sort of stares up ahead and gets quiet for a moment. "Sommer, before we go in, I have to warn you of something."

I know that look all too well. Something's bothering my friend. I gently squeeze Reya's hand for support. "What is it?"

Looking down at her lap, Reya goes, "My mom's been on one lately. So, yes, we're here on our own agenda. But be warned. She is, too."

I shrug. "I mean, the minute your mom called herself the Potomac Princess, I knew this wasn't going to be dipped in authenticity."

Reya doesn't laugh. "You don't understand. Mom has been acting funny about everything lately, and I don't know . . . I don't want her to—"

"Don't worry about it, Reya." I sling an arm around her shoulder. "I've been knowing your mom since forever, too, re-member? She's always been an eyes-on-the-prize sort of person. I mean, it's not exactly a bad trait. Everybody should be striv-ing for better . . ."

"Yeah, but . . ." Reya fiddles with her fingers a moment longer, then puts her game face on. "Come on, let's just go."

When we get out of the car, the sheer size of the mansion looms up at me. The double-door entryway lets us into a grand greeting room with cathedral ceilings and marble flooring. Off to the side is a gallery room leading into a vast mahogany library with more books filling the shelves than our entire inventory at the bookstore.

It takes everything in me not to shout, "*Daaaannng*, we should've been having parties up in *here!*" But I do have *some* couth, so I keep it cute.

Reya leads me down a hallway where the chef's kitchen boasts limestone flooring, a massive teak island and custom build cabinets showcasing expensive china and luxury cookware that looks like it hasn't been used once. Two more family rooms loom on the other side of the kitchen, one featuring floor-to-ceiling sliding doors that lead outside to the giant three-story deck.

I follow Reya outside where her mom is talking to a person I can only assume is a *Housewives* producer by the way she's waving her arms and demanding. "I'm not playing this game with you all this season. Get the scene I want or I'm not shooting. And another thing? That new Housewife? I'm not filming with her, so if she shows up here, I'm done for the day. I'm warning you now."

Finally, Ms. Angelica notices us. "Reya, baby, thank goodness you're finally here. We need to prep you for this dinner scene, and—"

She stops when she spots me. "Hey, Sommer, baby. I didn't know you were coming."

Her tone is singsong. But a certain something in her eye makes me question her words. "Reya told me it was okay to come . . ."

You used to make me peanut butter and jelly sandwiches, I silently plead to Ms. Angelica. *Please don't start acting brand new now.*

PRETTY GIRL COUNTY

Even though Reya warned me, a familiar feeling begins rising in the pit of my stomach. The ball of nerves I get when I window-shop at Tysons Corner mall without wearing designer. The loopy feeling I get when people ask, "Sommer with an *O*? Why on earth would your parents spell your name that way?" The overwhelming feeling I get when I know without a shadow of a doubt that everybody in the room has more money than I do. And I know that they know it, too.

Just as quickly as the anger rises up in my chest, Ms. Angelica's smile deepens. "Baby, I'm fine with you being here . . . Advance notice would've been nice." She tosses a look to Reya. "Because the glam I hired for today is going to have to work double time to get you two ready."

She grabs my hand and guides me closer to a little hair-and-makeup station set up in the yard.

I wait patiently for Reya to get her eyebrows redone. Then I sit down in the chair so the stylist can "slick these edges down better." Her words, not mine.

While I'm being primped, the Pretend Potomac Princess saunters back over.

"Reya, baby. Don't forget, we're going to sit around the table and discuss plans for your graduation party." She steps an inch closer into her daughter's ear. "And please don't forget to throw in a little tidbit about one of my cases. You know every time we mention my practice on camera, potential clients pour in."

Reya nods.

"And, Sommer, why don't you borrow one of my shirts?"

I frown but don't protest when the stylist hands me a designer blouse.

Soon enough, we're all seated around the table, mic'd up, and ready to roll. The red light goes on and I hide my nerves as best as I can.

Reya flashes her mother a big smile. "Is that a new bracelet, Mommy?" she asks. "How *grand*. But it keeps *rising* up your arm. Here, let me fix it for you."

It's all I can do to keep from laughing into my microphone. I guess this is Reya's way of easing her mom in.

Ms. Angelica fiddles with her arm candy for a moment, but seconds later she's whispering, "Don't forget the court stuff. Remember."

Reya nods, as if remembering her lines.

"Nothing beats your famous courtroom catchphrase, Mom: 'If the evidence isn't legit, you must acquit.'" She slips in the fakest laugh I've ever heard. "Tell me, Mommy. How many cases have you won with that line?"

Ms. Angelica, decked out in her finest silk Yves Saint Laurent floor-length kaftan, takes another sip of champagne. "You know, I like to say it's somewhere in the hundreds, but I was chatting it up with one of the judges the other day, and she mentioned we have to be nearing a thousand by now."

"*Grand* . . ." Reya says with a straight face. "*Rising* your clients up from the trenches of the prison system? Commendable."

I see my chance to jump in. "Clearing so many defendants

PRETTY GIRL COUNTY

from wrongful convictions probably gives them the free time to enjoy community spaces."

Reya turns to me. "Can you think of any great public spaces in our community?"

"Well, there's the Grand Rising bookstore, for one . . ."

I throw Ms. Angelica a sunny smile. But she's tossing back nothing but breezy shade. "Cut the cameras for a second," she demands. Then she turns to me and Reya. "I see what you're doing. But you better not mention that little run-down kiosk."

Her sudden venom bites into me harder than expected.

"*This* show is called Potomac . . . Let's keep it that way." She sits back up and pastes a smile on her face. "Okay, we can roll. Please remind the grips to film from my *good* side," Mom tells her producer, Shelby. "I can't suck in my cheekbones the *entire* dinner."

The red light goes back on, but I am too pissed to playact in this charade.

"Sommer . . ." I hear Reya say as I push the chair back from the table and stand up. I can't even look at Ms. Angelica.

"Don't apologize for your mother," I tell Reya. "She said it, not you." I rip my mic off and throw it down on the table. "I'll wait in the car until you're done."

"Sommer . . ."

I turn to face my friend. "No, Reya. I'm not going to stand around and be disrespected by a woman with champagne breath and an hourly rent-a-house. I'm out."

I finally look Ms. Angelica in the eyes. "My dad could sell

books out of his store, at a kiosk, or even at a fold-up table at the flea market. I still respect what he's doing a lot more than watching you prancing around this mansion thinking you're better than everybody."

I glance over at Reya and she's just sitting there, biting down on her lip and looking all speechless. You know what? I was wrong about her. She hasn't changed. And she's just going to let me stew while she films in her fake house.

I head for Reya's car, fuming. But then an arm reaches out to stop me.

28
Reya

MOM GIVES ME a sharp glance. "Sit back down, Reya."

I don't care. I've had it with my mother today. It was all supposed to be laughs and giggles. Fun and fakery layered over the persona my mother created for herself and our family. A silly afternoon spent with Sommer.

But that kiosk comment was too much. I won't be my mother's accomplice.

I glare at my mother. "You know what's so not Potomac, Mommy? Your nasty attitude today."

The camera's red light reappears immediately.

I'm not sure if Mom notices, but her left eye is twitching. "Now, hold on, Reya . . . don't forget this is your mother you are talking to."

Sommer puts her hands on her hips. "But it was okay to talk about me and my family any kind of way?" She pauses. "Respectfully . . ."

I can tell by Mom's facial expression she feels betrayed by Sommer calling her out. But she keeps that fake smile plastered on and doubles down on the sweetie-pie voice. "Sommer, I opened my *home* to you. I certainly didn't think we had any *issues* with each other."

"I didn't, either," Sommer says. "Until you started snapping on my dad's bookstore." She fluffs up Mom's borrowed shirt. "Also, not everyone has the cash to shop at Givenchy, Ms. Angelica. I can still remember when you loved a good sale at Ross."

Mom starts choking and darting her eyes around at the multiple cameras pointing in our direction. "Ross? Never heard of it." This time she looks directly into the camera. "Unless you're talking about the estate sale at Rick *Ross*'s house? That was a time, dah-ling!"

Enough is enough. "Mom, just stop it." Folding my arms, I narrow my eyes at my mother. "Bottom line, you made my friend feel unwelcome in our home." I take a look around me and have to laugh. "Our *fake* home, might I add. If we're going to be filming in this pretend house, you could at least play nice with my oldest friend. And stop insulting her family and where we used to live."

Mom notices a single camera sneaking a close-up shot of her reaction. Her Potomac face magically reappears. Letting out a soft laugh, Mom puts her hand to her chest. "Girls, is

PRETTY GIRL COUNTY

this why there seemed to be a little animosity at dinner? Let me explain. I was just *snapping*. Back in my day, we called it 'joning.' My parents called it 'playing the dozens.' Either way, it was all in good fun—a timeless Black tradition, really." Mom sashays across the yard, her silky designer kaftan slinking in the breeze, and cozies up to Sommer. "My silly jokes weren't meant to push you away, sweetie. As many guests as I've had out here for our many fundraisers and galas, there's certainly a seat at the table for our dear Sommer."

I'm happy Mom is trying to make things right with Sommer, but I'm still annoyed that things had to go this far in the first place. "I certainly hope you don't bring your joning, joshing, or other forms of disrespectful joking to my fashion show. Because that kind of unprofessionalism won't be tolerated anywhere near my event," I warn.

I'm so ready to stand up for the integrity of my show, I barely hear Mom sigh. Until she sighs and goes, "Well, I guess I can't put this off any longer."

"Put off what?" I ask, folding my arms.

Mom beckons for the cameramen to pause. "Well, due to unfortunate circumstances, production probably won't be able to film the fashion show, Reya."

"What?!" My heart drops. "Why not?"

Mom shakes her head. "I'm having problems getting certain clearances signed off."

"Well, what is it?" If I have to drop by the main office and get the principal's signature myself, I will. I *can't* lose out on this opportunity.

233

"I really don't think this is your fight, Reya," Mom says. "The school refuses to allow us to film there unless we showcase the name of the school."

My panic dissipates. "Okay, so let them show the name, Mom . . . Problem solved."

"Absolutely not!"

I stare at her open-mouthed. "Last time I checked, Academy of Health Sciences is one of the top high schools in the state. We graduate with high school diplomas and associate degrees. We're actually a flex. You're embarrassed of that?!"

Mom looks offended. "I'm not embarrassed of anything . . . but your high school is on the campus of Prince George's Community College. People can clearly see that's nowhere near Potomac."

"Who cares?" I don't mean to shout, but Mom's bringing unnecessary drama into an easy situation. "There are other Housewives who don't live in Potomac—you told me that yourself."

"Yeah," Mom agrees. "But they still live in other prestigious places, like McClean, Virginia, or Chevy Chase. No one else lives in PG County."

"*You do!*"

Mom sighs. "Reya, there are certain things about shows like this that you don't understand. The *Housewives* universe is supposed to be aspirational—showcasing houses and cars and jewelry that wow people."

"You drive a Rolls-Royce with the starlight ceiling interior—every time I stumble onto your IG page, you're leaning your

PRETTY GIRL COUNTY

head to the side so people can see the double Rs stitched into the headrest of your seats. People *know* we have money, Mom."

But my mother shakes her head. "Money doesn't mean anything if you aren't respected by your peers. These circles that the other Housewives run in—their kids wouldn't be caught dead hosting a Senior Skip Day at that *troublesome* Six Flags in Largo." She sniffs. "I'm certainly glad you had your priorities together and decided not to go."

Sommer and I exchange a look.

Not facts. I filmed with one of those *Housewives* kids last season. Not only did Little Miss Potomac try to sell me pills the second the cameras shut off, she was on her way to a party "in the trenches." Please.

"Mom, I don't know why you have such a complex about everything. A bunch of people have money in PG County. I don't see what the big deal is."

Mom makes a face. "It's a big deal to everyone else. No one respects new money, not in those *Housewives* circles. And watching our kids fight all over the news certainly isn't helping."

"They didn't even fight that day!" I tell my mother.

This doesn't sway my mother's judgment. "Maybe not your friends. But it's happened in the past. PG is a *Black* county, Reya. That kind of foolishness is not going to fly. You know the rules are different for us."

Her expression hardens. "You're growing up, Reya. Sooner or later, you're going to have to face the truth. People and what they think hold more weight than you know. If I were doing the show for fun, then sure, maybe I could be lax about everything. But the truth is, if the public decides I don't deserve to hold a champagne glass, I'm not coming back for another season." She sniffs. "The *Housewives* show may look like silly antics to some, but it's showcasing my law practice, it's funding the house we live in, and not for nothing, it's going to be paying for you to go to college next year. I can't afford to lose this opportunity."

Sommer comes over and grabs my hand as tears spring up in my eyes. "I can't afford to lose my opportunity, either. I was counting on filming to show FIT that I belong there. Without the show, I'm not coming off that wait list. What's the point of acting all fake and pretending to be 'Potomac' if there's no college to pay for?"

Mom looks like she feels sorry for me. But she doesn't budge. "I'm sorry, Reya. If everybody could get on the same page, I would be happy to film your fashion show. But I had to make an adult decision—the decision that's best for this family."

"Best for who?" I yell. "Your family . . . or your ridiculous reputation?"

Done with this whole charade, I look at my old friend. "Are you ready to leave, Sommer?"

Squeezing my hand, she replies, "I've been ready." She looks directly into the nearest camera. "Maybe we should swing by Grand Rising Bookstore on the way home, to grab our next great read!"

I smile at my friend. "That's in Seat Pleasant, right?"

"Right off MLK Highway. We stay open until eight."

Together, we march off toward my car.

PRETTY GIRL COUNTY

The last thing I hear is Mom snapping at production. "We're not using any of this film. And if you try, I'll film with my middle finger in front of my face the rest of the season. Don't cross me!"

"I'm sorry you had to listen to all that," I tell Sommer the second we get in the car. On the walk over, I worry about the status of our fragile friendship.

If Sommer doesn't talk to me the rest of the school year, I would honestly understand. I get stepping up your game to get noticed. But not if it means putting a big dusty boot print on a loved one to get there.

Uggghhh! Just when Sommer and I were finally reconnecting, now she probably hates me again.

"Don't sweat it, Reya. I'm not about to blame you for your mother's actions."

I slide Sommer a look as I start the drive back to PG County. "You're not mad at me?"

"I mean, I'm *mad* . . ." Sommer goes silent a moment. Then she sighs. "But no. I'm not mad at *you.*"

"You know what? We *should* have cameras film the store."

Sommer shakes her head. "Yeah, right. *Housewives* cameras are not coming to Seat Pleasant, especially after that."

"They will if Mom tells them to."

Sommer reaches out to check the temperature on my forehead with the back of her hand. "Good luck getting that to happen."

Sommer must have forgotten who I am. When Reya Samuels wants something, she makes it happen. Clearing my throat, I raise my tone an octave. "Ahem, yoo-hoo, producers, it's your favorite Potomac Princess on the line. Lace up those Sketchers and get your butts over to Seat Pleasant and film a bookstore for me. You're not there yet?! I said, *now!*"

I don't get my entire monologue out before we dissolve into a fit of laughter.

"Normally, I wouldn't be down for such fraudulent activities," Sommer says. "But in this case?"

I smirk. "We're calling this a good deed."

We high-five. Then we continue on down 495 toward home.

29
Sommer

IT'S FINALLY THE night of the fashion show.

For the last four days, Reya and I were basically a Disney Channel montage of "two heads are better than one" to get this fashion show down the runway. We did a few alterations to Bryce's old outfits, dressed up Azadeh's crutches and sent her down the runway for a few practice struts, and convinced Amara and Reed to film the fashion show instead of the big TV crew. Most of all, as lead consultant on the project, I checked and double-checked to make sure every design felt like a Reya original.

At the last minute, Reya and I reworked our vintage goose-feather vest look to send something hot and unexpected down the runway.

"You have to walk in this," Reya says now as we race

backstage getting everything ready for when the curtain goes up. On the other side of the curtain is the din of voices and laughter and scraping chairs, as our classmates and friends and parents and teachers settle in to watch this show we've poured our hearts into. I'm surprised to feel a nervous flutter in my stomach.

I look at the feathery vest Reya's dangling from her hand. "Excuse me, ma'am, you already know I'm more of a behind-the-scenes girlie."

"Yeah," Reya goes. "But this piece is special. Not just anyone can wear it."

And I know what she means—that vest says something about our friendship. And what it's taken to rebuild it, stitch by stitch, until it resembles what we had while being something entirely new.

I think on it a moment.

"I'm not walking in the show—" Reya's face drops immediately but I hold up a hand. "Since this vest isn't really a part of the overall collection, I think I should wear it at the end, when you walk out to take the runway walk as the designer. We can walk out together."

Reya smiles and nods her head. "Yeah, I like that idea."

"It's time!" Sauce says, checking his watch and peeking through a small opening in the curtain.

Reya looks grim for just one second, like every way that tonight could go wrong is flashing behind her eyes, but then she claps her hands and yells, "This is it! Fashion is forever.

PRETTY GIRL COUNTY

Make that runway your life for the next hour! And have fun!"

Then she starts lining up the models.

"Look at *you*," Sauce says when I line up behind him backstage. "You look so beautiful tonight." He brushes a lock of hair behind my shoulder.

Before he can say anything more, Reya stops him. "Get your little smooches in after the show, Sean. Sommer needs to hit this runway, makeup intact."

I'm grateful for the interruption. I've been so busy getting ready for the show that I haven't been able to spend any time sorting out my feelings for Sean or Octavius. Still, I can't deny how hot Sean is, especially in these outfits tailored to him. And a moment later, when Sauce glides down the runway, I find myself wishing I was the one by his side.

My heart bubbles with both excitement and sadness that just as everything's coming together, we're all moving apart. Me. Sauce. Amara and Reed. Octavius. And Reya.

For the next hour, it's a frantic frenzy of outfit changes, hair adjustments, and fixing smudged makeup. But model after model hits their mark, walking to the beat of the music, posing at the end before sauntering back. The crowd is loving every second and I feel proud of what we've done—of what Reya and I built together. The vision is hers, but this moment is undeniably ours.

All too soon, we're on our last outfit change, and when Sauce and Azadeh turn to start heading back toward the curtains, I take Reya's hand and squeeze.

Sauce and Azadeh barely have a toe backstage before Reya and I are off, moving down the runway like two gazelles in a clearing. Bright eyed. Showing off our individual looks. Showing off our friendship.

Finally, after five years of reeling from the fracture in our friendship, we are in perfect sync gliding down the runway together, me in streetwear, Reya in bougie couture. When we reach the end and do the spin Reya choreographed at the last possible second, we're met with thunderous applause from the audience.

I tell myself the clapping isn't about the spin at all—that everyone is simply happy to see us together again, that we've finally made things right between us.

There's a tiny bounce in my step on my return walk on the runway that I know might potentially earn me an elbow jab from Reya, but I don't care. How can we mess up at this point? We've done an amazing job pulling off this show and putting our friendship back together. There's still so much to fix regarding college and the bookstore in the upcoming months. But in this moment, everything is right in the world.

When Reya and I finally touch down backstage, everyone breaks out of their made-for-runway model personas to hug and congratulate each other. Then suddenly the sea of models parts, and Sauce is coming toward me.

"How did I wait so long to make you my girl?" he whispers. And in this moment I get swept away by it all—the success of the show, the thunderous applause, Sean's beautiful face. He

PRETTY GIRL COUNTY

leans down in front of the entire modeling club, swoops me into his arms, and kisses me like a prince who's come to revive his sleeping princess.

When I finally come up for air, it's not Sean's face I see but . . .

Octavius.

My heart freezes in my chest.

He is standing ten feet away, holding a bouquet of pink roses.

"You dragged us to this fashion show to get your girl, but your girl's already been got?" Octavius's crew, standing behind him, shake their heads and walk away.

For a second, all I register is pain on his face. Then he quickly recovers and bounces over. "You said y'all wanted a packed house, so I brought the whole Seat Pleasant with me." He turns to acknowledge his friends, but they've already vanished into the sea of fashion models, taking names and collecting numbers. He turns back to me and hands me the flowers he's holding. "I came back here to tell you that you did a good job. But I see your friend already beat me to it." He takes his time looking Sauce up and down before shifting his gaze back to me. "You did your thing, though. Congratulations, Lil Bookstore."

Sauce shakes his head slowly at Octavius's retreating back. "Honestly, I can't believe he played himself like that . . . Dude is *champ.* He's not even your type." He side-glances me, probably trying to get some verbal confirmation from me that he's hitting on the truth somewhere with his words.

243

But, to be honest, this whole back-and-forth is champ. I can't even hear myself think over Sauce's mouth right now.

When I don't say anything, Sauce keeps pressing. "Right, Sommer? That dude is the last person you would give the time of day to. He's broke AF. He's still riding around on a Huffy. He's—"

"He's my *friend*, Sauce!" I blurt out. "I'd appreciate you watching your mouth when it comes to him."

"Are you sure he's just a friend? I saw the way you looked at those flowers—at him." Sauce lowers his tone. "I know you like him, Sommer. Anybody with eyes can see that."

I throw my hands up. "How do you know that? I don't even know how I feel." I start pacing, thoughts going through me at a rapid pace. "All I know is that Octavius really listened when I was worried sick about my dad's store. He didn't just offer to help take the bookstore out of Seat Pleasant. He thought up a way to get the store to stay in the community." I look over at Sauce. "He cared about something that means everything to me."

Sauce's forehead crinkles. "But so did I. I texted my dad and everything."

"You told me to move the store."

His mouth falls open. "So me trying to help is a bad thing now? Do you even hear yourself?"

This is going in a direction I'm not ready for right now, and it's becoming too much. But now that it's out there, I have to say something. "Some things you're not going to get," I say carefully. "You've lived in Bowie your whole life." I pause a

PRETTY GIRL COUNTY

beat. "The best things in our city come from the people living there. Taking a community resource away is turning my back on my neighbors and my friends." I bite down on my bottom lip. "You know how you can't help jumping in for the people you care about? Well, I don't turn my back on the people I love."

An impossible silence takes over the moment.

"But you turned your back to take those flowers from ol' boy," Sean says slowly. "Yeah, I see what it is." He looks into my face like he doesn't even recognize me. "Okay, cool. How about I make this easy for you, Sommer?"

My heart drops when Sean turns his back on me. Then walks away.

30
Reya

PURE JOY IS running through my veins. We made it. Despite me almost giving up on this fashion show and my collection altogether, the audience oohed and aahed over every single one of my looks.

I can't take all the credit, though. My models were top tier, splashing onto the runway with the swimsuit looks, strutting in streetwear, and practically floating down the aisle in the grand finale prom looks like they were fighting for a spot in New York Fashion Week.

And, of course, I had Sommer.

I'm working the audience, thanking everyone for coming and encouraging them to interact with the different looks by downloading Sommer's latest digital drop, when Dean Willowbee appears in front of me.

PRETTY GIRL COUNTY

"You came?" I self-consciously smooth down the hemline of my skirt. The dean might have been a little intimidating before, but I stepped up and met her challenge. Now I can look her in the eye with a tiny bit of pride for seeing my work through to the end.

Dean Willowbee watches me preen with the corners of her mouth turned up. "I wanted to see for myself how you handle critique." She raises her chin. "Not *bad*. With the right training, the potential is there."

Before I can properly digest Dean Willowbee's delicious compliment, she's gone. And Carmen's walking up.

"How did you like the show?" I ask, hugging her.

"It was amazing, of course," Carmen says. "I'm glad you made me wait to see the final collection. My mouth dropped over every single look."

I hug her tighter, so happy we've finally settled into something real. "Make sure you let Sommer know how much you loved everything. She consulted on a lot of the changes."

"For sure."

Carmen hands me a bouquet of flowers. "I just wish the *Housewives* crew was able to come. Your looks are definitely worth the camera time."

That loss still hurts. But you know me. I'm always coming through with a backup plan. "Actually, Amara and Reed agreed to film the show. I'm going to throw the footage up on YouTube and cross my fingers it goes viral or something."

In fact, Amara and Reed are somewhere in a darkened computer room editing some clips for me to send in with my updated application. I make a mental note to send them on the *fanciest* dinner date at the Harbor when this is all over.

This makes Carmen smile. "*This* is the Reya I know."

Everything's turning out to be so lovely. Everyone around me looks really happy with the rollout.

Except . . .

"Sommer, what's wrong? We did it, girl!" I walk over to my oldest friend and give her the biggest hug. But she's not squeezing me back. And when I pull away, a strange look has taken over her face.

"There was some drama backstage," Sommer says quietly.

I narrow my eyes. "It better not be any of that neighborhood drama."

Sommer shakes her head. "You haven't gotten the update on that yet? Somehow, Cody and Bryce both ended up getting a job working at Smoothie King, and somewhere between mixing strawberry kale smoothies, they peaced it up."

My mouth drops. "So, Bryce could've walked in the show?"

Sommer shrugs. "I guess so." A dark shadow crosses her face again. "Anyway, the drama was between Sauce and Octavius."

My breath catches in my throat. "Octavius and Sean?! Hold up . . ." I pull Sommer to the side. "Tell me everything."

When Sommer starts giving me the specifics on her triangular entanglement, my heart returns to a normal pace and I wave the perceived drama away with my hand. "So they're both mad at you? Don't worry about it, Sommer. If I were you, I would give them both the boot. You're going to be moving

PRETTY GIRL COUNTY

on to bigger and better things next year at Spelman. Bigger school. Cuter boys. Fancier life. Trust me, leave these two in the DMV and keep it moving."

I put my hand up for a high five. You can't tell me I didn't just do my big one with *that* pep talk. But Sommer leaves me hanging harder than a teacher skipping over my waving hand in class.

"I mean, right? You're about to have your Hot Girl Semester at *Spelman*—Morehouse boys everywhere. You won't even remember these DMV townies next year."

Sommer doesn't look sad anymore. Wait. Why is her eye twitching like that?

"So that's how you feel? Moving on to bigger and better things?" Sommer shakes her head and looks away. "Now that I think about it, that's totally your motto."

I realize my mistake a touch too late. "Sommer, it's not even like that."

"Isn't it?" Sommer folds her arms. "You literally just laid out the blueprint on your move to Bowie. So you of all people can't say it's not like that, when it's *exactly* what you did."

My stomach begins bubbling immediately. Why do I always do this? Say the wrong thing on the cusp of everything going right?

Sommer shakes her head. "I'm not like you, Reya. I don't just leave people behind. I built friendships with Sauce and Octavius. Even if I get to go away next year, I'm not going to just forget everyone because I'm moving to Atlanta." She shakes her head. "I even planned to keep in touch with you . . . but maybe I should brace myself for the Boot 2.0, now that I'm done helping you with your collection."

This comment strikes a nerve with me, instantly taking me from regretful to annoyed. "Really, Sommer? Now you're just jazzing it. I've been doing the most these last few weeks trying to make up for my past mistakes. How am I still the bad guy?"

I don't even hide the fact that I'm heated, because for real, I don't deserve all this hate.

"You're going to stand there and act like you forgot how easily I got the *Housewives* producers to go exactly where I wanted? If I were selfish, I would have tricked them into coming here tonight, instead of sending them to the bookstore to film. But I'm fake and selfish, right? Wow!"

But Sommer isn't backing down. "Yeah, you're exactly what I thought, Reya. Fake and phony."

Before I can get another word in, a presence steps between us.

"You did what?!" Mom folds her arms. "Run that back, Reya? What will my *Housewives* cameras be doing at Grand Rising?" Oh no. She's mothering on high right now, and I'm cooked. "*Especially* since I specifically remember telling you, Reya, there's no way I would *ever* take my cameras into Seat Pleasant."

I have one second to make this right. Unfortunately, I'm unable to get one word out before Mom really lays into me.

"Don't bother explaining yourself, Reya. I know what I heard and let me save you the trouble. My camera crew absolutely will *not* be filming at Grand Rising. You can also kiss car

PRETTY GIRL COUNTY

privileges goodbye until you explain to me, how you—*a literal child*—found a way to convince an entire camera crew to go behind my back to film something I *specifically* told you I didn't want to do." Mom's eyes are blazing. "So, how did you pull it off? AI? *Please* don't tell me you used AI to fake my voice, because that is copyright infringement and—"

Sommer clears her throat. "She didn't use AI, Auntie Angelica. Reya's actually really good at *faking phony* voices."

Oh my god, Sommer, shut up, my insides scream.

"Is that so?" Mom steps forward. "Well, I can tell you one thing Reya is not good at these days. Impersonating my thoughts." She turns back to me again. "Because if you assumed for one second I would be okay with—"

"Mom, I know I was wrong. We don't have to go over every single detail," I grumble.

My mother raises an eyebrow. "Oh, we don't, huh?" She shakes her head. "Well *excuse me* for being hurt that my daughter, who promised to always keep it real with me, suddenly sets up an entire scheme behind my back that could literally cost me my spot on the show next season."

I look down at my shoes. "I really needed to help Sommer and her family. I knew you would never agree to filming at the bookstore, so—"

"You've got *that* right. If I wasn't comfortable with shooting the fashion show, what would make you think setting up an entire scene in Seat Pleasant was going to be cool?" Mom sighs. "You turned eighteen last month, Reya. It's time you started thinking like a grown-up."

I can feel Sommer flinching as Mom spews her venom.

"I see our move to Bowie has made you soft, Reya. You seem to think life is some fairy tale." Mom digs around in her purse, until her fingers connect with a little plastic key chain without a set of keys attached. When she hands it to me and I see the faded photo just beneath the plastic, I almost start crying.

It's a picture of Mom and me, a year before our big come up. I had been begging and begging all year to go on a family trip. We'd never been anywhere outside of Maryland, and I didn't care where we went, I just wanted to see what things looked like in another state. Mom wouldn't say yes or no to my constant pleading—I guess she wasn't sure she would have the money to take me anywhere and didn't want to get my hopes up for nothing.

It was a random day in July when Mom packed one of those Styrofoam coolers into the back of her ten-year-old Honda Accord, filled with sandwiches, bags of chips, and waters. She waited until we got to our first highway toll to tell me we were going to the big Kings Dominion amusement park in the middle of Virginia.

We had so much fun that day, riding the Scooby-Doo. We filled up on corn dogs and popcorn, and Mom even let me get one of those henna temporary tattoos. I remember when we first entered the park, and the photographer snapped this photo and told Mom she could purchase a copy for $23.99. "Nah, too expensive," she said, waving him off.

But on the way out the park, she walked back and forth to

PRETTY GIRL COUNTY

that photo kiosk three times, staring at our tiny photo and its price tag.

"You know what, YOLO," she told the photographer (because saying "YOLO" was acceptable back then). "I'm going to get it." Of course, the photo guy tried to upcharge her with like seven different sizes of the same photo. But Mom wasn't with all the extras back then. "No, just the key chain will be fine," she told him firmly. Turning to me, she smiled. "I want us to remember this special day. Who knows when we'll get to have another one like it?"

Mom was right. Even with the big house, and the fancy car, and more money on my debit card than I could've imagined back then, nothing's topped this special day yet.

Now, on the night of another special time in my life, I stare at the photo, still peeking through the scratched plastic, and then over at my mother with tears in my eyes. "I really am sorry, Mommy," I tell her.

I'm not sorry for trying to help Sommer, but I am sorry for going behind her back and for jeopardizing something she's worked hard for. I know she can see the sincerity in my eyes, and hear the truth in my voice, because she's struggling to maintain her tough demeanor. Her soft side breaks through anyway.

"Yeah, I know," she says. "But you need to remember how hard I fought to get us to where we are, Reya. *And* how much I have to sacrifice to keep us here. Being your mom has forced me to grow up. It's your turn now. You *can't* always act on impulse. You *don't* always get what you want. One wrong move can make your life a literal nightmare."

"But . . . it's *Sommer*, Mom. She's like family to us."

Mom stands in front of me, quiet and thoughtful. "I love Sommer and her family just as much as you, Reya. But you can't always take everybody with you on the way up, baby. It's not fair, but it's real."

"I can't live with that, though," I say quietly.

Mom nods. "Yeah, I can see that. But until you understand that my way goes—no car."

Dang.

When Mom reaches for the keys, I get desperate. I've been driving for a full year now—how am I going to make it without my car?

"But, Mom, I have to drive it home."

Mom waggles her fingers. "I'll have it picked up tomorrow."

"But how will I get home?"

Mom's expression is unyielding. "You miss our old life so much? Have fun taking the bus."

After plucking the old photo key chain from my hands *and* my set of car keys, she stuffs both in her purse, executes a perfect end-of-runway turn, and struts away.

Taking a deep breath, I turn back to Sommer, not even sure what I can say, but she's already gone.

31
Sommer

WHEN THE A12 lets me off on Martin Luther King Avenue, I cut through the gas station and head in the direction of my house a few blocks away.

The whole bus ride home, I think about everything that happened.

Octavius and the flowers.

Sean walking away.

Reya's run-in with her mom.

Reya telling me to go on to bigger and better things.

I thought Reya and I had healed our hurt, but it was still right there when she dismissed my feelings, when she told me just to move on and away. The old belief that I was replaceable. That being each other's day ones didn't mean anything if something shinier and brighter was around the corner.

Back when we stopped being friends, there hadn't been a big fight to end it all. It had been a gradual tapering off, which was almost worse. Like our friendship wasn't even worth fighting for. Then again, I hadn't fought for it, either—out of stubbornness. Out of pride.

All the thoughts are swirled up tighter than the stitching on Reya's outfits. And I don't know how to pull one thread without pulling them all. But when I close my eyes, when I sort through my anger and regrets, what I see is Octavius standing backstage, the smile falling off his face. I'm realizing—way too late—while Sean wanted to make me his girl, I didn't want to choose him. That even if he called me now to apologize for being in his feelings earlier, I would say no. I would tell him my heart is closer to home.

Even if Octavius doesn't want me anymore, I can't deny that I like him.

When I walk into the house, I find my parents standing in the kitchen looking worried and all my own drama falls to the wayside.

"What's wrong?"

"Hey, baby, how was the show?" Mom goes, kissing my cheek.

Kisses are cute and all, but based on the look on her face, there's no room for pleasantries.

"What's wrong?" I press.

Mom and Dad slide each other a glance, which angers me. "We're a family, right?" I ask. "I'm a member of this family, too. I want to know what's going on, so I can help if I need to."

PRETTY GIRL COUNTY

Dad sighs. "What did I tell you about being a kid? You're always—"

I put up a hand to stop him. "I'll be eighteen next month, Dad. You can try to protect me from the world, but news flash, I'm getting ready to step right into the middle of it this fall. When I'm down in Atlanta, you and Mom won't be able to shield me from obstacles—that's *life*."

They exchange another glance.

"Tell me what's going on," I demand.

Mom is the first to speak. "Didn't you go to see the Bowie State campus last week with Rey-Rey?"

"Yeah . . . ?"

"What did you think about it?"

I think back on that day, touring all the new-looking buildings and the bright, green campus. "I mean, it was cool. A little closer to home than I would prefer, but it seems pretty legit."

"What if we had to put Bowie back on the table, as an option?" Mom asks.

"Just for a year or so," Dad follows up. "Until we get everything squared away with the closing of the business, looking for work, finances . . ."

Oh. So this is what those faces are about.

When I was little and begging for Happy Meals, Mom would say, "We don't have McDonald's money, Sommer. We're eating at home."

Now it's my turn to make a grown-up decision.

"You know I would do anything for my family." I turn to

Mom. "If we don't have Spelman money, I'm staying home." I give both of my parents hugs.

As I make my way into my bedroom, I justify my quick decision.

I mean, it only makes sense, right? We'll save money going to school in-state. And Bowie's a great school—I saw that with my own eyes.

Everything about Bowie State should make sense right now.

There are times to put yourself first. This isn't that moment.

So, why can't I stop these tears from slipping down my face?

The next morning, I wake early to leave the house before my parents wake up. I walk every block of my neighborhood. I go up Drylog Street and cross over to 72nd. I walk down Seat Pleasant Drive and cut through the Best One convenience store parking lot, passing Church's Chicken to get to Martin Luther King Jr. Highway.

When I finally make it to Grand Rising, I see Octavius, straddling his bike, in the bookstore parking lot, staring at Dad's display window.

"What are you doing out here?" I ask him.

When he turns back to look at me, his eyes are a little red and hazy. "I'm minding my business," he says in a flat tone. "I don't owe you an explanation."

"And you're literally in the parking lot of my business," I snap back. "I have a right to know what's up."

A stroke of silence passes over us.

PRETTY GIRL COUNTY

"So, um, are you mad at me now?" I hate to ask. Everything's so awkward. But I have to know.

He turns back toward the display window, shaking his head. "Nah, more like mad at myself."

"For what?"

His neck tilts down. "For doing too much."

I move closer to him. "Why did you do that?"

He gives me a sharp look. "Don't even play with me like that, Sommer. I know you've been on your little preppy girl stuff ever since you switched to that gifted program, but don't talk to me like I'm that lil rich Ken doll you're running around with. I don't toss *my* hair back to get the sun out of my eyes."

I raise an eyebrow. "Um, neither does Sauce."

The mention of the third person in this weird triangle seems to annoy him. But if there's any chance something could still happen between us, I have to be honest with him.

"Whatever I had with Sauce is over."

I don't know what I expect. A warm hug? A passionate kiss? Instead, I get Octavius's back and silence.

Then? "You should choose the rich boy, anyway."

"What? *Why?*" Did he even see how extra good he looked dressed up in his Chrome Hearts tee with the Cuban link last night?

Octavius shrugs. "Rich Boy can fly out to see you in Atlanta next year. I won't even be able to afford bus tickets. Nobody's trying to have no FaceTime relationship." He finally turns around to look at me again. "Sometimes, to get ahead, you gotta look out for you first, Lil Bookstore. And sometimes"—his eyes dampen—"you gotta let people you care about do the better thing, even if it means having to let them go."

"Sauce *isn't* better than you," I tell Octavius. "And . . . and you aren't better than Sauce . . . I don't look at things like that. Plus, there's a good chance I'm staying right here." I put a hand on his handlebars to steady him. "Regardless, *you* understand me—what it's like growing up here. *You* don't treat me like some poor charity case. You see *me*."

O scrunches up his face. "Dude isn't looking at you like no charity case, Sommer. You look good. You're also cool. Every one of my boys has tried to holler at you, but you always walk so fast, with your nose stuck up in the air or down in some book, you don't give nobody a chance to post up and talk to you."

I suck my teeth. "Yeah, right. And when was this?" I can't recall anyone around here ever flirting with me.

"All the time, Sommer. But you wasn't trying to give none of us the time of day." He looks me up and down. "That's part of the reason I liked you, too. You finally slowed down enough to give me a little of your time—I figured you must really like me."

He drops his head. "I guess I was wrong, though."

My heart aches when he peers over at me with those sad brown eyes.

"No, Octavius, you're wrong . . . about being wrong." I trace my finger along his fiberglass handlebars. "Anybody can give me a ride in their big, spacious car. But somebody making

PRETTY GIRL COUNTY

room for me on a bike *they* barely have enough room to ride? That means something."

I meet his gaze. "So, what's up?" I ask him. "You going to give me one last ride on your bike?"

He takes one look at my outfit. "Nah, you can't be all up on my handlebars, dressed like that. It's windy out here."

"Okay, so I can ride behind you."

He smirks. "That's not going to work, either. You gotta be my girl to sit that close up on me like that . . ."

I take a step closer. "So, what if I was your girl?"

"What?"

"You heard me . . . I've been fighting my feelings for you for weeks."

Octavius gazes at me. "So your heart's telling you to take a chance on a dude from the Seat?"

"Right now, my heart has a giant letter *O* stamped right in the middle."

Octavius raises an eyebrow. "You sure that's not the beginning of heart disease? You know high cholesterol is a thing in the Black community."

"Boy!" I push him away, then bring him closer. Then, right here, in front of Dad's Some Personal Favorites display window, we kiss for the first time. His lips taste like sweet perfection.

"You ready to hop on the back of my bike?" Octavius whispers into my ear when we finally come up for air.

Instead of answering him, I kick my sandals off, carry them

in my hands, and hop onto the seat of his ten speed. When my arms are wrapped safely around his waist, he nudges the kickstand back and takes off down the block, back into the heart of our city, where kids playing in the street dart closer to the curb as we ride by. Moms laugh together on porches. Dads are outside fixing their cars, or gathered around a fold-up table playing a quick game of cards. A car, with the music cranked up loud enough to make my teeth chatter, moves gently around us to keep moving down the street. When we pass a red-and-white house, O calls out to Jada, who is leaning up against a tree with— Is that Santana? Well, okay, I didn't know *they* were a thing.

When Octavius pedals harder up the hill leading to my house, I pretend I'm a stranger, or an older version of myself returning to my neighborhood for the first time in a long time.

Yeah, it's still there. The beauty, which has always been known to those living in our community, is still visible from the outside in.

A few seconds later, O drops me safely in front of my door.

"That was too short," I complain, nestling myself into the warmth of his back.

Octavius wraps my arms tighter around his midsection. "Trust me. We have all summer."

32
Reya

A WEEK LATER, on Saturday morning, Mom pokes her head into my room. "You're still mad about me taking your car?"

"Yes." I hope my mother knows I plan on sticking to my word. Until I get my car back, I won't be going anywhere. So she'd better get used to *this* face around the house. Because I'll be right here. Laughing extra loud during her shows. Asking questions. Eating up all the food in the refrigerator. Maybe taking a nap in her bed.

Except I've had my plan in motion all week and Mom actually seems to welcome my presence around the house. She even asked me to join her on the couch to watch *Bridgerton* with her last night. Ick.

"Come join me in the kitchen, sweetie," Mom goes, smiling. "I want to talk to you about something."

See what I mean? I need to turn the oven up on this master plan and really get annoying. Because at this rate, she's going to realize I'm best friend material and take my car away for good.

When I make it into the kitchen, Mom is looking more like a housewife than she does on any of her episodes on Bravo. Today her borrowed jewelry has been returned to the safe, and her perfectly contoured makeup has been washed off. Her hair is in two braids behind her shoulders; a small kitchen towel is hanging over her left shoulder.

The first thing she says when I join her at the massive kitchen island is "The producers just sent me the dailies from the last scene we shot, and you know, I think I let that show turn me into an ass sometimes."

If I ever want to get my car back, I'd better not agree with that statement. "So, why do you do it? You're a lawyer. We're far from poor."

Mom sips a little water from her Stanley cup. "It takes more than one salary to keep this house running, Reya. I need as many eyes as I can get on my law practice so I can bring in more clients." She sweeps her arms around her. "To keep this life I've built for us."

She gazes at me. "Do you know what people told me when your dad died while I was pregnant?"

I shake my head.

"They told me to hurry up and get on public assistance. That life as a single parent was a dead end. That I was going to struggle the entire time raising you. And to not let people

PRETTY GIRL COUNTY

calling me a welfare queen get to me, because at least I was keeping food in my baby's mouth . . ."

Mom's eyes travel back decades. "Everyone acted like my life would be the same forever because times were hard for a while. But I never believed our hard times would be permanent. Not with a daughter on the way. Not for one second." She finally looks me in the eyes again. "Money or not, I always have a plan. I signed up for every type of public assistance the county was offering. WIC, a SNAP card, Medicaid. All those programs helped me, and I'm not ashamed to say it." She drums her nails on the kitchen island. "Out of all of them, though, financial aid was the public assistance that saved me the most."

The faraway look is back in her eyes. "Being able to take classes and work toward a degree gave me another path. I had a chance to break the cycle of poverty I'd been born into."

Now is probably not the time, but I can't help myself. "I wish there was some public assistance available for Grand Rising. Sommer and her family could really use it right now."

Mom pats my hand. "Sommer and her family will be fine, Reya. Don't worry. I've known the Watkins family a long time. They're scrappy like me—they'll find a way. Now . . . I was having a *moment* here?"

A sad chuckle escapes Mom's lips as she slips back into her moment again. "Imagine finishing school, becoming an attorney, moving your child out of the hood and giving her everything you never had, only to have everyone still consider your life not good enough."

I wrinkle my nose. "Who says our old life wasn't good enough all along?"

Mom twists her lips. "Come on, Rey-Rey."

"I mean, we didn't have fancy jewelry or expensive cars back then, but we still had fun."

Mom makes a face. "We went to Kings Dominion *one* time."

"And you built Slip 'N Slides in the backyard out of Hefty bags, and you played hide-and-seek with me and Sommer. And you taught me to play Go Fish and Tonk and Spades. Everything you've done for me has been good enough—because you were right there with me."

I'm not jazzing it to get my car back, either. Every single word came straight from my heart.

And I think my mom realizes it, too.

Mom and I are sitting around eating the "From the Runway to Your Dreams" sheet cake she was supposed to surprise me with if I didn't tick her off with my schemes the night of the fashion show when the mail truck pulls into view, just outside the kitchen window.

Licking frosting from my fingers, I stand up and walk outside to the mailbox. Most of the bundle the mail carrier slipped in the box is junk mail, but two envelopes peek out at me.

I throw the junk mail back into the box and walk the two envelopes back into the house.

"Who still sends snail mail?" Mom asks, wrinkling her nose.

PRETTY GIRL COUNTY

"Colleges," I say, staring at the envelopes in my hand.

One is from the Fashion Institute. The other is from Bowie State.

This gets Mom's attention enough that she puts her cake down.

"Well, are you going to open them?" she asks.

I stare at the envelopes, unsure of what to think. "Hold these for me." I slide the letters in Mom's direction. Then I pull out my phone.

"Can you come over?" I ask Carmen when she picks up. "I can't come scoop you, *because someone still won't give me my keys back*." I give Mom a look. "But I still need you here."

"I do know how to Uber, Reya. Or I can just get on the bus."

I shudder thinking of that hour-long bus ride just to go fifteen minutes up the road. "Please catch an Uber. I can't wait that long."

I want to call Sommer next and give her the same instructions, but she's left me on read since the fashion show. So instead I scream across the yard for Azadeh to come outside.

When most of my important people are assembled around the kitchen island, I get back to the business of these envelopes, bitterness rising in my throat like bile. "I probably didn't get into FIT," I say. "And this is probably a letter from Bowie State banning me from the campus for trying to get mentorship out of Dean Willowbee without paying the enrollment fee."

"Reya, stop it." Carmen says, shaking her head. "Don't be so hard on yourself. Bowie's probably begging you to reconsider after the dean saw that fashion show. Come on, open that one first."

I grab the envelope, slide my coffin nails under the flap, and lift out a folded-up letter.

I quickly scan the handwritten note. "It's from Dean Willowbee," I say.

"See?" Carmen goes. "Read it out loud."

"Reya. Thank you for inviting me to your show the other night. I love the improvements you've made to your collection. There are many designers destined for greatness, but in my thirty years wandering through the world of fashion, I've found that the *best* designers all have a singular trait in common: the thirst to become better. You trust your talent, but you are also willing to listen. I am confident you will make the right decision in regard to your educational plans for the fall, but I would like for you to know that our initial offer of acceptance still stands. You are always welcome here at Bowie State. It would be my honor to walk by your side on your journey to greatness."

"O-*kay*," Carmen goes, snapping her fingers. "See, that's the kind of love you get when you roll with an HBCU . . . personalized letters." She and Azadeh slap five. "Wow. That's incredible."

Even I'm impressed. "This was really nice of her," I say quietly, reading and rereading the words. I can't believe an actual dean, with her big office and fancy degrees on the wall, took time not only to come to my show but also to send such a thoughtful note.

PRETTY GIRL COUNTY

"Now, you already have an HBCU on your side, so you're already winning," Carmen says.

"No matter what FIT says," Azadeh adds. "So, hurry up and open it!"

Here we go. I take the letter from FIT from Carmen's hands as everyone around the kitchen island gawks at me.

A storm is raging inside me as I slowly pull the white paper from the envelope. I take my precious time peeking at the results, since I've never been a fan of bad news.

When I finally turn the letter around and stare at the tiny print, my bottom lip trembles.

"Congratulations! It is our great pleasure to offer you admission to Fashion Institute of Technology for the fall . . ."

I close my eyes and press the letter to my chest. "I made it," I whisper.

"You what?" Carmen polishes off the last of her cake and jumps into my arms. She only pulls away to grab the letter and read the words for herself. "Babe!" she yells. "Arrrrrgghh! You bodied this wait list!"

This gets everyone else started up with a round of hooting and cheering and celebrating my win. Mom screams so loud, Azadeh's dog starts barking from inside her house next door.

"Will you *please*?" I glare at my mother until she simmers down—slightly. "You know the HOA doesn't mess around about noise complaints."

When Mom finds her way back to her island stool, I'm alone with my thoughts again.

I only updated my new portfolio days ago. There's no way

269

FIT looked at all my new materials this soon. I don't know if I made it off pure luck or if I was always meant to go to this school.

But I made it.

"Wow!" Azadeh smiles at me with wonder in her eyes. "You actually did it, Reya. You made your dream come true."

"I did," I say.

So why doesn't it feel as good as I thought?

I look around the kitchen island again, at the faces of the people I love.

Maybe because going to FIT means leaving Carmen behind just when things are starting to get good between us. Maybe because FIT means being away from Azadeh for the first time since we became friends. Going to FIT will mean leaving my mom—which I don't even want to think about right now, because it'll make me start crying.

And then I think about the person who's not here: Sommer. And how leaving for New York means possibly never getting the chance to prove to my oldest friend I'm not fake or selfish— that I've grown past the young girl from all those years ago.

Most of all, going to FIT will mean not going to Bowie and having Dean Willowbee's eagle eye in close proximity. I stare at FIT's letter again, wondering how I ever got to a place where I'm even considering another program.

But now that I'm here, standing between two letters, each promising a different path toward the same goal—I don't know what to do.

PRETTY GIRL COUNTY

I look at the enrollment due dates on each letter and realize I don't have a lot of time left to make my decision.

As if reading my mind, Carmen suddenly lifts my chin with her hand. "Hey. I think there's someone else you should tell about this acceptance. It might make you feel better."

"My . . . followers?" I ask weakly, even though I know exactly who Carmen is talking about.

"Don't think I don't know who gave you the advice to make it right with me after our disaster of a date," Carmen says. "So, it's time I return the favor. This beef with Sommer? Apologize for your part. Your friendship is too important to leave on the cutting room floor."

And even though I know she's right, even though Reya Samuels has done the impossible over and over, this time, I have no idea how to make it right.

33
Sommer

AGAINST MY BETTER judgment, I'm standing in Reya's room, reading acceptance letters from FIT and Bowie State.

Reya has been texting me all week, and I've been leaving her on read, but when she sent me the pictures of both letters with a simple text that said, I don't know what to do, I found myself calling an Uber and arriving at the front door of her Woodmore McMansion.

I don't know. I guess I saw the old Rey-Rey in those words, the nail-biting beneath the bravado. And I would be lying if I said that every time I've left her on read, I haven't been wondering if I've done the right thing. Like, am I right to feel old wounds can't just be fixed with goose-feather vests? Or am I jazzing it right now by keeping the drama going?

PRETTY GIRL COUNTY

"What's the problem here? How could you even consider anywhere else?" I shake Dean Willowbee's letter at her like smelling salts—just in case she needs an extra wake-up call. "I saw how you felt on that campus. You *liked* it. The option is back on the table. You're lucky to have *options*," I say, saltiness coating my words. Thinking how my options have basically narrowed to zero.

Reya's expression is agonized. "But it's FIT. I've been dreaming of it for years."

"Name a dean at the Fashion Institute," I demand.

Reya shrugs. "I'm not in New York yet. I'll probably meet them when I get there."

"Yeah, but you know Dean Willowbee already. And she knows you. I'm not sure that happens everywhere."

"It's easy for you to say, you're going to your dream school," Reya says dismissively.

My heart starts to harden. "No, I'm not. I'm working on getting my scholarship back from Bowie. We can't afford Spelman with the store closing."

Reya's expression is stricken. "I'm so sorry, Sommer. I know what Spelman meant to you. There's nothing else you can do? Maybe there's some other scholarship somewhere that could help?"

"This is the real world, Reya. There's no secret money fund to unlock, or some rich dead relative leaving me millions. I can't just Disney Channel my way out of this one like some people."

"What is that supposed to mean?" Reya asks, narrowing her eyes.

"Let's just say that I learned long ago that I can't just get what I want all the time. And I can't just pay people whatever amount so they help me."

Reya looks wounded. "Really, Sommer? Paying you was my way of using every resource I had to reach my goal. I wasn't about to blend in with everybody else on that wait list. When I really want something, I fight with everything I have."

"Oh, you're a fighter, huh? Then why didn't you fight for our friendship?" I say.

See? Like I thought. Reya has no comeback for that.

"The way I remember things back then, you got yours and you got out."

"Well, if *that's* how you feel, maybe there's nothing left to fight for," Reya says, crossing her arms over her chest.

"Maybe," I say, staring right back. "These past few weeks have been nice, pretending we're friends again. But let's just stop all the faking. I got a paycheck, and you got FIT. It is what it is, right?"

"I guess so," Reya says flatly.

With that, I turn to leave, desperate to get home before the tears fall. But as soon as I make it to the winding staircase, Ms. Angelica calls from the kitchen. "Reya, is that you?"

I should've kept pushing down the stairs. But thanks to good home training, I feel the need to go on into the kitchen to speak.

PRETTY GIRL COUNTY

"No, Ms. Angelica. It's me, Sommer," I say politely as I enter the kitchen.

"Oh." She goes quiet a moment. "I'm glad you're here, actually."

I stand there, feeling awkward, while she takes a moment to find her words. "Listen, Sommer, I didn't mean to hurt your feelings the other day. But you know how messy things get when you're extra focused on the goal."

Don't I know it.

Ms. Angelica reaches over the kitchen island and places a hand on my shoulder. "I'll be more careful with my words next time. We've been friends a long time—family almost—and you and your family didn't deserve that kind of disrespect."

"Thanks," I say quietly.

"Well, now that the uncomfortable stuff is out the way." Ms. Angelica smirks.

She's trying to lighten the mood, but something's still bothering me. "Why do you care if the other Housewives know you're from PG County?" I blurt out.

Ms. Angelica walks over to her six-burner stovetop to check on something peculiar bubbling in a smaller pot. "And let them call me ghetto? I don't think so . . ."

I watch her grab the handle of the pot off the stove and carry it over to the sink. "I just need a tiny little snack so I don't pass out before my casserole is done," she tells me. Using a fork, she drains the water from the pot. Then she dumps the noodles into a bowl, pours in a powdered sauce packet, sprinkles in some hot sauce, and mixes the whole thing together.

While all of this is going on, I'm still stuck on her flagrant use of the word *ghetto*. "But you're okay with your castmates calling you a backstabbing social climber?"

Ms. Angelica shrugs. "Well, that's just a little *Housewives* hazing, Sommer. Every newbie gets called *that* their first season."

She carries her bowl of noodles over to the kitchen island. Then, like she's remembered I'm standing here watching her, she holds her bowl out to me. "My bad, Sommer. You want some? You can grab an extra fork from the drawer."

I shake my head. "No, thank you. I can't stomach those things anymore."

She stares at me, like *I've* changed. "*Whaaaat?!* You used to love the beef flavor back in the day."

I laugh a little. "That was then. Now my stomach clenches up at the sight of those things."

I can't stop staring at Reya's mom slurping up those noodles. Those aren't penne noodles, or even pho. I can't believe I'm sitting here at this quartz countertop, in this million-dollar kitchen, watching Mrs. Housewives herself slurp up a bowl of Oodles of Noodles.

If you're unfamiliar with this sodium-filled treat, let me give you a quick rundown. For the very affordable price of ten cents, you can get yourself a hot, steaming bowl of the most flavorful mix of noodles you will ever come across. Though you might be hungry again in an hour, right after you eat this saucy treat, you are full, packed with sodium, and satisfied.

PRETTY GIRL COUNTY

"Tuh. You better get ready. I hear noodles are a college delicacy." She leans over the kitchen island. "Where are you going in the fall, again?"

"Well, I was supposed to go to Spelman, but probably I'll be heading to Bowie," I say with a sigh. I can't wait to get to the part of my life where we never talk about college acceptance again.

She nods. "Spelman. Hmm. *Okay* . . ."

For a minute I'm a little offended. "What's wrong with Spelman?" I ask folding up my arms.

"*Nothing.*" Reya's mom slurps up her last noodle, then carries her bowl over to the sink to rinse the leftover juices down the sink. "When I was a kid, there was this show called *A Different World.*" She gives me a look. "That's before your time, baby girl."

"With Dwayne Wayne and Whitley Gilbert. I've seen a few episodes."

Ms. Angelica's eyes light up. "Right! Well, I watched every episode of that show when I was kid. And I always wanted to go to a college like that." She shrugs. "But I didn't."

"Why not?"

"No money," she says simply.

"What about scholarships and financial aid and—" But the words ring false as soon as I say them out loud. What good did those do me?

Reya's mom stares at me a moment. "Trust me, Sommer. When I was your age, going away to college felt impossible. I didn't even have bus ticket money to get myself down to

277

Atlanta. There was no way I was going to be able to pay for books and room and board. And I didn't even have the right clothes to be going down there with all those rich girls whose parents were paying their way."

A soft smile appears on her face. "I eventually took night classes once Reya got older, and got my house and white picket fence anyway . . . So it all worked out."

The look on her face and the pride in her tone find their way to my heart, making me wish everyone got to see this side of my friend's mom.

Then she ruins it by tacking on "Yep, shook all things ghetto like an all-star running back."

"My dad always says ghetto is a place, not a person," I snap. "You grew up in a poor area, big deal . . . You made a good life for yourself, despite not having much. Why wouldn't you want to share that?"

She fans away my question with her hand. "And be laughed off TV?"

But I refuse to back down. "You think most of America is walking around dripping in diamond earrings and staring at their Picassos all day? Most people watching your show are still trying to make it themselves." I shrug. "The *Housewives* is supposed to be aspirational. So, why not show viewers what's possible by showcasing your own come-up story?" I chuckle. "Even Drake claims to have started from the bottom . . . You know why? Because people love rooting for the underdog. It's easier to see themselves in you when you aren't so high above them."

PRETTY GIRL COUNTY

This gets Ms. Angelica's attention. "I've been thinking of adding a little razzle-dazzle to my storyline this year. What are you thinking?"

"Show the world how you were. Then show them who you've become. Your audience will root for you."

Ms. Angelica stares at me. "You think so?"

I nod. "Yeah. People connect better to authenticity and they *love* a come-up story. Take them to Seat Pleasant. Show them where you come from—why money and security are so important to you now. Humanize Seat Pleasant so the world can see our town isn't some down-and-out, hopeless place. Show them a city that can be so much more, with just a little more support."

I watch Ms. Angelica think on this awhile. "I won't promise anything," she finally says. "But I'll think about it, okay?"

A moment passes. Then she asks, "What is your family going to do once the bookstore closes?"

"I don't know," I say. "But I'll help my family however I can. I've been saving my own money, too."

Ms. Angelica reaches over to smooth back my hair and places a hand on my shoulder. "Things are going to work themselves out for you, too. I promise. It just takes the universe a minute to catch up with the real go-getters." She smiles. "But I see you, and I'm proud of you, Sommer. Really. You're doing your thing, baby girl."

For the first time in a long time, her words feel genuine. I guess under all the bravado and *Housewives* persona . . . Reya's mom is still like me. Willing to do what it takes to make her situation better. I still don't agree with her chasing everyone else's approval. And I personally wouldn't take the champagne-throwing route to gain money and fame. But I can respect her hustle.

Before I leave, I pop back in on Reya, who is sitting at her desk, typing out an email to Dean Willowbee.

"Hey," I call out softly. "Can we fix this for real this time? I don't want to keep going back and forth with you. We love each other, but we fight like sisters. And while that's annoying, I still don't want to go another five years not talking to you."

Without confirming or denying our constant bickering, Reya gets up from her desk and jumps into my arms.

"I love you, Sommer."

"Yeah, I love you too, Reya."

34
Reya

THE FOLLOWING SATURDAY is Seat Pleasant Day. I haven't been to the annual city celebration since my move to Bowie. But this year is different. Since my visits to the bookstore have increased, it only makes sense that I attend the all-day festival. Plus, I have something special planned.

My last conversation with Sommer didn't sit right. After she left the other night, I went downstairs to the kitchen to find Mom washing her bowl out in the sink.

"We *have* to help Sommer," I told her. No more excuses. Friends can feel like family if the bond is there. And once upon a time, my family and Sommer's family were neighbors, turned friends, turned family. I would never leave my mom hanging. Just like she would never leave me out in the cold.

If the Samuels and the Watkins families were ever really as

close as we claimed to be, it would be unthinkable to turn our backs on them in their time of need.

"Okay," Mom finally said after I laid out my bullet points. "You're right. Let's do this."

Now, if Reya Samuels can make the impossible happen, just imagine what it's like when Reya and Angelica team up.

Which is why we're walking around the Seat Pleasant Day festival with the *Housewives* camera crew behind us. Along with Ms. Johnson, from the book club. Adding her in at the last minute was my idea, of course. Just like I knew a well-dressed church lady would, she just so happens to have connections to city hall.

Ms. Johnson brought the council members to Mom. My mom used her attorney skills to appeal our case. Now? The ball is in motion. We've organized an *event*. A very important announcement is coming. One that I can't wait for Sommer and her family to hear.

"Here, give me your face, sweetie," Mom says, pulling an eye drops kit from her purse. "This isn't a simple dinner table scene," she goes, dropping clear liquid into my eyes. "To stand out, you have to look *alive*. Exude *confidence*. Smize!"

"You don't want a few drops, baby girl?" she asks, pointing her eye dropper at Carmen, who's walking with me for moral support.

"No, thank you," Carmen tells her. I give my mother a don't-embarrass-me look.

"I'll take a few of those drops," Ms. Johnson says, hold-

PRETTY GIRL COUNTY

ing her face out. "I've never been on television before." She is beaming like she is on the cusp of her big break into show business.

And maybe she is—you never know. Miracles are about to start cropping up everywhere, according to my top-secret information.

While Mom is getting camera ready, I'm looking out over the crowd for my friends, who all promised to come for my very special announcement. But so far, only Carmen's here. I don't see Sommer anywhere.

"She's coming, sweetie," Mom goes, dropping liquid into Ms. Johnson's eyes. "No one from around here ever misses Seat Pleasant Day."

Time whips by and before I know it, the parade to kick off the start of Seat Pleasant Day is gathering at the top of Seat Pleasant Drive and Hill Road.

I look around once again for Bryce, Azadeh, Marlon, someone. Still no one.

Suddenly, a terrible thought hits me. What if my friends don't care about my announcement? Maybe they feel like they won't ever live around here, so only what goes on around Bowie matters.

I'm so close to sharing my worries with Mom. But she's barely paying attention to our little group any longer. She's busy craning her neck and looking out at the crowd gathering.

283

"Have you guys seen Kevin Durant anywhere? I was hoping the cameras could get a shot of him." She slips the eye drops kit back into her purse. "I mean, I didn't know him personally from back in the day—but we practically grew up together . . . I'm sure he won't mind reminiscing about the old days for a minute or two."

Mom suddenly raises her palms to gesture to the camera crew behind her. "Cameras up!"

When they follow her command, she thrusts her shoulders back, jostles her hair around a bit, and flashes a toothy smile at the camera lens before sashaying away from us.

But when she gets to the edge of the sidewalk, the heel of her stiletto gets stuck in a random crack, she trips on the curb, and now she's sprawled out in the middle of the street, with a scraped-up knee.

"Cameras down!" she yells from the asphalt. But the cameras don't move. They remain fixated on the scene in front of them. A few pockets of laughter come from the gathering crowd, and I almost get mad, because I don't care what she's doing, no one laughs at my mother and gets away with it.

But from the crowd emerge Amara and Reed, who help her off the ground.

"I'm fine, I'm fine," she grumbles, shaking loose pebbles from the crevices of the tulle of her skirt. But when someone randomly mumbles "Kevin," her skinned knee is instantly forgotten as she dashes into the crowd, yelling "Cameras up!" behind her.

PRETTY GIRL COUNTY

I don't have the heart to tell her the Kevin in question is not the NBA superstar but actually the owner of the Sugar Shack corner store down the street.

"You two made it," I go, once Mom disappears in the crowd.

"Yeah, we come every year," Reed says. "I usually come to hear the Go Go bands. And stay awhile for the free food."

"Free," Amara adds, "is where we're trying to be."

I smile at that. "Have you two seen Sommer?"

They look at each other. "Not yet," Reed says. "But I'm sure she's coming."

"She's probably helping her dad set up a vendor table in front of the store," Amara adds.

They stand with Carmen and me as the parade gets started.

The marching bands from the various high schools in the county lead the parade, followed by the mayor waving from the sunroof of his car, and a few key city council people. Residents of Seat Pleasant, along with anyone else who wants to check out the show, line up on both sides of the street to cheer, wave, and Swag Surf as the high school bands drop the melody.

Finally, as the parade passes through Seat Pleasant Drive, anyone who wants to can join the back of the parade line. I pull Carmen by the hand.

"Um, I'm okay standing on the sidelines," she goes nervously. But I continue to pull her along. "Come on," I tell her. "From what I remember, it used to be so much fun joining the parade. Plus . . ." I crane my neck to look up ahead. "It might help me spot the rest of my friends."

I'm right. By the time the parade snakes its way to the end of Seat Pleasant Drive, I've collected Marlon, Bryce, and Azadeh.

"Anybody seen Sauce?" I ask.

"Not yet," Azadeh responds.

"I texted him," Marlon says. "But he's been a little MIA in the groups chat lately."

"Yeah, ever since your girl . . . you know," Bryce says.

Azadeh yanks his arm. "Don't bring it up. You *know* that's an awkward subject."

When the parade line finishes, the crowd disperses. Some head over to Goodwin Park to see the live bands. Some head over to the food trucks pulling up in the Family Dollar parking lot. And others, like me, head over to Grand Rising for the big announcement.

Mayor Grant and County Executive Alsobrooks are already there, standing near a long, fancy blue ribbon. Mom is next to them. Along with Ms. Johnson and . . . *Octavius?* He wasn't originally a part of the plan, but I mean, I'm not about to tell him where he can and cannot stand in his own neighborhood. If he's up there with the movers and shakers of the community, then that's obviously where he's supposed to be.

Octavius nods at me, then goes into the bookstore and comes out with Sommer and her parents, all of whom look beyond confused.

Despite all the people gathering in front of the store now, we find each other and lock eyes. Sommer breaks away from her parents and walks over to me.

PRETTY GIRL COUNTY

"What the heck is going on, and why is your mom standing over there with the mayor?"

"Cameras up!" Mom calls out, and all the cameras are pointing at the group standing in front of the bookstore.

"You said I didn't fight for you," I tell her. "It took me a minute to get it, but I'm here now with my boxing gloves on." I nod toward all the Bravo cameras. "Or at least I'm here with cameras and a councilwoman."

"Shhh," Ms. Johnson says, turning around. "They're about to get started."

When County Executive Alsobrooks holds a microphone to her lips, the crowd goes quiet. "As a proud champion for *gorgeous* Prince George's County, Maryland, I am ecstatic to share with everyone all over the region our plans to build a phenomenal play space for the city youth in Seat Pleasant."

The crowd gathering begins to clap—which convinces Mom to lean into Ms. Alsobrooks's mic and go, "Go, Seat Pleasant!"

Okay, I'll give her a little moment. She *did* help make this happen.

Someone pushes a random kid to the front of the crowd, and while he's being mic'd up, Sommer looks more closely at him. "That's Noah, the same boy who spray painted Dad's window," she says.

"Tell me, young man," Mom coos into her microphone. "What will having this new recreational park mean to you?"

Even though he has a mini mic now attached to his shirt, Noah grabs Mom's mic and leans in. "Uh, it's going to mean a lot," he says, flashing a smile at the camera. Bright lights

287

pop as the local newscaster gives him a thumbs-up.

"And what will be the first thing you do with the space?" Mom asks.

Noah takes a moment to think. "Well, uhhh, I'm a big fan of board games—"

"Awww," goes the crowd.

"But let me get one thing straight." Noah mean mugs the camera. "If my guy DeAndre starts stealing out the bank like he usually do, he's out of the game—"

"Boy!"

Out of nowhere, an arm pops out of the crowd and snatches Noah. He breaks free, hands Mom her mic back, and does the Harlem shake for the camera for a second or two before his grandmother snatches him back into the crowd.

"Can't take you nowhere!" she says, but even she's smiling.

"But part of community is honoring what makes a community special in the first place," Ms. Alsobrooks continues. "And that's making sure to preserve cornerstones like Grand Rising Bookstore."

Sommer's jaw drops open. Her mom brings her hands to her mouth in surprise, and tears shine in Mr. Watkins's eyes.

"This young man here," Ms. Alsobrooks says, pointing to Octavius, "had a great plan to build over the store. And my good friend Ms. Johnson"—Ms. Johnson waves elegantly to the crowd—"and Seat Pleasant's very own respected lawyer and Housewife, of course, Angelica Samuels, spoke very persuasively to keep this neighborhood gem in place."

PRETTY GIRL COUNTY

My mom grins proudly. Sommer looks at me in astonishment and throws her arms around me.

"You did this?" Sommer asks as Ms. Alsobrooks continues talking about the redevelopment.

"You were right that I left," I say simply, taking her hand. "But you showed me the way home. *Thank you.*"

35
Sommer

REALLY, REYA, REALLY?!

This is the best surprise. And I can't believe my friend somehow made all of this happen, especially after I had to go off on her a little the other day.

I guess when the friendship is true, there's room for squabbles—and maybe even breaks. Maybe real friends will always find their way back to each other, even through the deepest misunderstandings.

After the ribbon-cutting ceremony, when my parents and I rush over to Ms. Angelica, Reya's right by my side.

My dad shakes his head, tears still glistening in his eyes. "How did you do this, Angelica?"

"Well, it turns out that Reya's friend from book club, Ms. Johnson, is almost as well-connected as I am. We put our heads

PRETTY GIRL COUNTY

together, and you would be surprised how fast the county can reverse demolition plans when a certain Housewife storms into county offices with plans to film her protest of the only bookstore on this side of PG County closing in a few weeks."

Dad's eyes immediately snap in my direction. But Mom still has questions. "So, the county just went for that?"

Ms. Angelica casually shrugs. "Like I told my good friend County Executive Angela Alsobrooks, we can either make bookstore activism my newest storyline next season, or together we can stage a cute little 'book talk' here where I talk about my memoir and she talks about her run for state senator next election."

Reya's mom digs around in her Fendi bag before handing Dad a thin paperback. "Now, this isn't the final version—I'm still tweaking some things. But the finished cover is cute, right? I think it'll look perfect front and center in the store."

I watch Dad turn the book over to look at the front. "*From Housing Projects to Housewife: The Aspirational Angelica Samuels Story?*" he reads aloud. He raises his eyebrows. "When did you write this?"

"I've been working on my memoir for a while now, Keith." Ms. Angelica narrows her eyes at him.

"Well, I usually like to read over the books I add to my collection before stocking them." Dad catches the look on Reya's mom's face. "But since you've kept the bookstore alive, I'm sure we can devote a whole table to your memoir."

When Dad disappears to thank Ms. Johnson as well, I look over at Reya's mom with pure disbelief in my eyes. I mean, my friendship with Reya goes way back. But Ms. Angelica is technically just my friend's mom.

"You would do all this for me?"

"There are three areas in life where you should never settle, Sommer." She puts her hands on her hips. "Quality shoes. Love. And"—she gently grabs my chin—"chasing your dreams."

She looks me in the eye. "You're my baby girl, right? We're practically family, and I never, ever turn my back on family." She gets this faraway look in her eyes, like she's taking this moment to remember her own past dreams. "Once I pay off Reya's college tuition, I have big plans to see the world." She comes closer. "But you, baby girl? You have a chance to do it now—so *go*. First stop, Atlanta. No excuses now. Then next stop? Anywhere you choose."

Mom, who's been smiling ear to ear nearby, comes over to rub Ms. Angelica on the shoulder. "It feels good seeing you back around the way, Ange. Now, don't take so long next time to pay your friends a visit. This was a really wonderful thing you did for the bookstore . . . and our family."

Face-to-face with my mother, Reya's mom couldn't plaster on her *Housewives* persona if she tried. "Of course, Naomi!" she says, giving Mom a tight hug.

When Mom pulls away, she sidles up to me and whispers in my ear. "Looks like you're headed to the McDonald's in Atlanta."

"With extra chicken nuggets and endless packs of barbecue sauce?" I ask, wrapping an arm around her waist.

PRETTY GIRL COUNTY

Mom smiles. "Plus a Happy Meal, with a bonus toy inside."

No one has to tell me twice. I already know what's in my heart. And now that the bookstore's staying open, nothing else is in my way. "Okay," I tell her. "I'm going."

Dad is so excited over the surprise he dips into the store and comes out with one of those old-school stereo speakers. He hooks it up to our in-store sound system that usually plays Erykah Badu or Jill Scott for our patrons. In minutes, hip-hop is blasting through the speaker into the parking lot.

Now, I don't know about you and your neighborhood. But anytime someone from around *my way* hears good music playing, we're sliding right into a line dance, the Tootsee Roll, the Dougie, you name it. The older crowd will group up and get the Soul Train line started, and everyone in earshot will be down to create a party right on the spot.

I didn't even know Octavius danced, but he's right in the mix with his hands up, hyping up the crowd and inviting Ms. Johnson to do the Cha-Cha Slide with him.

I'm not doing too much dancing. I'm having a good enough time just people watching. This is exactly what I'm doing when I see him. *Him.*

"I'll be right back," I tell O.

I break through the crowd and head straight over. Things might always be awkward between us, but I can at least pretend they're not. Despite everything, we formed a true friendship and I miss hanging out.

293

"You? In Seat Pleasant?" I let out a chuckle. "Now I've seen everything."

Sauce tries to play it cool, but he can't hold back a grin. "I dropped you off plenty of times over here. Don't act like that!" He shrugs. "Plus, my mom wanted me to check out Ms. Samuels filming here. She's thinking of joining *Housewives* next season to promote our Mumbo Sauce line, but she doesn't want to pretend to live in Potomac."

Now that would be interesting. I immediately wonder how Ms. Angelica would react to sharing the spotlight with another PG County Housewife now that she's finally repping her county. Maybe I'll tune in next season to see that.

"If she does join, tell her I already have the perfect tagline," I tell Sauce. "Like my Mumbo Sauce, I'm here to spice things up!" I do a spin and smize that cracks Sauce up.

"You'll have to text that to me, so I can show it to her later."

We meet each other's eyes again, and all the things we're not saying in this moment hang in the air. Finally, Sauce grabs my hand.

"Hey, we're going to be cool," he says. "I'll admit I was disappointed that night, but we're graduating in a few days, and I don't want to leave school with any bad memories."

Squeezing Sauce's hand, I smile and mouth the words *thank you*.

Can you believe, while I'm trying to have a moment with my friend, some random girl runs up, steps between Sauce and me? "You're dating Tate, right?" she tosses back to me. Eyes shining, she bats her lashes at Sauce. "Boy, you are too fine.

PRETTY GIRL COUNTY

Take this!" She hands him a slip of paper before dashing off.

Noting the ten digits written on the slip of paper, I smirk. "It looks like you're going to be just fine."

Sauce blushes, but I don't miss him slipping the girl's number into his pocket.

We hug goodbye and promise to text this summer. Then I head back over to Octavius, and Sean goes looking for his number one fan. Just like that, we've friend zoned each other. And that's fine. Friends are a good thing.

Octavius finally gets me to dance, and while I'm busy doing the Cupid Shuffle, I spot Reya engaged in a scene with her mom. No drama—just the cameras rolling on the dynamic mother/daughter duo. My heart warms over Reya finally getting her moment—the very thing she's been working so hard to get this whole time.

When she's done, she comes rushing over. "They said they are going to slip in a sentence or two of me discussing one of my outfits as long as they can air Mom falling on the ground back there, and Mom agreed!"

"If this airs, the scene will be pinned to my socials for all eternity." She leans back and cups her hand around her mouth. "This is the best day ever!" she yells out.

Yep. It truly is.

The joy of this festival carries with it a reminder that towns aren't built on reputation—but on the backs of their people. That bookstores are just shelves with books without the local bookseller getting to know the customers and hand selling their next favorite read. That fights only spread and worsen

295

until the people behind the beefs come together to try and understand each other. That hopes and dreams are rarely realized without your people—your *supporters*—backing you up and lending a helping hand where they can.

"If Reya did all this for Seat Pleasant Day, I wonder what she has planned for Bowie Day in a few weeks," Azadeh says, walking up, eating cotton candy from one of the food trucks.

"She's probably going to skydive into the festival to announce she's finally chosen to attend Bowie State," I reply, giggling.

From Seat Pleasant to Bowie, the people of Prince George's County should be proud of what we've built so far. A county full of Black wealth. But also, a community of great hope. A space to dream. And a place to create something beautiful, straight from the hearts of its people.

There are a lot of girls like Reya in PG County. Wealthy. Pretty. With a whole *lot* of rizz. Watching it all play out, it can feel like those are the girls who get everything. Then there are girls like me, coming straight out of Seat Pleasant. Palmer Park. Bladensburg. We may not have the most. Things may not come as easy. But we dream just as big. And sometimes? Girls like us, the underdogs—no, the *people's champs*—get exactly what they deserve, too.

Some Personal Favorites

For Young Readers

Brown Girl Dreaming by Jacqueline Woodson

Concrete Rose by Angie Thomas

The Davenports by Krystal Marquis

Long Way Down by Jason Reynolds

Monday's Not Coming by Tiffany D. Jackson

Nigeria Jones by Ibi Zoboi

Revolution in Our Time by Kekla Magoon

For Adults

72 Hour Hold by Bebe Moore Campbell

Afeni Shakur: Evolution of a Revolutionary by Jasmine Guy

The Autobiography of Malcolm X by Malcolm X and Alex Haley

Becoming by Michelle Obama

Black Girl Lost by Donald Goines

The Black Rose by Tananarive Due

Cane River by Lalita Tademy

The Coldest Winter Ever by Sister Souljah

The Collected Poetry of Nikki Giovanni by Nikki Giovanni

The Color Purple by Alice Walker

The Darkest Child by Delores Phillips

Douglass' Women by Jewell Parker Rhodes

Family by J. California Cooper

Flyy Girl by Omar Tyree

I Know Why the Caged Bird Sings by Maya Angelou

Invisible Life by E. Lynn Harris

Kindred by Octavia E. Butler

Mama by Terry McMillan

Manchild in the Promised Land by Claude Brown

The Misadventures of Awkward Black Girl by Issa Rae

Perfect Peace by Daniel Black

P. G. County by Connie Briscoe

"Recitatif" by Toni Morrison

Redefining Realness by Janet Mock

Roots by Alex Haley

Silver Sparrow by Tayari Jones

Their Eyes Were Watching God by Zora Neale Hurston

The Vanishing Half by Brit Bennett

The Warmth of Other Suns by Isabel Wilkerson

The Women of Brewster Place by Gloria Naylor

ACKNOWLEDGMENTS

Thank you to Kelsey Murphy, Lanie Davis, and Kat Jagai for all your editorial wisdom. Thank you always to my literary agent, Melanie Figueroa, for advocating for me and my career in the best ways. Thank you to every single person at Penguin Young Readers who helps bring my books to life. You are appreciated. Thank you to my family, especially my mom, who cooked for my family for many weeks so I could keep writing and revising uninterrupted. Thanks to my dad, who helped her drive all that food over to my house! Thank you to my partner, who will reach out to anyone to advocate for my books and will also bring me juice when I've practically evaporated into the couch during long writing sessions. Thank you to my son, who, along with his friends, provided lots of the inspiration for my characters. I should also thank him for bravely allowing me to peek into his group chats a time or two, ha! Thank you to my daughter, an alumnus of the Academy of Health Sciences program at Prince George's Community College, for sharing her experience attending this amazing high school program.

Finally, thank you to every person who does their part to make Prince George's County, Maryland, a great place for young people to grow and thrive. To the faculty and staff at Prince George's Community College and Academy of Health Sciences at PGCC for making quality education accessible. The librarians of Prince George's County Memorial Library, who advocate for young readers. County Executive Angela Alsobrooks, whose public service includes investing in education and expanding access to healthcare. The Prince George's County chapter of the NAACP—especially Brenda Lipscomb for championing my books. The mayor of Seat Pleasant during my childhood, Eugene Grant, and the current mayor, Kelly Porter, for all you do to keep our smart city reaching new heights. Kevin Durant and the Durant Family Foundation for your tireless work creating college track programs for the youth, building recreational spaces and revitalizing retail space in Seat Pleasant, throughout Prince George's County, and beyond. Finally, from the summer camp counselors at the Sports and Learning Complex to the lifeguards watching over the wave pool at Six Flags: Thank you all for keeping our county *Gorgeous Prince George's*.

For more sparkling romance
from Lakita Wilson, check out
LAST CHANCE DANCE,
available now!

READ ON FOR A SNEAK PEEK!

Prologue

THE FIRST MAJOR chance I ever took on love paid off big-time. And that's surprising, because before high school, I never really had a solid example of what *lasting* love looked like. Sure, my parents were married for close to thirteen years. But by eighth grade, they were giving me and my younger sister, Riley, the *divorce* talk and splitting assets.

I was obsessed with reality TV dating shows in middle school, but it seemed like *that* love only lasted through the taping of the season. By the time the reunion episodes aired, the couples were always sitting on opposite sides of the host debating over who was at fault in the breakup.

Still. I wanted to believe in a forever kind of love. And I needed to experience it for myself to truly believe it could exist. Then fate stepped in.

Three days before freshman year, Mom and I were walking out of Target with all my newly purchased back-to-school supplies—at the same time, the most gorgeous boy I've ever seen is walking in. His brown skin resembles a freshly scrubbed penny, only a few shades darker than my own honey-brown skin. His thick, bushy eyebrows hover over the biggest brown eyes. His sideburns and full pink lips send me over the edge, and before I know it, I'm thinking: *This has to be fate.* Cute boys *never* shopped in this particular Target.

Now, there's two major rules when it comes to reality dating shows. The first rule? Speak up for what you want, or get cut in the first episode.

So I stop Mom from walking out of the double exit doors. "I think I forgot something," I tell her as the cute boy grabs a shopping cart.

Mom holds up two shopping bags and raises an eyebrow my way. "Whatever you don't have, you can order later from Amazon." She lets out a long, exaggerated sigh. "Besides, my feet are tired."

But I can't take no for an answer. The boy, who's wearing a crisp white polo shirt, slim fit jeans, and the freshest Js I've ever seen in my life, is turning the corner and disappearing from view.

"But, Mom, I need a graphing calculator in my hand to*day*. Bree heard from Eva, who heard from Ashli, that if we don't have everything by the first day of Pre-Calc, we're basically headed down a slippery slope of flunking out of school."

LAST CHANCE DANCE

At this point, I'm sure Mom knows I'm full of it. But she's probably tired of standing there holding the heavy shopping bags, because she digs in her purse, hands me her debit card, and goes, "Make it fast, Leila. We have to be out of here in time to pick your sister up from summer camp."

I blow my mom a kiss and say, "Back in a second!" as I dash back into the store.

Because reality dating show rule number two? Never let go of a promising prospect too soon. Because they'll only show up on the reunion episode looking ten times better than the first time you laid eyes on them. And you'll wish you had taken the chance on them when you could.

I couldn't risk losing sight of this cutie only to have him show up in one of my freshman classes, already taken and looking one hundred times better, on the arm of some thirsty girl from an earlier class period.

So while Mom walked off to find the car, I beelined my way through the back-to-school shopping extravaganza. I ducked past the five-dollars-or-less sand trap, ignored the jewelry display case, and followed the giant yellow cardboard pencil cut-outs down the middle aisle, to the back of the store where all the school loot was on full display.

I know what you're thinking. *Leila, are you taking a chance on love? Or are you just a tad thirsty, chasing some dude you've never met through a store loaded down with security cameras?*

But look, Mom had Tinder and a well-manicured swiping finger to meet her latest dating conquests. If there were apps for teen girls who wanted to browse boy candy from the comfort of their couches, it would be predator city.

So—I saw an opportunity. And I took it.

I finally found him lurking in the office supplies aisle, biting his fingernails and comparing brands of Scotch tape.

"Double-sided *sounds* like a good idea, but it tends to stick to everything except your paper—just go for the regular stuff," I told him, trying hard not to sound all out of breath from the running I just did.

When the boy looked my way, the fluorescent megastore lighting bounced off the little flecks of gold in his light brown eyes and—*whew*—he was fine. Initially, I thought he was Black like me, because we shared the same brown skin. But up close, I noticed his hair didn't have a curl pattern and his shade of brown was closer to copper than mahogany. I wanted to ask him what his background was, but like—how do you ask something like that? Asking "What are you?" is just rude. Even fresh out of the eighth grade, I knew that. So I waited for more clues to fill me in.

"You in one of those Instagram fandoms, or something?" he asked. "You obsessed with all things tape?" Then he barely chuckled—like some sort of *tuh* sound mixed with a breath, like he was too cool to laugh at his own corny joke.

His smart mouth didn't throw me off. If anything, it made me go at him harder. Because if reality TV taught me anything, it was how to flirt like a boss.

"No fandoms over here. I just suckered you into doing me a favor."

LAST CHANCE DANCE

There's no real way to look sexy leaned up against a shelf full of staplers, but I tried to make it work.

"Oh yeah? What's that?" he asked. At around five foot seven, he didn't completely tower over me, but he was tall enough for a kid fresh out of middle school. I'd have to stand on my tiptoes to kiss him. If I wanted.

"I need help finding the right graphing calculator."

"A TI-84? Oh, that's nothing. I could actually give you mine. I'm going into advanced math this year and won't need it."

Okay. I peeped the door he'd just opened.

"I've never turned down free," I told him, helping him seal the deal. "But are you sure you want to lend an expensive calculator to some girl you barely know?" I propped a couple of fallen binders back up on the shelf. "How do you know I'm not into flirting with cute boys for their expensive math goods?" I stepped closer to him until I was right under his chin. "What if I borrowed your calculator and disappeared? For the rest of your life you'd be wondering—"

The boy looked down into my eyes. "I'd find a way to track you down." His breath smelled like one of those giant Fireball candies and made my nose hairs burn a little. But I didn't mind. He was one of the few boys my age around without pimples. Fair trade-off.

He plucked the green three-pack of Scotch tape off the hook on the shelf. "For one, by the time we finalize the terms of this calculator loan, we'll know each other's names." He stuck his hand out. "I'm Dev. It's short for Devrata, but—"

"Leila—"

"Right. *Then*, I would make sure I got your number before handing over anything math related." He stepped closer to me. "Since you're possibly a calculator bandit and all."

And just like that, we were exchanging numbers. Like he promised, Dev delivered on the calculator the next day, when we met up at Sweet Frog for ice cream. And before my first day at Baldwin High, Dev and I were a *thing*. Junking up Mom's living room with our laptops, pens, journals, and backpacks during our *homework and chill* sessions. Making matching Halloween costumes inspired by '90s Saturday morning cartoons. Dev teaching me to drive and then offering to drive me places when I accidentally hit a fire hydrant and vowed to never get behind the wheel again.

Lighting the candles during Diwali. Tossing colorful gulal during Holi with Dev's extended family. Riding the Metro train downtown to see the lighting of the Christmas tree on the National Mall. Easter egg hunting on the White House lawn with my mom and little sister. FaceTiming with my dad for my sixteenth birthday when his flight from Houston was canceled.

Dev was there for the regular boyfriend stuff. But he was also *there*, in the real kind of way that makes me cringe every time one of my well-meaning aunties refers to our relationship as *puppy love* or Dev as *Leila's little friend*.

Dev was *there* when I didn't get the SAT score I wanted last year. And again, when I got an even *lower* SAT score the second time around. My friends were supportive, of course, but it was

LAST CHANCE DANCE

Dev who missed every Friday night football game, even after our high school went to the playoffs, to help me study until I finally scored high enough to apply to the really good colleges.

Last October, for my birthday, instead of grocery store cake and cheap perfume, Dev secretly signed us up for a visit to my dream college, Brown University. While I hopped around squealing like the last bachelorette standing at a rose ceremony, Dev kicked his logical side into high gear. He found a chill day on the school schedule, printed off *very* realistic permission slips for an overnight field trip to Colonial Williamsburg, and took his mom's old minivan in early for a tune-up so there wouldn't be any mishaps on our way up I-95.

After Dev bought a case of Capri-Suns, and I made tuna wraps, we hit the highway, riding for seven hours and thirteen minutes up to Providence, Rhode Island. We toured the campus and sat in on a world literature course. I mostly kept quiet, leaning forward and chewing on my pen cap, while basking in the ninety-minute discussion on character motivation and word choice. But Dev—as a birthday bonus—raised his hand and asked a surprisingly insightful question that made the lit professor raise an eyebrow of approval. We took pics with the Brown Bear, the school's mascot, watched a few pirates walk by singing a cappella, and ate in the Ratty, aka the cafeteria— which Dev pointed out was false advertising, since the food was surprisingly delicious.

"Too bad we can't see the dorms," I said as we finished the walking tour.

"I'm sure you'll give me a private tour when I come up to visit," he whispered, planting a kiss on my lips.

Fate had brought me the perfect boyfriend. Because, when it came to things that really mattered, Dev was my rock. Through the good times and the hard moments, like when Brown had rejected me back in December, shattering me for a solid two weeks, Dev was always there for me.

Until, suddenly, he wasn't.